MIKE GAINE

Gripping his rifle firm, thrust it forward and drove the tip of the bayonet into the Laotian's back. The man screamed with pain and lost his footing in the jungle underbrush. Mike was upon him in a flash.

Using the rifle as a primitive spear, he drove the bayonet deep into the man's chest. Mike pulled the bloody dripping weapon out of the Communist soldier's body.

The American mercenary looked at the crimson-bathed stainless steel blade and the cut-open lifeless rag doll at his feet. Mike Campbell had not forgotten how dirty war could be. It was just that he had hoped this mission would be different.

ATTENTION: SCHOOLS AND CORPORATIONS

WARNER books are available at quantity discounts with bulk purchase for educational, business, or sales promotional use. For information, please write to: SPECIAL SALES DEPARTMENT, WARNER BOOKS, 666 FIFTH AVENUE, NEW YORK, N.Y. 10103

**ARE THERE WARNER BOOKS
YOU WANT BUT CANNOT FIND IN YOUR LOCAL STORES?**

You can get any WARNER BOOKS title in print. Simply send title and retail price, plus 50¢ per order and 50¢ per copy to cover mailing and handling costs for each book desired. New York State and California residents add applicable sales tax. Enclose check or money order only, no cash please, to: WARNER BOOKS, P.O. BOX 690, NEW YORK, N.Y. 10019

THE POINT TEAM

J. B. Hadley

WARNER BOOKS

A Warner Communications Company

WARNER BOOKS EDITION

Copyright © 1984 by Warner Books, Inc.

All rights reserved.

Cover design by Gene Light
Cover art by Morgan Kane

Warner Books, Inc.
666 Fifth Avenue
New York, N.Y. 10103

A Warner Communications Company

Printed in the United States of America

First Printing: October, 1984

10 9 8 7 6 5 4 3 2 1

Over North Vietnam, 08:22 hours, December 12, 1972

THE pilot knew it was way too late for him to take evasive action. The surface-to-air missile corrected its trajectory, wobbled for an instant on its stabilizing fins and then homed in on the exhaust of his starboard jet engine. He hadn't seen the goddamn thing in time.

He was flying a solo mission—no crew, no radio contact—north of the DMZ. He was a goner.

Except no man ever believes that.

He waited with one hand on the seat ejection mechanism in the hope that through some failure of infrared heat sensor technology the missile would miss its target. This delay might cost him his life by trapping him inside the burning plane, but he would take a chance on that rather than eject early and hang from his chute only to see his plane fly away on automatic pilot after escaping the missile.

He felt the impact of the missile's exploding warhead shake the plane out of control, and almost simultaneously he blasted himself clear of the cockpit. He spun end over end at high speed in the cold, thin air, clear of the flaming wreckage and its lethal debris. The green jungle turned crazily and then righted itself far beneath him as he began his slow parachute descent. The burning jet fighter plunged into the trees a few kilometers to the north, and a lead-colored plume of smoke marked its final resting place.

He hit the tops of the jungle trees and was fortunate not to break an arm or a leg as he crashed down through the branches. The parachute canopy and its lines became entangled in a treetop and left him dangling in his harness, swinging to and fro sixty feet above the jungle floor.

He swung harder until he caught the slender tree trunk with his arms and legs, released his harness and shinned down the trunk. He hit the ground and looked around him. Five peasants pointed automatic rifles at him and stared at him in silence.

Finally, one let his rifle hang loose on its sling. He made gestures of taking off his clothes to the airman, who obeyed and then stood naked before them. The North Vietnamese peasant fetched a spade lying on the ground nearby. He handed it to the flyer. The spade was carved skillfully from a solid piece of valuable hardwood and would have fetched a fancy price in a Western curio shop.

"Dig! Dig!" the peasant screamed at the pilot in Vietnamese.

The flyer leaned casually on the wooden spade. He asked in excellent Vietnamese, "Why do you want me to dig?"

The foreigner's knowledge of his language seemed to increase the peasant's frenzy.

"Spy! Infiltrator! You have come to monitor our activities!"

The airman smiled. "Look, I wouldn't even be down here if some of your friends hadn't sent me an invitation by way of a missile—"

"You came to bomb us!"

"You know the difference between a bomber and a fighter."

"Dig! Dig! Here!" The peasant grabbed the spade from him, pressed down on its blade with a sandaled foot, dug up a chunk of jungle soil and put it on one side. He handed back the spade. "Dig like that."

"Why?" the airman asked truculently.

"Your grave."

The others laughed heartily at this.

The flyer took the spade and decided to dig. Chances are, he guessed, they're trying to psych me out. His mind resolutely shut out another possibility. Almost.

He pressed down gingerly on the hard wooden spade with his bare foot and heaved aside a wedge of soil. The moist, soft earth was heavy to lift but easy to cut through. Three of the peasants watched silently as he dug. The other two went through his belongings, and one began to write with a ballpoint pen and paper that he found.

It was only as the hole assumed the shape of a grave and got to a depth of a couple of feet that a full realization of what he was doing hit the flyer. The horror of his situation swept over him, and he stopped digging and faced the three peasant watchers. They looked back at him without expression—he could see neither hate nor pity in their eyes. He threw the spade on the ground.

The one who had ordered him to dig pointed at the edge of the hole. "Kneel!"

The airman looked at him with contempt. "Americans kneel only to God."

All three sprang on him in a rage. One kneed him in the groin, and the flyer doubled over in agony. They forced him down on his knees, held him by his hair and pushed his face into the dirt in front of him. The peasant who had spoken raised a machete and swung the blade down on the back of the unprotected neck of the flyer. He hacked the head clear of the man's shoulders and put it in a rice-straw bag. The other two kicked and rolled the body into the shallow grave, then scattered soil over it with the spade.

One of the two peasants who had been examining the airman's belongings held up the sheet of white paper upon

THE POINT TEAM

which he had laboriously copied some meaningless English symbols with the ballpoint pen. Still in his teens, the peasant looked very proud of his achievement. Had they understood what he had copied on the paper, they would have read: Lt. Frank Vanderhoven, USAF.

Chapter 1

THE ornate mansions stood in walled compounds, visible through high, decorative iron gates. The French colonials had lived in them when they had ruled Indochina and the city had been called Saigon. Now it was Ho Chi Minh City, and the elegant buildings of this residential section had new masters and rotted gracefully in the tropic heat. All emblems of colonial rule had been removed where possible. The name of one mansion, Les Pleiades, still remained, engraved too deeply in the cut stone of the gate piers to be easily effaced.

In this house's garden, which was about two acres in area and still bore traces of the obsessive geometrical neatness of French horticulture, two dozen children labored over vegetables in the soil. They thinned out lines of seedlings and weeded between the rows, bending over their work earnestly as drops of sweat fell from their faces onto the earth at their fingers. A few had Western shirts, jeans and sneakers, but most were clothed in rags and wore sandals.

As they stooped at their work, the hair color of the children marked them as being different. Even those with black hair did not have the glossy jet black of Vietnamese children. Many had brown hair, and one had a shock of curly red hair. They looked up only when the front door of the mansion slammed shut after a Vietnamese woman and two children. The woman glanced disdainfully at the Western faces of the children working in the garden. She hurried her own two children before her and unlocked the tall iron gate opening into the street.

"Commie bitch!" one of the children in the garden called after her.

The child's use of English and his American accent caused the woman to wince. She would never get used to these little monsters. Her husband often said it would have been better for everyone if all of them had been shot. Not just these, but the thousands of them all over the place fathered by American troops. The ones who looked Vietnamese could get by. Not these Western-looking ones. No one wanted them.

She locked the gate after her.

The boy who had shouted at her spat onto the ground. He was thirteen years old and was the only one of the children who had crossed over into adolescence. His voice had broken, and something of the belligerent adult male could already be detected in his stance. His hair was brown, as were his only slightly almond-shaped eyes, and his skin was sallow. In a Coca-Cola T-shirt, blue jeans, and sneakers, he could have been a kid on any American street.

The others looked up from their work, waiting for what he would do next. It was evident from the way they waited for him that he was their leader.

"His goddamn crap cousins from up north!" the youth growled. "I'm sick of 'em!"

He carefully cultivated the tones he imagined belonged to a GI tough guy.

"Vo Veng is watching from the window," a girl warned.

The youth looked up and saw the small, skinny figure clad in black pajamas standing at a second-floor window looking down at him. The youth grinned insolently up at the man and glanced at his bare left wrist as if looking at a nonexistent watch. The man at the window involuntarily glanced at his own expensive Swiss watch on his left wrist, grimaced at the trick the youth had played on him, and stalked away into the interior of the room out of their view.

The youth laughed and said, "Now, I wonder what a dedicated communist cadre like Vo Veng would want with a rich capitalist's watch?"

"Or with all the other watches, TV sets, radios, tape decks and other stuff we get him," another boy added.

"One of the stupid kid cousins was wearing a blue T-shirt this morning," a girl said.

They curled their lips in disgust at the thought of this. They could accept any kind of behavior from the adults, but they kept their special scorn and hatred for the kids their own age who were part of Vo Veng's extended family. Once they had lived inside the mansion with Vo Veng as orphanage supervisor, his wife as cook, and his two children as classmates in their schoolroom run by an outside teacher. Things hadn't been too bad back then.

Vo Veng was from North Vietnam and felt himself superior to the South Vietnamese, who he claimed were corrupted by Western values. After a while the teacher from outside ceased coming, and their schoolwork came to a stop. Vo Veng put them to growing vegetables instead. Then more and more of his cousins arrived from the north. The men built two huts out of sight at the back of the house. The walls were constructed of bamboo, and they had galvanized zinc roofs which rattled like drums in heavy rain. But the cousins didn't move into these two huts. They moved the children out of the big house and put the girls in one hut and the boys in the other.

Vo Veng's wife no longer cooked for them. Nor were they supplied with any food. They ate vegetables they grew in the garden and rice they bought in the market with surplus money from what they called their "business."

THE POINT TEAM

Their "business" was where the orphanage's supervisor's watch had come from, which was why he had started guiltily when reminded of it by his insolent ward. Smuggled consumer goods from the outside world were at a premium in communist Vietnam. Items such as watches and tape decks, once cheap and taken for granted in Saigon, had become expensive status symbols in Ho Chi Minh City.

Most of the smuggled goods came overland from Thailand, across communist Cambodia or Laos into Vietnam. The rest were brought in by fishermen in their boats at lonely spots along the coast.

The kids at Les Pleiades held what was almost a franchise for their part of the city in the sale of this contraband. They were outcasts. They had nothing to lose, no one to embarrass by their antisocial activities. It was Vo Veng who had to be careful. Party zealots did not take kindly to one of their members trading in Western luxury goods. Was he still receiving a salary from the government for their nonexistent teacher? The children were long since aware he was spending money meant for them on his cousins from the north and as capital to buy smuggled goods to resell at a profit.

As the orphanage supervisor's weaknesses became more evident to his wards, he grew increasingly distant with them and allowed them to run their own affairs so long as they caused no trouble. His way of saving face at their insolence and lack of respect for him was to pretend they were not there. It was understood on both sides that any effort on the part of the children to force him to acknowledge their existence would have unpleasant results for them.

They were unwanted. A breed apart. They had the stigma of foreign blood. There was no place for them in Vietnam's new egalitarian and fraternal society forged by the glorious revolutionary fighters. The only hope they would ever have was to perform tasks that all good party members had to shun.

None of this was ever put into words. The children knew these facts of life instinctively, and accepted their lot. The more adventuresome of them watched and waited for any opportunity offered.

The youth in the Coca-Cola T-shirt had not resumed his work on the vegetables. He dusted off his hands thoughtfully and fished an expensive digital watch from a pocket of his jeans.

"We ought to be going," he said to the boy next to him.

"Can I come too?" a girl asked.

"Maybe next time."

Four boys washed their hands and faces with a garden hose, then climbed a plum tree alongside the wall of the compound, sat for a moment atop the wall, and dropped down into the street outside.

Katie Nelson was still in high school when the Vietnam war ground slowly to a halt. Back then, cheerleading for the school football team had been more important to her than American military policy in Southeast Asia. She still wasn't quite sure what it had all been about, but didn't worry overmuch since political or military analysis was not what the TV network expected from her. They paid her to do "human interest" stories.

And she was damn good at them. Good enough to move from a local station in Spokane to St. Louis, to Cleveland, to network TV in New York. She handled cats up trees, bears and coyotes in suburbs, chronically ill babies, skiing octogenarians, vandalism in cemeteries . . . she could wring a tear or a smile from any assignment—and build a newscast's ratings overnight.

Katie Nelson was also ambitious. She knew that the anchormen, with all their bullshit contacts in the White House and Congress, did not take her seriously. She was

THE POINT TEAM

light relief in their eyes. Tinker Bell lost among the hard facts of men's deeds. They hardly noticed her demanding, and getting, choice assignments. What they did notice was that she helped get them ratings. They'd peddle their mothers for ratings.

Katie lay on her back on the bed, looking up at the plaster decorations on the ceiling, and smiled her famous smile. People all across America knew that smile. She reminded a lot of people of a 1980s Mary Tyler Moore. Cute, pretty, bouncy, smart. Folks liked that.

She'd done a lot of coke late the previous night and early in the morning. Jake, the sound man, had brought it in with his equipment. She giggled. Here they were in Southeast Asia where most of the world's heroin originated, and Jake smuggled in cocaine. Jake was a nut.

She looked at his naked body beside her on the bed. He was perspiring as he slept. The air conditioner didn't work—it probably hadn't since the evacuation of Saigon. When other media people in New York heard she was coming to Ho Chi Minh City and was going to stay in this hotel, they'd regaled her with stories of the wild days (when she had been a cheerleader in high school). She checked out the bar. It was still the same as they had described, except there were no loaded Western journalists, blitzed American and ARVN officers, no hostesses, no good bourbon. Now it was vodka, Russian technicians, and Viet bureaucrats. She guessed it just wasn't like the good old days anymore.

They'd eaten strips of fried gray meat, bamboo shoots and rice, drank plum wine and vodka, then retired to her room, where Jake produced the coke.

She turned away from Jake, over on her side, and ran her fingers down the muscular back of Roger, the cameraman. If only the viewers out there in TV land USA could see her now, lying nude in bed between two snoring, naked men with a slightly anesthetized nose and a sore crotch. She'd given both the guys a real workout!

THE POINT TEAM

She poked Roger in the back. He groaned. Then Jake in the side, who muttered something incomprehensible.

"Come on, fellas," Katie said. "It's almost eleven o'clock. We gotta meet our little friends at midday."

Lt. Tranh Duc Pho gestured his men forward. His fifteen-man unit held their Kalashnikov AK47 assault rifles at the ready and advanced slowly through the undergrowth. The jungle was silent except for their bodies brushing against the thick undergrowth. The lack of light beneath the canopy of huge trees and their camouflaged fatigues and careful movements made them almost invisible from beyond a hundred yards. The unit eased its way down the jungle-clad slope to the slow, muddy river.

The river flowed southwest out of Vietnam into Laos and emptied into the Mekong. Here, fifteen miles inside the Vietnam border, nearly four hundred miles north of Ho Chi Minh City, the lieutenant and his crack unit fought a continuing war on several fronts. They subdued rebellious Montagnard clans, and intercepted smugglers on their way into Vietnam and refugees on their way out. When an area party cadre was not toeing the Hanoi line, the unit paid his headquarters one warning visit. Second time, it was discipline. After only a few punitive missions, the reputation of Tranh Duc Pho's unit spread so that now even the mention of the possibility of a warning visit was enough to tame the most erring local leader.

Tranh Duc Pho took things personally. These were his mountains, his jungles, his rivers. He said who went where. The tribal villages in the mountains and the Vietnamese farmers in the foothills supplied him and his men with women, food, and shelter. His father and brother unloaded ships at Haiphong. Tranh Duc Pho was the star of the family—a miniature warlord!

The green-brown water of the muddy river slid silently by twisted roots of giant trees on its bank. The lieutenant and his fifteen men reached a pathway that wound among

THE POINT TEAM

the tree trunks alongside the river. They carefully checked a section of the pathway and withdrew to cover.

The lieutenant briefed his men in a low voice. "This was one of the branches of the Ho Chi Minh Trail that supplied the area around Da Nang during our war with the American imperialists. Unfortunately, heroes no longer walk on it today. It's the only trail around here that the hill tribes don't booby trap. So, apart from the river itself, it's the only line of transportation. They wouldn't dare try the open river in daylight. And they were moving overland when spotted yesterday. Unless we've already missed them, chances are they'll be along here in the next few hours."

He arranged his men in a long line on higher ground above the trail. The men covered themselves with green mosquito netting and settled down to wait.

Katie Nelson and her crew were at the meeting place on time, along with their three Vietnamese "guides." The three Americans had found that they were free to wander alone in the city so long as they had no video or sound equipment with them. When they were set to make tapes, they found themselves accompanied always by "guides" who appeared from nowhere to escort them to "suitable locations" or chased away certain individuals from them.

Jake and Roger took all this passively, being used to this kind of treatment all over the world, from Lebanon to Guatemala to Indonesia. But Katie was not going to stand for it.

"I want to film ordinary people eating their midday meal," she told one of the Viet guides, who all spoke a smattering of English. She pointed down a street of ramshackle houses. "Down there."

"No, no, madam," the Viet said. "Dirty, lazy people down there. I bring you nice place."

"There!" Katie insisted.

The wiry Viet, a few inches shorter than the pretty

THE POINT TEAM

American woman, eyed her for a moment and then spoke rapidly in Vietnamese to his two colleagues.

"You wait here," he said to the three Americans. "We find you a house to film in."

The three Viets went down the street a way, peering into houses as they went. Then all three entered one newly painted house.

The Americans were alone less than a minute when they heard a call. The voice came from a shady lane overhung by large-leafed, flowering trees. Katie pushed her way past some of the branches.

"Follow me," an American boy about thirteen told her. He was dressed in a Coca-Cola T-shirt, jeans, and sneakers.

"Eric," Katie called after him, "where are you taking us?"

"You'll see," he said shortly, and nodded to three other American boys his own age.

They brought up the rear behind Jake and Roger.

"Follow me," the youth repeated. It was a command.

They trailed him down the lane, turned into a rocky roadway lined with shacks, and then followed the bank of a filthy river that stank of sewage. Shacks and boats lined the muddy bank, and children played at the edge of the offal-strewn water among clouds of flies.

"You want to stop and film this?" the youth challenged Katie.

"No, Eric. This is poverty and ignorance. I don't have to come to Vietnam to shoot scenes like this."

Eric sneered. "I think maybe you're too friendly with the communists here to show something they mightn't like. Otherwise they'd never have let you, as an American, come here in the first place."

"I want to be fair," Katie said firmly. "Deliberately searching out a place like this is not fair. I could do that in any country."

"This isn't what I brought you to film," Eric told her.

"What I'm going to show you near here, you won't find in any old country."

Roger changed his video camera from one shoulder to the other, glad of the pause, and wiped the sweat from his forehead with a handkerchief.

"You speak real good English, all four of you," he said. "How do you manage that?"

One of the other boys pointed to Eric. "He makes us talk it all the time. The people who watch us talk Viet and French perfectly, but they don't understand our English when we talk fast and use slang."

"It's our badge," another said.

"They don't want us, so we show we don't need them," Eric summed up the conversation abruptly. "Let's go."

Eric set out along the riverbank again, beyond the last shack, along a path among rank eight-foot-high weeds and saplings. Katie followed him, then Roger, then Jake, with the three other boys behind them. Although they could see nothing because of the huge weeds, they smelled the river nearby.

The cameraman and sound man lugged their equipment through the midday heat uncomplainingly. As long as they weren't being shot at, they had nothing to gripe about. However, Katie Nelson had led a more pampered existence up till now in her TV career and was becoming increasingly agitated.

She suddenly froze. "I think I saw a snake! Over there! A large green one!"

"Leave it alone," Eric told her. "I got worse to show you than snakes."

Katie shuddered and obediently scampered past the reptile's lair.

Jake and Roger exchanged a look. They had no need to say to each other what they felt about this damn insolent kid dragging them around. Yet both felt amused that he was pulling such a number on Katie. Neither of them had managed so far to get the upper hand with her. They were *her* crew. She let them know that. Now here was this kid leading her into who knew what kind of shit... But Katie had a nose for a story. Maybe this would be one. They respected that, kept quiet, and trudged after her.

Eric, in the lead, held up his hand for them to stop and went ahead himself to investigate. He came back in a moment and waved for them to follow. Around a turn in the path the weeds began to thin so they could see the river again to their right. Ahead of them was a huge clearing in which stood a compound, seven or eight feet high, of bamboo stakes with sharpened tips. More than two hundred women sat on the bare earth within the compound, without shelter from the blazing sun. All had children. The oldest were two or three years old, and the youngest, a few months old, still being suckled at the breast.

Roger had already taken cover in a forward position among the weeds. He had no idea what the hell he was filming, but he knew a striking picture when he saw one. They could put words and sense to it later. He used his zoom lens for close-ups, panned across the sea of women and children, did retakes after making adjustments to the camera. Jake tried for sound. The women were raising an eerie, mournful keening, not outright wailing, but a sound very far from the chatter of women in a marketplace. Jake shook his head in disappointment to Katie and held up a meter.

"I need to get closer in," he said.

"What's going on here?" she asked Eric.

"What happened to me when I was three years old," the youth said. "My mother and I were separated. I never saw her again. She died in a reeducation camp."

"Will they take these women's children from them?" Eric nodded.

"But why?"

He shrugged. "They are judged by the state to be unfit as mothers to bring up communist children."

"That's inhuman!" Katie said.

"When the trucks arrive, you'll see it happen. We'll wait here." Eric glanced at his watch. "They'll be here in the next half hour."

Katie examined the thirteen-year-old carefully as they sat hidden in the weeds near the compound. She had met him the previous day on the street, and knew only his first name and that he was an orphan.

"Do you know where your father is?" she asked, phrasing her question more bluntly than she meant to.

Eric met her gaze angrily. "My father was married to my mother. I'm not a war bastard. Look at this." He fished out a sheet of paper from his pocket and handed it to her. "A letter from my father to my mother. It's a copy. You keep it. He's dead. He was a pilot."

Katie glanced at it without reading its contents. The letter was typed and signed by someone with the last name of Vanderhoven.

"You're Eric Vanderhoven?" she asked.

The youth nodded. "I hate it here. You got to get me out."

She smiled. "Is that why you came up to me on the street?"

He nodded. "I suppose you are a leftist. That's why you're here. Those are the only Westerners they let into Vietnam."

"I'm not anything political," Katie said vehemently. "I'm just interested in people."

"Sure," he said, with veiled sarcasm in his voice.

Katie turned on him angrily. "You know something? You're a kind of snotty unpleasant kid."

"This is a kind of unpleasant place. I have to survive. You want to make a real film? About how we live? What it's really like here when you have no foreign passport and no food?"

"I didn't come all this way just to put Vietnam down," Katie told him.

The youth looked at her with scorn on his face and

moved a little away so that she could no longer talk with him.

In a little while eight army trucks with canvas coverings bumped their way over the open ground and raised a cloud of red dust by the far side of the compound. Unarmed soldiers piled out of the vehicles and into the bamboo compound. They went to the nearest group of women and children and led the women to one truck and their children— even the babies, which they carried gently—to another. The women being separated from their offspring screamed, thrust out their arms, struggled, collapsed . . . It was no use. They were led, carried, or dragged to one of the trucks. When that truck was filled, it drove off, and the soldiers began to load another.

The women crowded into the compound backed away from the soldiers and protectively clutched their young ones to them. Their voices rose now in a high-pitched, continuous wail.

Jake was still having trouble picking up the sound on his equipment.

Roger returned from his forward position among the weeds and loaded a new video tape in his camera. "I need an unobstructed view of the trucks, but there's no way for me to get any closer without being seen."

"This sound quality is shit, Katie," Jake complained. "I got to take the mike in closer."

"There's no way you two can do that," she said. Jake and Roger were six-footers, and very, very conspicuous.

"I know how to work the camera," Eric volunteered, his sullenness suddenly evaporated. "Mitch and Red can do the sound if you show them how. They won't spot us. I guarantee it."

Roger and Jake's expressions showed their unwillingness to hand over their equipment.

"This is too good to miss," Katie pointed out. "You got to let them."

While they were making up their minds, there was a big

THE POINT TEAM

outburst near the trucks as women struggled with the soldiers. Roger and Jake knew they had to cover the news, no matter how. They handed over the camera and sound gear. After a brief lesson on what knobs and dials to turn, all four youths crept forward through the weeds around the edge of the clearing. The three Americans watched anxiously as the boys maneuvered into position and filmed the scene at the trucks.

Roger said, "They seem to be doing OK. But his camera movements are jerky, and he's zooming in and out too fast."

Katie grinned. "You're both afraid the kids' stuff will be better than yours."

Roger laughed. "So long as the union doesn't get to hear of this, I don't care."

They saw the boys creep forward, practically out into the open, as the soldiers lost their original patience and pushed, battered, and kicked the hysterical women. Some carried a baby, hanging by an arm or a leg, in each hand and tossed it for another soldier to catch inside a truck. They might have been loading heads of cabbage, for all the care they showed.

They saw Eric take the video camera off his shoulder and give it to the boy with him. He came back alone to the three Americans, stooping as he ran through the weeds.

"Bring back my camera!" Roger growled before Eric had a chance to say anything.

"Tomorrow at seven in the evening. Same place as we met you today."

"To hell with that!" Roger snarled and went forward.

The three boys had already disappeared with the camera and sound equipment.

"We'll make you a film that'll show you how we have to live," Eric promised with a sneer. "Not some pinko tourist crap like you would have shot."

He sneered at them once again and disappeared among the weeds.

THE POINT TEAM

* * *

Green mosquito netting concealed each of the still forms of Lt. Tranh Duc Pho and his fifteen men as they waited in a line on the jungle slope above the muddy river, nearly four hundred miles north of Ho Chi Minh City and fifteen miles inside Vietnam's border with Laos. They stared down from higher ground at what once had been part of the Ho Chi Minh Trail. Occasional Montagnard tribesmen passed by, then a group of Vietnamese peasants, then seven armed Montagnards with heavy backpacks—the lieutenant did not stop these smugglers since he had bigger game in mind. He and his men lay concealed in the jungle for four hours—fighting off the fierce tiny wildlife that bit and stung them even under the protection of the netting—before they saw what they had been waiting for.

Two Montagnards with American M16 rifles at the ready walked abreast along the path, scanning the forests to either side of them. They didn't spot the men hidden above them.

A minute behind them came the first of the bicycle bearers. Each bicycle was laden with goods wrapped in cloth. So much was tied to the frame of the machine that each bike looked like a bloated maggot with handlebars and wheels. The lieutenant counted thirty bicycles, each steered by a man walking alongside it. Twenty men walked beside the bicycles, unburdened except for their M16 or AK47 rifles. He knew there would be a rearguard of three or four more men. So he and his fifteen men would be up against at least twenty-five men with rifles, plus another thirty who probably carried pistols at least and perhaps could reach easily for a rifle in the baggage on the bicycles. There was only one way for him to do it.

As the Montagnards wheeled the laden bicycles along the path, the lieutenant's men sighted along their rifles and waited for the signal to fire. They were outnumbered but had the advantage of surprise. With bated breath, they held

THE POINT TEAM

their fire. The lieutenant would be the first to shoot. That would be their signal to let go with everything they had.

Tranh Duc Pho's rifle was on full automatic. He found the front sight's post in the notch of his rear sight, settled on one man's chest, pressed his finger on the trigger, and swept the gun barrel to the right. The thirty 7.62-mm rounds in the AK47's magazine emptied out of the muzzle in a matter of seconds. The first man collapsed like a wet paper bag, and those behind him were cut down before they knew what was happening as the gun barrel swung to the right. Two bicycles fell as the men sank in the hail of lead from this single rifle. Then the rest of the unit joined in.

Some of the Montagnards died as they raised their rifles in self-defense. Others were zapped in the back as they turned to run. Most of the rest were butchered as they cowered behind the laden bicycles or simply stood without moving, immobilized by shock.

The unit's fifteen AK47s sang out together like a crazed hive of killer bees before the lieutenant's burst of fire had finished. Their burst of fire was equally short, lasting just a few seconds before they had to replace the box-type magazines. The line of men wheeling the bicycles and their accompanying guards crumpled under fire. Their shouts of fear turned into screams of agony as the lead projectiles burrowed into their flesh and shattered their bones.

Seven Montagnards unaccountably remained standing, untouched by this sudden holocaust. They fled panic-stricken down the path, back the way they had come. The lieutenant had completed loading a fresh magazine into his rifle and sent a burst after them, bringing down the last two.

"Get after them," he yelled to his sergeant. "Take half the men and bring back at least one alive."

As they ran down the path after them, Tranh Duc Pho brought the rest of his men down to examine the dead and injured.

"Finish them off," the lieutenant ordered.

THE POINT TEAM

The men used handguns to deliver a single bullet to the forehead of each fallen man. They were well trained at this kind of thing and left nothing to chance.

"You want this one to talk, Lieutenant?" a soldier asked, dragging a Montagnard to his feet from beneath a bicycle. "He's wounded in the arm only."

Tranh Duc Pho answered, "Hold him till we catch one of those who got away."

In a short while the sergeant and his men came back with two of the escaped Montagnards walking in front of their guns with hands clasped behind their necks. The lieutenant indicated where the two men were to stand.

"Do you understand Vietnamese?" Tranh Duc Pho asked.

"I do."

"So do I."

Tranh Duc Pho turned to the man wounded in the arm. "And you?"

"Yes."

Pointing to the wounded man, the lieutenant said, "What's in that baggage tied to those bicycles?"

The man hesitated a moment and saw no reason for not parting with information which the lieutenant could easily get for himself simply by stooping and ripping the cloth covers.

"M16 rifles, M60 machine guns, and M79 grenade launchers," the man said. "There's ammunition for the rifles, not for the others."

"All American weapons," Tranh Duc Pho jeered.

The wounded man nodded.

"Where did they come from?" the lieutenant demanded.

"I suppose they were left behind by the Americans."

"For their Montagnard friends," the lieutenant continued in a jeering tone. "The Green Berets left them for you and you kept them hidden, even after we had liberated you from the imperialists and their puppets in colonial Saigon. I have only two questions for you, and you had better

THE POINT TEAM

answer them if you want to live. I know these weapons are going from one hill clan to another. Who sent them? Who was meant to get them?"

The wounded man remained silent.

The lieutenant nodded to the soldier guarding the man being questioned. He hit him with his fist on the blood-soaked part of his tunic sleeve. The man hardly reacted.

Tranh Duc Pho scowled. "He's in shock. He won't feel a thing. He's of no use to us."

The soldier guarding him drew his bayonet from its scabbard and sank it into his prisoner's side, a single deep thrust. He let the falling man's weight pull itself off the length of sharp steel. The man lay on his face on the ground, bleeding from the side into a great pool of blood, twitching and moaning.

The soldier wiped the bloody blade on the fallen man's shoulder, smiled, and said to the lieutenant, "I think he felt that, comrade."

"You," Tranh Duc Pho said, pointing to one of the two uninjured Montagnards. "You will feel more than he did. Where were the arms going? Who sent them?"

This man too remained silent.

The sergeant beckoned to two of his soldiers who had taken a large metal cooking pot from one of the bicycles and filled it with river water. The soldiers placed the pot in front of the Montagnard under questioning. They forced the man to kneel before the pot and glanced at the lieutenant for approval. He nodded to them. One soldier lightly hit the Montagnard in the solar plexus, causing him to expel his breath, and before he could refill his lungs with another breath of air, they forced his head into the pot of water.

They held his head under for a full minute as the man's arms and legs threshed in desperation. They pulled his head up, and he puked water and sucked air into his waterlogged lungs. His eyes were round with terror.

Keeping his face close to the river water in the cooking

THE POINT TEAM

pot, they let him partly recover. But he could see what faced him again if he refused to answer questions.

"Can you talk?" Tranh Duc Pho asked him.

The man said nothing.

The lieutenant kicked him with the toe of his boot in the ribs.

The prisoner yelped in pain. "Yes," he gasped, "I can talk."

"Good. Where were the arms going?"

Silence. The soldiers slowly lowered his face toward the water. They paused to give him a last chance. The man took a deep breath. They forced his head into the pot so that water slopped over its sides.

This time they kept him down for three minutes and pulled him out half drowned. He wouldn't speak. They kept repeating this until, during one immersion, the man's arms and legs went limp. They took their hands from his shoulders, letting him lie head first in the pot of water, and turned expectantly to the remaining live Montagnard.

"Will you answer my questions?" the lieutenant asked. "None of your clan will ever know. We will release you and you can say you escaped."

"I will tell you," the man said in bad Vietnamese.

"Where were the arms going to? What clan?"

The Montagnard named a tribe three days south of them.

The lieutenant's face twisted into a mask of rage. "Those are our friends. You taunt me."

He struck the Montagnard a sidewise swipe with the heel of his hand above the man's right cheekbone. The Montagnard's right eye popped out of its orbit and remained hanging there by its optic nerve and six muscle strips. The Montagnard stood at attention as if nothing had happened.

"Who sent the arms?" the lieutenant barked.

The Montagnard named a tribe friendly to the Vietnamese two days to the north.

"This one is having fun with us," Tranh Duc Pho said

THE POINT TEAM

through clenched teeth to his sergeant. "I want him to die slowly."

The lieutenant strode away. He could not afford to lose more face before his men.

Chapter 2

KATIE Nelson had no time even to recover from jet lag on her return to New York. There were the producers' questions to answer for her one-hour special on Vietnam, the tape editors' questions to answer, the voice-overs to record, the publicity and promo takes, talk shows—by the time the show aired, she was prostrated from exhaustion. The special was a big winner with an even higher audience share than anticipated, so that the network and sponsors were delighted. After it she went to Martha's Vineyard for a few days of peace and quiet, which as usual turned into a round of parties—she even put a couple of celebrity interviews on tape while she was there. Then back to New York City and the everyday pandemonium and chaos of TV newscasting.

Katie hated loose ends, and began to clean house after the project. She called her cameraman and sound man to thank them for the great job they had done on backup equipment after their best gear had been stolen, but Roger was already on assignment in South Africa and Jake in France. She carefully alphabetized and filed all documents she had, in case the authenticity of anything on the show was questioned later. These days a news reporter was expected to verify what he or she said if it was challenged. Katie was patient and methodical. She came across a battered photocopy of a typed letter.

Cher Eugénie,
My typing is godawful but you cant read my wriiting. Here in Okinawa on top secret meeting. Waste of time as usual I suppos. Damn machine. I can spell better than it can. Hope to see you in a couple of weeks or so, dear wife. In the meantime be careful of my son and heir (will it be a daughter? I wish I could run my fingers over your beautiful big tummy right now and feel the baby kicking. If it's a boy, we must call him Eric after my brother who drowned. I suppose you will want to give a girl a French name like your own. Id prefer her to have a real Vietnamese name. Think of the arguments we will have....
                                      Be careful, love.
                                               Frank

"Lt. Frank Vanderhoven, U.S. Air Force," Katie mumbled as she gazed at the top of the sheet of paper. "Vanderhoven... I wonder."

She put in a call to the network's library and in three minutes had a reply.

"Son of William V., shot down over Vietnam in late 1972, one of the last of the American flyers to be killed, had married into a wealthy Saigon family, fate of wife and son unknown. Need anything else, dear?"

"Please. The address and private phone number of William Vanderhoven."

Katie called the number she was given and was told curtly by a male voice that Mr. Vanderhoven did not give interviews to the media.

"Then we'll have to do a piece on his Amerasian grandson without giving him a chance to review it," Katie threatened. "You sure you want to take responsibility for that, Mr.—what's your name?"

"Boggs. K. V. Boggs. I will review the matter with Mr. Vanderhoven and contact you directly."

He hung up on her. She only smiled. She had slapped down the officious bastard. Old Vanderhoven would see her, she had no doubt of it. Not even a crusty old billionaire was beyond the reach of national TV if they found a chink in his armor.

One of the newscast backroom staffers filled her in on old William's bio. He was a real billionaire, who held the controlling majority of shares in the family's chemical and banking businesses. Known for his personal viciousness and lack of ethics in his business dealings, he had just divorced his seventh wife. She was twenty-six, he eighty-four. One son had been drowned in a boating accident at Princeton, and the other had been shot down over Vietnam. There were no known direct descendents apart from a grandson who had been left behind in Vietnam at the fall of Saigon. The old man was known to have made no will and to have energetically opposed anyone who presented himself as a possible successor in any of the family businesses. In fact, the old man's insistence on maintaining entire personal control caused a major drain of top executives who finally gave up hope of ever getting due recognition and took their skills and knowledge to rival firms. She didn't have a chance of talking with him. More important people than she had tried and failed.

Her office phone rang. Her assistant had just varnished her nails, so Katie picked up the phone herself.

"K. V. Boggs here. Mr. Vanderhoven has never heard of you or seen you on television, Ms. Nelson. I'm afraid I can't say the same for myself. I explained to him who you were. Will you be on the news this evening? You will? With what subject will you deal?"

"Tobacco smoking in public places."

"Oh dear," Boggs said with mock sympathy, "I'm afraid that will be a touchy subject."

The phone went dead.

Ten minutes later Boggs was on the line again. "Mr. Vanderhoven recognizes the freedom of the press and the media, I must stress that, Ms. Nelson. However, in your commentary this evening, he would appreciate it if you mentioned the fact that cigar smokers have civil rights, too."

Katie laughed, "Sure."

"It's no laughing matter with Mr. Vanderhoven, I assure you," Boggs' voice primly answered her. "He will expect you for dinner tonight. Please wear something suitable, Ms. Nelson. Will 8:15 sharp be suitable?"

"Sure."

"Be punctual."

The phone went dead again.

Perhaps old Vanderhoven had a heart of gold and needed a crud like K. V. Boggs to protect him from the world. Somehow she doubted that.

Katie decided not to change the blue dress she had worn for the newscast. The producer had given her flak for its neckline being too low, but old Vanderhoven would probably enjoy a glimpse of her boobs. He was eighty-four, so she hadn't much to worry about.

Her taxi dropped her at the canopy of the Fifth Avenue apartment building north of the Metropolitan Museum. A uniformed man opened her taxi door, and she paused a moment to listen to the breeze in the trees of Central Park across the avenue before she swept through the glass doors held open for her by other uniformed doormen. Two more assisted her to the elevator as another phoned upstairs about her arrival. The apartment door was opened by a severe-looking man in black tie.

"Mr. Boggs?" Katie said, and offered him her hand.

"Mr. Boggs has gone for the day, madam. I am Simmons. A servant." He had not taken her hand.

A little flustered, Katie was shown into a huge dark-paneled room with Old Master oils and a crystal chandelier. A fierce-looking old man with bulbous eyes and large white mustaches stood before blazing logs in a huge stone fireplace.

He had a drink in his hand and nodded to a sideboard of bottles and glasses. "Help yourself, girl."

Katie did. To a hefty Jack Daniels and two ice cubes.

"I met your grandson in Ho Chi Minh City." Katie always believed in strong opening lines.

"A little Marxist, I suppose, singing hymns to Lenin?"

"Quite the opposite, Mr. Vanderhoven. He hates it there and wants to get out."

"Every damn relative I have wants something. Sons die on me. Wives cheat and rob me."

Katie smiled "You might be luckier with grandchildren. A new generation."

The old man guffawed. "I liked what you said about cigars."

Katie was a bit nonplussed about this sudden change of subject, as well as the fact she had stated her belief that cigar smokers had no special rights in enclosed spaces with other people.

"I don't smoke," Vanderhoven added.

"I thought you smoked cigars," she said.

"You were meant to." He crossed the room and poured himself another drink. "Do you expect me to play Daddy Warbucks to this Orphan Eric from Vietnam? I think you have me miscast in your script, young lady."

His body was frail and his skin was wrinkled and discolored, but his movements were quick and his dark, piercing eyes were those of a young man. His eyes!

"You have the same arrogant, contemptuous expression in your eyes as your grandson, Mr. Vanderhoven. I could have told you were related by that appraising look you give a person."

The old man seemed genuinely interested. "If that's the case, the boy is a throwback. His father looked more like his mother. My second boy also. Cold English eyes. I'm from Dutch farming stock on Staten Island—almost next to the Vanderbilts. We were here when this was New Amsterdam!"

"I've never heard of the Dutch being known for burning, fierce eyes," Katie said.

"Burning? Fierce? Woman, you are flattering me."

"Only a little."

"Tell me about this grandson of mine while we eat."

She followed him into a dining room, where they sat at opposite ends of a long, narrow table with almost twenty feet of mahogany between them. Katie sloshed down wines and swallowed leek soup, snails, veal, asparagus spears—let herself go. She noticed that when she described Eric in a tear-jerking, sentimental way, the old man looked bored, and that when she called the youth boastful and overbearing, the old man laughed and said the kid sounded like a Vanderhoven. She kept Eric's theft of her video and sound equipment for a grand finale. Vanderhoven admitted to being mightily impressed.

"You know, Katie, I'll be damned if my collection of ex-wives are going to inherit my fortune. And they very well might if I don't make some provisions for it."

"I would be more than willing to go back to Vietnam and locate the boy for you, Mr. Vanderhoven."

"Very kind of you, Katie."

"In exchange for exclusive TV rights on the story. We'd need that in writing in advance."

"I'll think about it."

Katie decided not to overplay her hand and left soon after dinner.

As soon as she was out the door, the old man punched numbers on his phone. "Boggs? Who runs Vietnam these days? You don't know his name? Well, find out and get in touch with him."

Chapter 3

"MITCH, you fool, you've messed it up again!" Eric Vanderhoven turned in anger on the other boy beneath the heat radiated from the galvanized zinc roof of the bamboo hut in the compound of Les Pleiades. "Look, it's completely out of focus. You couldn't see their faces because of the shadows on the last take you did. What the hell's wrong with you?"

Mitch stared at the TV screen attached to the videotape player and twisted his mouth miserably. "I tried my best."

"Say 'I done my best!' You don't even speak good English." Eric gave him a push.

"I done my best," Mitch said contritely.

"It ain't good enough."

Mitch and Red exchanged a glance behind Eric's back. But they did no more than that. Even together they were no match for Eric, and each knew he would be readily betrayed by the other for just a nod of approval from Eric. The fourth boy had chickened out of the venture after Eric had received death threats over the videotape player. The smugglers had given them two days to pay. Now they swore they would kill Eric for cheating them.

"When we're finished with it, we'll sell it and give all

the money to them without taking our cut," Eric explained. "That will satisfy them. In the meantime we gotta be careful."

Things had not gone as smoothly or as quickly as they had thought. Even when they had filmed a sequence they were happy with, bad lighting or a poor shooting angle often made it impossible for a viewer to figure out what was going on. They did not have a videotape editing machine and would not have known what to do with it if they had. So Eric shot and reshot, bought more blank videotapes on the black market, and picked up skills by trial and error. In spite of all their mistakes, they were building up a documentary of life in Ho Chi Minh City which no Western journalist would ever be permitted to even become aware of.

"Listen," Eric would tell Red and Mitch, "we're not doing this just to entertain people in America. One of us is in most of these scenes. When the American public see how half-American, half-Viet kids have to live here—especially us three—they'll put pressure on Hanoi and we'll be rescued."

"How are we going to get these tapes to America?" Red asked.

"When we finish filming, we'll sell off the equipment and watch the hotels for Western reporters. Katie Nelson might even come back. I guess we owe them to her. Although I think she's kind of dumb. What she wanted was pictures of cute kids in funny straw hats planting rice with a big smile on their faces. You know, even in America they have dumb people—not just here. Anyway, we can't choose. Whoever we come across that we think we can depend on, we give him the tapes to get to America. We'll worry about that when the time comes. First, we gotta finish the tapes. Here, give me a hand putting this stuff away."

They lifted sections out of the earth floor of the hut. A few inches of earth covered a framework of wooden slats which covered a shallow hole excavated in the floor. They packed the videotape player and TV set in plastic bags and covered them. The camera and sound equipment were in another hole. Red unplugged the long cable that carried electricity from an outdoor outlet of the big house to the hut, wound it carefully, and stowed it in another hole.

Eric asked Red, "Are the others still working in the garden?"

Red nodded.

"You explain to each one of them what happens if they breathe a word about any of this?"

Red drew his finger across his throat. He was not smiling.

Mitch asked, "You still want to film something about the way we live in these huts?"

"Of course," Eric said. "Americans will be upset by that. They've never heard of people living in huts. They all have big houses with huge plate glass windows."

"What about the way they treat black people?" Mitch asked. "Hanging them in trees and not letting them live with whites."

"Do you believe that crap Hanoi puts out?" Eric asked incredulously. "That's propaganda. Everyone in America can do what he likes. He has a big car. A big house. Lots of dollars. If we three were in America, we would all have Cadillacs."

"I'd prefer a jeep," Red said.

"If that's what you wanted," Eric assured him.

"You mean we're thirteen years old and we could drive our own cars?" Mitch asked a little doubtfully. He suspected that Eric at times exaggerated a little when he was talking about America, but Eric talked with such authority that Mitch never quite had the courage to voice his doubts.

"In America you get your driver's license at twelve," Eric told him.

"Twelve!" Red repeated in awe. "Over there I could have been driving for a year by now!"

THE POINT TEAM

"Sure," Eric said. "You could pick up your telephone and call one of your girl friends and take her to a drive-in movie tonight with a case of beer in your Cadillac or jeep."

Mitch and Red looked at him, silenced and overawed by the possibilities of their lives in America. As Eric had explained, all they needed to do was complete these videotapes . . .

"Do you think we should take the chance?" Mitch asked on the way. "They'll be on the watch."

"No one will expect three kids to have video equipment," Eric answered. "They won't look at us twice."

"This is different," Mitch said. "Before this we've been filming local militiamen or Vietnamese Army soldiers harassing civilians. But these are Russians unloading a Russian ship. We don't even know what we're going to film."

"Grow up," Eric told him. "We got to face the fact that one military secret in our videotapes will get us more attention than a thousand bleeding-heart shots of kids living in huts and mothers being separated from their babies. We got no choice."

"I'm more scared of those smugglers who promised to kill you than I am of the Russians discovering us," Red said. "We'll be right in their territory down on the docks."

They pushed a homemade barrow constructed of odd pieces of lumber and two bicycle wheels. It was loaded to overflowing with vegetables from their garden.

As they neared the dock area, Eric went over his instructions again.

"Remember it's the Russian ship with all the odd-shaped crates that we want the best view of, including crates piled up on the dock. We'll need to shoot from several angles and make sure any lettering on the crates is photographed. The Soviet ship next to it seems to be unloading mainly pipes. We'll give them a quick look-over

THE POINT TEAM

with the camera, but it's all them odd-shaped crates that we got to concentrate on. You two just stand and watch them working and move the barrow along every now and then."

"We get it," Mitch said.

When they reached the dock area, in a deserted alley between two windowless warehouses, the three boys removed the vegetables from the barrow, exposing the video camera beneath. Eric climbed into the barrow, set the lens of the camera in one peephole, and looked out another peephole with the viewfinder.

"It ain't great," he said, "but I can hardly miss if you point the barrow directly at what we need to film."

The other two threw the vegetables in a mound on top of him and resumed their journey.

They could not read the Cyrillic characters on the stern of the Soviet ship, but the red flag with a hammer and sickle was identification enough. The wooden boxes were being unloaded over the side by derricks and slings. Teams of sweating stevedores freed the boxes on the dock and stacked them by hand.

"Look at the way it takes four men to lift even the smaller ones," Mitch said. "I bet there's rockets and such inside them."

"Nuclear warheads," Red suggested.

A voice rose from beneath the vegetables: "Shut up, you assholes, and get a move on."

At first they kept a distance away. Then they got bolder when no one paid any attention to them. Apart from one dock foreman who yelled at them to keep out of his crew's way, they could move about as they needed to get clear shots of the crates. When four Russian crewmen came up on deck and started down the gangplank, they pointed the barrow at them. A Vietnamese was with them, talking in Russian. The Russians were laughing, and one was so unsteady on his feet he nearly fell off the gangplank. His comrades caught him, and this made them laugh even louder. One of them pointed to the barrow.

Red and Mitch started to wheel it away fast. They ignored the shouts of the Viet who was with the Russians. The man was anxious to please the foreigners and ran after them.

He said in Vietnamese, "They won't steal your vegetables. They'll give you a good price for them."

One of the crewmen said something in Russian.

The interpreter translated it for them into Vietnamese. "They've been at sea for weeks and want to buy everything you have for the ship's kitchen. They'll pay you well."

"No," Mitch said. "We have to deliver them to an important party function. The cadres will be annoyed if they don't get them."

The drunken Russian sailor almost toppled over the barrow as he grabbed an armful of vegetables. Then he started singing and grabbed a huge double armful out of the barrow. Eric looked up at them from the bottom of the barrow with a bright smile on his face and tried to cover the video camera with his body.

The three youths stood before an elderly man sitting at a table. He was their judge at the District Action Committee Against Youthful Delayers of Socialist Progress. Their prosecutor was an energetic young man whose eyes seemed to sparkle eagerly behind his glasses. The judge was tired and weary by comparison.

"Is there any evidence to show that the American television crew hired these youths to film antisocialist lies?" the judge asked the prosecutor.

"No. They seem to have stolen the equipment and done this on their own."

The judge nodded. "Have they shown any understanding of how their actions run counter to the people's wishes?"

"They show no repentance for their crimes or even much understanding of the new order of society that is everywhere springing up with such abundant energy. Particularly the middle boy, Eric Vanderhoven..."

The prosecutor made a mess of the pronunciation of the Western name.

The judge interrupted, "Why hasn't he been given a Vietnamese name?"

The prosecutor consulted his papers. "It appears that this is his legal name. He refused to change it. He's the one who insists, despite our records of his birth in this city, that he is a CIA agent who parachuted last year into the Mekong Delta."

A flicker of amusement crossed the judge's wrinkled face. "I think we might give our young CIA man an opportunity to get to see Vietnam close up, so to speak. Perhaps a season of work in the rice fields would make it clear to him and his two friends here what it means to be patriots in a workers' republic." He looked at the three severely. "Have you anything to say for yourselves?"

Mitch and Red were silent.

Eric ground out, "Better watch out how you treat me. I'm a personal friend of President Reagan."

Chapter 4

THE trailer camp was an oasis in the dusty, scrubby Arizona landscape. Folks watered miniature lawns in front of their mobile homes. You could tell how long people had lived in the park by how pretty and settled their little gardens looked. They planted shrubs to remind them of back home. This made some others mad. They claimed they had come out here to the clear desert air to get away from pollen and allergies, and now these clowns were spoiling everything for them. Those who liked the shrubs that reminded them of back home saw no reason to plant prickly pears in their lawns because of some invalid's psychosomatic hang-ups.

Michael Campbell was not involved in this dispute, since all he did was throw empty bottles and cans in front of his trailer and kill plant growth by urinating on it in the middle of the night. His girl friend Tina always cleaned up after him the next day, and no one complained too much since word got round about him practicing out in the desert with a machine gun. More than one person said that they could "feel" enormous reserves of violence in Campbell. And he was definitely peculiar.

A tall, lean man, tanned, lined, and scarred, restless,

maybe in his late thirties, but it was hard to be certain—he could be in his early forties—gray eyes, calm, helpful. Friendly, except for going off and sitting on a rock for hours or walking off into the desert in the midday sun. Or he might read for days. Or live on yogurt and do exercises for a week.

The occasional booze-ups and empty bottles were a lot less alarming to his neighbors than these less familiar pursuits. It was recognized that his eccentricities were in some way linked to his days as a Green Beret in Vietnam. Everybody in the trailer park had seen TV shows about how Vietnam vets suddenly hop up and slay everyone around them because of a sudden delusion these easy-going Americans are Cong attackers. More than a few in the camp mentioned the possibility that they all might fall victim to Campbell in some evil way.

When word of this got back to Mike, he laughed and said to Tina, "If only they could sometimes look into my head, they'd hitch up their damn trailers and move on."

Tina was small, dark, and shapely. She lapsed easily into Spanish when excited or annoyed; mostly she was cheerful and busy and apparently unaware of Campbell's moods and doings. When Campbell disappeared for months on end, as he did occasionally, she never betrayed the least anxiety and assured those who asked that he'd be back soon, just as casually as if he'd driven into town for the afternoon.

The residents of the trailer park had their own sinister interpretations of his absences. For the most part, they were retired people who now looked back with fear and suspicion at the world from which they had been superannuated. For once, this kind of lurid gossip fell far short of the bloody actuality of Campbell's doings while he was away. The park residents' imagination did not go much beyond trucking marijuana and illegal aliens across the border or being a hit man for a New York "family." Most of them would never have heard of the countries which employed Campbell for his very special talents. The problems of Namibia, Costa Rica, Bahrein, or the Sudan were not everyday conversation topics in this Arizona trailer park.

But now Campbell had been home for many months and was growing restless. His treks across the desert became more numerous, his fitness regimens came and went more often, he was seen practicing his marksmanship with a variety of weapons—including throwing a knife against the side of his trailer one morning... He was primed and ready to move. With nowhere to go.

Campbell's tossing and turning in his sleep had woken Tina. Once awake, she had not been able to go back to sleep again. She climbed out of the bed, over his sleeping form, and flicked on a reading lamp in the dining area. Settled in an easy chair and puffing on a Vantage, she turned the pages of *People* magazine. Outside, the lights of the trailer park shone on empty cars and patches of grass. A few places had left a string of lights burning along the edge of a canopy. She tapped her cigarette ash into a white cup with a blue castle and the words *Walt Disney World*. She looked up when Campbell moaned and thrashed about on the bed. He steadfastly refused to see anyone about these dreams. Like going to a shrink. There was nothing more she could do about it, except put up with them. Like he did.

Col. Michael Campbell, known as "Mad Mike" to his men in the Special Forces, looked at the sergeant. "What's wrong with Green?"

Sgt. Harper responded, "You know what they be saying about the lieutenant?"

Campbell grinned. "That the NVA haven't read the same military textbooks as him?"

"I'm just repeating hearsay, sir. I wouldn't bad-mouth an officer."

"No, but you might frag the bastard if you thought he was going to have you all killed. You saying that this is one for you and me and leave the kids at home?"

The sergeant nodded.

"You got it," the colonel said. "How many men can you raise?"

"Nineteen, including me."

"Call the choppers."

They went airborne in two Chinook gunships which would give them air-to-ground support after they were landed.

"We got one green smoke, sir," the pilot of Campbell's chopper said, "but it'll be nearly an hour old when we get there. The flare will be dead, but I know the place without it. Maybe when they saw no response right away, they relaxed again."

"Or maybe they've had time to arrange a welcome for us," Campbell said.

"We got a hundred-plus North Vietnamese regulars according to the sighting," Sgt. Harper clarified.

"Too far for artillery to be accurate," Campbell growled.

"Yeah, sir, at this distance they got as much chance of hitting us as them, even with exact coordinates."

"Mortar teams, Sergeant?"

The sergeant looked at the colonel. "They been called in, sir."

Both knew this was a bullshit conversation—that twenty Green Berets were going into the jungle after a hundred or more North Vietnamese army trained men. These were no farmers-by-day and guerrillas-by-night Cong. They would be combat-hardened troops fighting for their lives. And a hundred-plus could mean a thousand! The mortar teams would not be in time. The helicopter gunships would have to pull away under ground fire. They would be on the ground by themselves. Which of course was why Sgt. Harper wanted Campbell along in the first place instead of an inexperienced lieutenant. The fact that the colonel always volunteered to go on this kind of mission was part of the reason he was called Mad Mike. The rest of the reason was how he behaved in actual combat.

"Landing zone is that clearing at two o'clock," the pilot radioed to the other one. "I'll go in first while you cover me."

The chopper lurched and lost altitude fast. They went down into the clearing, the men tumbled out on the ground, and the Chinook was lifting off again in seconds with the gunner anxiously searching the treetops through the open side door. Nothing. Either the NVA had moved on or the landing had taken them by surprise.

The second chopper went in fast also, but came under fire from a machine gun a couple of hundred meters southeast of the clearing. The bullets ripped a few holes in the fuselage without causing serious damage. The men jumped out, and the machine took off northward from the clearing and drew no further fire.

The nineteen men now lay in the cover of knee-high grass at the edge of the trees. The helicopters were circling about trying to locate the machine gun to fire a rocket at it. The NVA were not wasting ammunition on them.

"All right, Sergeant," Col. Campbell said, "at least some of them are southeast of this clearing. Wanna go see?"

The sergeant designated a man to stand point in a five-man scouting party and sent them ahead of the main group. The men spread out in a single file with about twenty yards separating them and slowly worked their way forward through the trees a little way in from the perimeter of the clearing. These were all experienced men and needed no last-minute exhortations or warnings.

The NVA would guess that the landing party would not stay put on any account, Campbell thought as he made his way, but they could not tell on which side of the clearing they might approach or whether they would head off in some other direction. On their part, they would know that

THE POINT TEAM

he, Campbell, had no idea or only the sketchiest notion of their deployment and numbers. Campbell was fairly sure of just one thing. Their strength and intentions would be tested by the enemy fairly soon. Like any moment now.

As they moved, they searched the trees for snipers, scanned the ground for trip wires and sharpened sticks, peered through the undergrowth ahead and on the side for shadowy forms, glanced back over their shoulders to make sure the man behind had not died silently... They clutched their M16s in sweaty palms, the selectors switched to full automatic. Frayed nerves had cut their reaction time down to almost zero. At that moment, anything moving in the forest and not instantly recognizable would have bought it in a big way with at least ten pounds of lead.

The man at point dropped to the ground, and those behind him broke for cover. In a few minutes, the man at point crawled back, and the colonel and sergeant crawled forward to meet him.

"They haven't seen us," the soldier said.

"How many of them?" Campbell asked.

"Five. And same as us, they're spread in a file, about a hundred yards front to back. Coming right at us."

"Are they coming fast?" Campbell asked.

"No. They're on tiptoe. Scared as shit. We got three or four minutes."

"We got to take 'em, sir," the sergeant said. "We need the room to move."

"Take charge, Harper." The colonel pulled his machete from its scabbard and crawled rapidly forward with the point man.

As he passed each of the forward men, he gestured to his machete and whispered, "Let 'em all come through. I make the first move."

Campbell brought the point man with him to the advance position in case, as he said, "There's more than five of them."

There were no birds or animals in the midday forest heat

to give away their hidden presence. The men simply lay in the silence, waiting, making neither sound nor movement.

The North Vietnamese army scouts came into view, taking one step at a time, looking around them, skittery as deer in the hunting season. Campbell could see the taut face and neck muscles of their man at point. His eyes darted here and there beneath his peaked cloth cap, and he held his AK47 in one hand for a moment as he beckoned the others to follow him. After only a few paces, he paused to listen. He probably figured that since Americans were big and noisy, if he couldn't hear them they weren't there.

He passed only fifteen feet away from Campbell. Another man in the colonel's position would have sworn he'd be visible to the North Vietnamese, but Campbell knew better. As long as he made no movement, his camouflaged fatigues broke up his outline enough to let him merge into the background. The NVA regular passed him and the American point man, passed the next man, and moved on, watching and listening, listening...

Those following forged ahead more confidently than their leader, reassured that when the shit hit the fan their point man would be the first to go—they would have a chance to duck, shoot, or run.

The fifth man approached Campbell. The colonel's long, lean body suddenly extended up out of the undergrowth like the deadly strike of a pit viper. Campbell swung the machete as he came, and the bright steel curved in an arc and whacked into the soldier's skull with the sound of an ax sinking into a log. The only other sound was the rattle of the man's equipment as he fell.

Swift, silent, and lethal, the other Green Berets nailed their victims seconds after the colonel disposed of his. Except one man. Campbell looked back at the sound of the struggle. The North Vietnamese soldier had fended off the blow of the machete with his AK47 rifle. When the American tried to raise the machete blade for a second blow, he found it embedded in the wood stock of the rifle. As they struggled, the North Viet fell backward, with the American on top of him. The Green Beret released his hold on the machete, gripped the AK47 at either end, and forced it down across the throat of his opponent.

The North Viet tried desperately to push the rifle up but could not. As the weapon pressed firmly down, constricting the man's windpipe, he clawed wildly at his attacker's eyes. He only succeeded in scratching his face before his own death throes canceled out his counterattack. His eyes protruded and his tongue stuck out as his body convulsed, and he made an inhuman croak in an unsuccessful attempt to suck in air.

Campbell stood over the dying man and said to the Green Beret killing him, "You call this a professional job?"

The Green Beret glanced up without releasing pressure on the rifle. "No, sir. Sorry about that." And returned to finishing him off.

They left the five bodies half-concealed by the undergrowth and pushed on again in the direction from which the machine gun had fired at the chopper. As before, the five-man scouting party preceded the main group. Progress was slow—however, no one criticized that, since one oversight or mistake made in a moment of eagerness or bravado could cost the lives of all twenty Special Forces operatives there on the ground. The only reason all these men were alive and fit to walk around was that they weighed all the chances before they took them, and paused for a second look before jumping in.

Campbell's strategy was simple yet effective and familiar to all the men. They had to locate the main body of North Vietnamese troops, engage them from a distance, and call in the gunships to soften them up with rocket and machine-gun fire. Then the Special Forces would overrun their position, wipe out as many as they could, and head back to the clearing fast to be evacuated. When such hit-and-run tactics worked, they were devastating to the enemy. When something went wrong, it was usually a big disaster for the attacking force.

The Viet Cong would have faded into the forest and would not have stayed to fight it out. But the North Vietnamese army regulars had more men, better weapons, and a different style of fighting than the Cong. Campbell knew they would never have sent a scouting party against him if they had intended to run. They meant to fight. He listened. Nothing. Both sides were maintaining a radio silence. They had disposed of the five enemy soldiers without a shot being fired to warn the main body of North Vietnamese. They now had some room to move in.

"We'll keep moving in a straight line," he whispered to the sergeant. "If they spot us and we don't see them, they'll probably cut around behind us to take possession of the clearing so we can't be lifted out by air. With the clearing as a landmark, the airstrikes will be easy."

The sergeant said nothing. He knew that if the North Viets were all that predictable, the colonel wouldn't be bothering to explain things to him. An officer, even one like Mad Mike, never bothered to justify his actions if he thought everything was going to be easy.

They moved on slowly through the forest, every man watching the man in front of him, glancing back at the one behind, peering into the green depths at something that might have moved, avoiding a small mound of leaves that might conceal an antipersonnel mine... A gunship passed overhead and was gone—they could hear it circle in the distance. Their footfalls in the dead leaves were strangely loud, and all about him Campbell felt the huge, alien, hostile world of Asia in the heat, the leaves, the unknown...

The man at point raised a hand for those behind him to stop. Then he suddenly wheeled about and ran wildly back through the trees! The other scouts zigzagged through the growth right after him. There could be no doubt they had been seen and were getting their asses out of there as fast as possible. The sergeant called up the men behind him so that the long line of men now formed into a knot of solid resistance.

Right behind the escaping men came a horde of NVAs in full charge, bayonets fixed to their AK47s. Their officer had obviously spotted only a few of the Americans and had wanted to take them out silently so as not to warn the others. Campbell waited till the last of the five forward men got back to them and opened up on the NVAs who were now no more than thirty yards away. Other Green Berets opened up with their automatic rifles and grease guns, and the first few rows of North Vietnamese were almost sawed in half by the Special Forces fire power.

"Hell! There's got to be sixty, seventy of 'em!" the sergeant howled as the NVAs kept coming in a solid wave, many of them firing now from their AK47s, but still intent on skewering the Americans with their bayonets.

Campbell pushed a fresh magazine into his M16 and sprayed it into the chests of the oncoming troops. Men fell, but the rest came jumping over them, eyes wild, their bayonets like a mouth of shark's teeth. Campbell changed magazines again as they were almost within touching distance of him. He pulled on the trigger. Nothing happened. His M16 had jammed. He dropped the rifle and hauled out his machete.

He swung it two-handed in a circle over his head, gave a loud yell, and came at the NVAs.

When Campbell came to, he picked himself off the ground and looked about him.

Tina was looking up from her magazine at him, blowing cigarette smoke out her nostrils.

"You fell out of bed," she said. "Which dream was it this time?"

"Bayonet charge," he answered.

She smiled sympathetically. "Get yourself a beer and sit down with me."

He took a bottle of Dos Equis from the refrigerator, bit the metal cap off with his teeth, and swallowed half the contents. He put the bottle on the table.

"Guess I woke you earlier on, kicking and shoving?" he asked.

"You got it, Colonel."

"Sorry."

He kissed her on the cheek and ran his palms over her bare shoulders, looking down at her breasts beneath the fabric of her loose-fitting nightdress. She put down the magazine she had been reading, clasped his wrists, and guided his hands down over the smooth, warm orbs whose nipples hardened to his touch.

He kissed her for a while and then reached down to lift her effortlessly and carry her to the bed. He exorcised the demons from his mind in the pleasure and beauty of her body.

Chapter 5

"A long distance call, sir," the manservant told William Vanderhoven. "It's Mr. Boggs, from Switzerland."

The manservant placed a telephone on the side table beside the old billionaire, lifted the receiver, pressed the lighted extension button, and said, "Mr. Vanderhoven will speak to you now."

He wiped the ear- and mouthpieces with a white linen cloth before handing his boss the receiver.

"Boggs, where the hell are you?"

"In Bern, sir. That certain party has refused all direct contact. All communications have to be through the Swiss."

"I remember. I'm not senile yet, Boggs."

"No, sir. Of course not."

"Well?"

"Not good news, sir."

"Stop shilly-shallying! Give me the details, man!"

"Certainly, sir." Boggs paused before doing so. "The particular party I've been referring to refuses to cooperate on two grounds. The first is the attitude of the subject—"

"Boggs, talk straight! You mean Eric?"

"I'm worried about security over the phone lines, sir."

THE POINT TEAM

"To hell with security. What's wrong with Eric's attitude?"

"They say he is unrepentant for his crimes against Marxism and he did something else against Leninism—I couldn't quite follow the ideology involved. When you listen to all the intellectual crimes with which he is accused, it's hard to realize he's only a thirteen-year-old."

"That's their style, Boggs. What's the second ground for their refusal?"

"Eh—eh, you, sir."

"Me!"

"They claim your companies made napalm and other war-related substances which were used against them by the U.S. Armed Forces."

"So?"

"Before they are willing to consider Eric's release, they insist that you make a public apology to them for this and make financial reparations to the present communist government."

Boggs waited and heard only a sputtering noise. He added quickly, "I'll tell the intermediary, sir, that you will not tolerate such impertinence."

"Be sure you do, Boggs."

Boggs felt relieved by the cold, grating tone in Vanderhoven's voice, which told him the old man had regained control of himself. "Might I make a suggestion, sir?"

"Go ahead."

"I think it's a waste of time trying to deal with these Vietnamese communists, sir, especially here. Perhaps I would do better than before if I return to Washington, though I have my doubts."

"That's a waste of time, Boggs."

"Yes, sir. That's what I think, too. Which is why I checked into a possible backup—an alternative, so to speak—"

"Get to the point, Boggs."

50

"Yes, sir. I meant sending in a group of your own, sir, if you get my meaning."

"What the hell are you talking about, man?"

"I've left an envelope marked 'alternative' on the top shelf of the wall safe, sir. You will find all the details there."

"Come back to New York without delay, Boggs."

"Yes, sir."

Mike Campbell peered out of the plane window as the aircraft veered around the end of Manhattan. The twin towers of the World Trade Center were off by themselves a little away from the rest of the Wall Street skyscrapers. A foggy haze hung over the middle of the island, just above the midtown group of tall buildings—the Empire State Building and the Chrysler were still the most individual and recognizable among all their younger neighbors.

The elderly woman in the window seat commented wistfully, "It all looks so orderly and peaceful from up here."

"That's the view from heaven, ma'am."

She sighed. "I think you may be right. There's times when I think the Good Lord just can't be aware of what's going on."

Since Campbell had already heard of her daughter's second failed marriage and her son's lack of attention to her, he didn't need a dissertation from her on street crime. He got one anyway. Her energy and indignation, all the way from Phoenix to New York on an early morning flight, amazed him. For some reason Campbell could never fathom, people unloaded their worries on him in planes, in buses, on park benches—even at the trailer park, where they daily expected him to run amok and make coyote food of them all, individuals would come up to him from time to time and unfurl some sad tale without an ending.

The plane flew north in a line directly above Fifth

Avenue and then swung east over where the Harlem and the East Rivers separated Manhattan, the Bronx, and Long Island. They touched down at La Guardia Airport on Long Island Sound. Mr. Vanderhoven's limousine was waiting.

Campbell was ushered into the study of the huge Fifth Avenue apartment.

"Colonel Campbell," William Vanderhoven said by way of greeting, and shook his hand.

"I'm retired," Campbell said. "People don't call me by my rank anymore, except by way of a joke."

"I see. What is it they call you now—yes, I remember. Mad Mike. Do they call you that to your face?"

"No."

"But you are popularly known as that by your . . . associates?"

"I suppose so." Mike grinned, completely unfazed by the hard time the old man was giving him. "I just can't think what I've ever done to earn a name like that."

"Let us say you wouldn't be here today if you didn't have your name and reputation. Mad Mike. Indeed. I like that. Know what they call me? The Old Bastard. My name is William—but no one has ever called me Wild Bill or Crazy Willie. Just the Old Bastard. Mad Mike is much better than that, don't you think?"

Mike laughed at the old man's poker-faced brand of humor. He could easily imagine this man's employees putting a lot of feeling into it when they called him the Old Bastard.

Then Vanderhoven tried to sound him out on his views on Namibia.

"If I was into making bets on political stability for business ventures, I'd be sitting in a glass-walled office somewhere," Mike told him. "I'm a soldier. I deal with the present. A soldier can't heal the past or foresee the future. He's like a repair man. He tries to fix something that's not working right. What the other people do with it the next day is something he doesn't control so long as he remains a soldier and stays out of politics. And out of business."

The crusty old billionaire obviously didn't like to be told what Mike was and was not going to discuss. His mouth tightened and his manner became cold. Mike watched this drama with detached amusement. He could imagine how this sudden change of mood in the old man would cause one of his employees to quake after saying something that displeased him. Mike never gave a shit for generals when he was in the armed forces, and right now he didn't need money so bad that he had to give a damn about the moods of a wealthy old carpetbagger who wouldn't even be talking to him if he didn't need to hire him for some dirty work. The Old Bastard sure as hell wasn't hiring him to play polo or race a yacht to the Bahamas. Mike was determined to betray no curiosity about what Vanderhoven had in mind and had received no clue yet as to what his mission might be. His five-thousand-dollar consultant's fee, whether he took the job or not, was enough to persuade him to take a short trip to New York, all expenses paid.

"I understand that you have pursued a military career of sorts since you left the Special Forces."

"I've been a mercenary, soldier of fortune, call it what you will."

"Where?"

"Africa, the Middle East, Central America—I'd prefer not to get too specific."

"I understand," Vanderhoven said. "How long were you in the Special Forces in Vietnam?"

"Four years. Not all in Vietnam, of course. There were forays into Laos and Cambodia."

"I'm sure you don't want to be too specific about that, either. Have you been back in Southeast Asia since the war ended?"

"No."

"Care to go back?" the old man asked casually.

Mike hesitated. "I imagined you had something in Africa for me..."

"You are avoiding my question."

Campbell shrugged. "I'd have to give it serious consideration."

"Good. I'm pleased to hear that. Because I don't want any gung-ho amateurs or reckless heroes in my affairs. What I tell you now I expect you to keep confidential even if you are not interested. Agreed?"

"Agreed."

Vanderhoven began to speak in a dry neutral voice. "I have a grandson in Vietnam..." He told Mike the whole story in as few words as possible and without emotion until he summed up his narrative by saying, "These totalitarians demand that we *both* apologize. Vanderhovens apologize! I hadn't realized I'd treated the boy unjustly—I'd never considered him a *real* Vanderhoven—until Katie Nelson described his attitudes to me and then my assistant Boggs confirmed the fact that the boy is standing up alone—at the age of thirteen—to these... these inhuman communist robots. I want him out, Campbell! I want you to go in there and bring him out! I don't care how you do it, and I don't care how much money it costs. Understand? Bring him out, and I'll leave him every penny I possess."

The force and passion in the octogenarian's voice took Campbell by surprise. He said, "People you suddenly develop an affection for after not noticing for years may not live up to your great expectations."

"I am used to people falling short of my expectations, Campbell," Vanderhoven said in a flat, ironic voice.

"You're certain that this boy Eric wants to come? That it will be a rescue, not a kidnapping?"

"I'm absolutely certain."

Mike shifted in his chair. "If money's no object, I can bring a team into Vietnam for you and bring the boy out again. The part I'm not happy about is making contact with him. A unit of heavily armed Westerners can't wander about looking for an American youth. There's no tourist trade, so we can't wander about with cameras and Bermuda shorts, either."

"Katie Nelson is more than willing to return to Vietnam. I understand the communists were very pleased with her American TV program and will let her back in anytime she pleases."

Campbell shook his head. "The media will blow the whole thing. They'll put us on the seven o'clock news while we're still behind enemy lines and announce to the world exactly what we're doing and where we're going. Forget her."

"She knows the boy, Campbell. And she can move inside Vietnam with much more freedom than you can. You can't do without her help. Plus she demands the exclusive TV news rights to your escape story in exchange for her cooperation."

Mike laughed. "You can't be serious! Not only do you want us to go into the middle of communist goddamn Vietnam and grab one of their citizens, who happens to be a minor and may not want to come for all I know—not only all that, now you want me to take along a TV crew to cover the action. What do we do, pause for commercial breaks? Coming to you live from Vietnam, via satellite, Mad Mike Campbell abducts a rich American's grandson from under the very nose of Russia's puppets in Hanoi. Our own Katie Nelson is providing a live commentary, and we'll be back with Mad Mike after this word from Budweiser . . ."

"It's very possible that Miss Nelson has such a scenario planned," Vanderhoven replied. "However, I'll leave it up to you to make arrangements with her. I recommend that you promise her whatever she wants. What you actually deliver would be your concern. I don't care."

"Money?"

"What will you need?"

"For me alone, one million."

"I see." Vanderhoven paused. His face was expressionless. "Very well. The full amount if you succeed, half if you fail."

"OK. I'll also need a hundred thousand each for five men, plus another half million in expenses. That will include weapons, training, transportation, bribes, the lot. This kid will cost you a total of two million."

"Each of my seven wives has cost me twice that."

"Eric is all you have left?"

"Right. One of my boys was drowned while still at school. The other, later Eric's father, I tried to keep in school and out of the war with a student deferment. He was having none of that, particularly because the peace demonstrators had already begun to picket our factory that made napalm. I got him nominated to the U.S. Air Force Academy out in Colorado Springs. He was delighted— never saw that I was sticking him in school for four years anyway. He came out of there a second lieutenant four years later and the damn war still hadn't finished. He was out there less than a year when his plane was shot down south of the DMZ."

"Missing in action?"

Vanderhoven shook his head sadly. "Not even that hope. No, they found his body. He's buried in Arlington."

"So are a lot of good men."

"My son was a better human being than I am, Campbell. Seems as though my mean personality must have skipped his generation and been inherited by this young fellow, Eric. You think that's possible?"

"I couldn't say, sir. When I bring him back, you'll find out for yourself."

The old man brightened. "You'll go then? We've got a deal?"

"A million dollars up front. I run everything, you ask no questions."

Vanderhoven offered him his hand and over their handshake gave him a crafty, jeering look. "Good luck, Mad Mike."

"Thank you, Old Bastard."

"You've put on weight, Harper."

"I'm fit as you any day, Mike."

They threw a few playful punches at each other, and the burly black man in a well-tailored business suit gestured to a cream and chocolate-brown Lincoln pulled up near the airport entrance.

"Come on, before I get towed away," he said to Mike.

On the drive across Detroit along the Edsel Ford Freeway, Harper began to sound Campbell out. "You know I ain't going to help some jive-ass white farmers in Africa because they claim the Zulus is communist."

"This is nothing like that."

"Better not be. Now that time we was in South America. That was OK."

Campbell laughed. "That's not what I remember you saying while we were there."

"You're right. We were lucky to escape out of there alive."

That mission had been the only one on which Campbell had persuaded his former sergeant in the Special Forces to go along as a merc. Harper could not be persuaded to go near the continent of Africa with a white mercenary group under any circumstances, although several other black soldiers who had served with them both in Southeast Asia had gone along.

Campbell gave him a quick rundown of the mission, omitting all names and actual locations within Vietnam. If Harper agreed to go, it would cut his work in half. Had he thought it would make any difference, he would have offered him a higher cut than the hundred thou. But Harper was already a millionaire—the only one of the old unit who had hit it big moneywise after returning home. Campbell waited for his answer.

THE POINT TEAM

"I want you to see my latest place," Harper said, pulling the Continental onto an exit ramp from the freeway. "Just opened it a couple of months ago."

"How many does this make?"

"Eleven."

"Not bad," Campbell said admiringly.

The Continental pulled into the parking lot of a large, spread-out, single-story restaurant.

"Same formula as the others, except this one's much bigger," Harper explained. "Family places, reasonable prices, nothing real fancy, not expensive—just real American food that hasn't been frozen or kept in a can for a year."

They were well into their meal before Harper announced that he would go on the mission. They discussed the other possible members, all of whom had served with them in the Green Berets and had been along on one or more of Campbell's later merc missions. The men were given an order of preference—the first four available would go. Harper would take care of this. Campbell would come back to Detroit again in a week and they would finalize a timetable together.

Harper looked about his big, thriving restaurant as if he were seeing it for the first time. "I got a wife. I got kids. I got this. Yet I agree to go back to Nam with you. That's crazy."

"Probably."

On their way back to the airport along the freeway, Campbell kept glancing back over his shoulder. He said finally, "We're being followed."

"Mike, you're getting uptight. I been watching you just now. You were eyeballing that blue Regal that left two exits ago. Now you think it's that tan Plymouth. Right?"

"Damn right," Campbell said. "And I bet the Plymouth peels off a few exits from now and we'll have something else on our tail."

Harper laughed at this but kept a wary eye in his

rearview mirror. The Plymouth left the freeway as Mike had predicted. It could have been replaced by any of three cars behind them, none of which followed them into the airport turnoff.

Campbell shrugged.

"This is Motor City, Mike," Harper joshed. "Don't get paranoid about cars in this place."

"I wasn't paranoid on my way here. I was sure I wasn't being followed. What worries me is that the guy who's backing this mission told me he first tried to get action in Washington and then in Switzerland. That would have put them onto him. I knew none of this when I went to see him. We'd have done it differently if I had. So someone saw me, maybe."

"Maybe not," Harper put in.

"My imagination."

Three days later Campbell, back at the trailer park in Arizona, got a phone call from Harper.

"I got a phone call from the Internal Revenue Service yesterday afternoon," Harper said. "When I called them back this morning, a dude said they *might* want to discuss my last seven years of finances with me. Said they were looking into the situation. He'd let me know. Next I get a call from Washington. Fella says he wants to fly up to review my hiring practices—equal opportunities for women, how many blacks, whites—he wants to know how many people of Asian background I employ; I thought he kind of leaned on that one a little. Why the hell would a black man serving Middle Western food in Detroit hire Asians? Yeah, you got it. The state and city health departments may recheck my places, I've heard from the city fire department—and this is all in one day!"

"And the others?" Campbell asked.

"All four have heard from the IRS yesterday or today. Also, Nicholls heard from his parole officer, although he's not on parole anymore."

THE POINT TEAM

Campbell knew that Harper was giving him this information deliberately over a line they both knew must be tapped. Harper had realized that his own involvement was finished, as was that of the four men he had contacted. All he could do now was provide Campbell with the opportunity to realistically cancel everything.

Campbell said, "Abort the mission."

He hung up quickly and hoped that whoever listened to the tape in Washington would believe him.

"I'd swear these things have been moved around," Tina said when they got back to the trailer from having dinner with friends forty miles west of there.

Mike opened a drawer. His .38 Smith & Wesson revolver was still there. He checked the shells in the chambers and tucked it in the front of his belt. The rifles and shotgun were still locked in the gun rack on the wall. Then he checked the secret compartment in the floor of the trailer. The seals he had made with solder were broken. He unscrewed the cover. Inside, intact, were his submachine gun, ammo, M16, and pistols. Nothing had been taken. But the compartment had been discovered and opened. Whoever did it knew what they were doing. Yet not even they could escape Tina's sharp eyes.

"They've been through everything," she said, "from recipes and electricity bills to cups and saucers."

"Stay here," he told her. "I'm going to take a look around outside."

He slammed the door after him and walked up the lighted pathway past three other trailers before he cut between them, away from the lighted center of the park, out into the pitch-black, scrubby desert that surrounded them on all sides. He stood motionless out in the open land until his eyes grew accustomed to the dark, and what had once been blackness now assumed different shades of gray and black in the starlight.

Campbell moved slowly and gently, carefully placing

each foot as he made his way back to the rear of his trailer. Out here, only twenty yards from the tattered lawns and light bulbs of civilization, it was a different world. Things slithered along the ground at his feet, and small dark shapes ran swiftly and noiselessly in his peripheral vision. Every time his legs pressed against plants in his way, their thorns pierced his skin and sank into his flesh. There were no daisies or lambs out here, only lean spare creatures and plants that could defend themselves.

He had eased his way almost directly behind his trailer before he noticed something unfamiliar, almost like the column of a cactus, quite near him. Campbell knew there was no cactus in that place. Then his brain sorted the information his eyes fed it. It was a human figure, standing rigid, pointing something at his trailer.

Although he knew he should creep away to check the area further before acting, sudden anger overwhelmed Mike. He covered the ground between them in a few giant springs and leapt into the air so he hit the dark figure in the right shoulder with both his feet, flexing his legs to deliver a powerful double kick.

In spite of the darkness, Campbell's timing was good. He felt the tremor as his frame absorbed the shock of his jackhammer double kick, and he felt the sudden release as the man's body lost its resistance and footing. It hit the ground with a dull thud, and before it could make a move, Campbell had thrown himself knees first onto the back of the prone figure, squeezing the remaining air out of the lungs in a long wheeze. Mike grabbed the man's hair, hauled his face out of the dirt, and gave him a chance to breathe.

"Who are you?"

"Kelleher, FBI, Phoenix office," the man gasped.

Campbell did not budge. "What were you doing?"

"I was holding a directional microphone toward your trailer."

"You know who I am?"

"Campbell, get off my back, you big lug."

THE POINT TEAM

Campbell got to his feet, pulled his Smith & Wesson .38 from his belt, and let the man feel its muzzle against his forehead. "Your ID," he demanded.

He had to reach inside the man's jacket himself to get the ID, and noted warily the revolver in the right hip holster on the man's belt, the position favored by FBI men. The ID checked out, so far as he could see by the light of a trailer window.

"Where's your backup?" Mike asked.

"Other side of the trailer camp. Asleep. I was going to wake him and go after you'd gone asleep."

"You wanted to hear whether we'd spotted your break-in, eh?"

The FBI man said nothing. Mike picked up his listening gear and handed it to him. Kelleher left without a word. Which was sporting of him, Mike figured, since he could have trumped up all sorts of charges. But then he'd have his own illegal break-in to answer for. No, Kelleher went quietly because he was under orders to go quietly.

Campbell walked around the trailer and climbed the steps to its door. He found himself looking into the unwinking big eye of a shotgun barrel inside the door. Tina was at the other end of the gun.

She took the weapon from her shoulder, dropped the hammer on her thumbnail, and set about unloading the gun. "Thought I heard something out back."

"It was me."

One of Campbell's unbreakable rules was for him not to involve Tina in anything. No matter what he got himself into, he wanted her to be innocent of it. She'd spot the FBI men soon enough herself if they kept hanging around—and since she knew nothing, she had no reason to be careful of what she said over the phone or elsewhere.

He fetched himself a bottle of Dos Equis from the refrigerator and sat down to think. Tina found something on TV so that he could sit there staring at the screen and let his mind concentrate on the decisions he had to make.

THE POINT TEAM

Harper, his old sergeant, was out, along with the four men he had contacted. There were others from the unit, and some he had met later as a merc. All good men. Little to choose between any of them. But all known to Washington as soldiers of fortune, and known to be associated with him.

Campbell knew what the attitude of the Washington bureaucrats would be. A lot of the top politicians there would privately be supportive of Vanderhoven's mission to get the kid out, but the desk-bound know-it-alls of the State Department would lay the law down. *They* were taking care of everything through diplomatic channels—which was bullshit—and all anyone else could do was make them look bad if they succeeded or "embarrass" the American government if they failed. So far as Mike was concerned, so much crap had gone on in Washington in recent years, he doubted very much if he could come up with anything new to embarrass anyone.

The only idea Mike had come up with since receiving Harper's phone call had been to recruit total unknowns in unexpected places. A classified ad in local newspapers would be one way to go. He'd have a lot of traveling to do to check the applicants, but expenses were no problem, and it would take him no more than a minute or so to decide whether he wanted a man along. It was a cumbersome way of doing the job, yet probably the most effective. Chances were better than good the FBI wouldn't spot it if he kept the newspapers he used widely scattered and in fairly densely populated areas.

He'd have to be careful of the wording. "Combat-hardened veterans..." He liked that, and it almost certainly meant service in Vietnam without mentioning the name. He'd put it under the first word VETERANS, then "combat-hardened only, big-money enterprise." That was as near as he could get to making it sound legit and fast money at the same time. Then a box number. He would probably get some law-enforcement officers answering to check him out. He figured he could spot them fast, or at least not recruit anyone he had the least doubt about. He'd drive into Phoenix tomorrow and find the names and addresses of newspapers in the library.

Chapter 6

JOE Nolan was in Youngstown, Ohio, and out of work. Not only had they closed the steel plants, they were even knocking some of them down. Takes an optimistic man to believe a plant will open again after it has been demolished. Some of his friends had taken off for Texas and other places. Others just hung out. All this was no great calamity to Joe. He always did wander from job to job, woman to woman, drink to drink... It was a guy in a bar who showed him the ad in the paper.

"Joe, you was in the Green Berets?"

"Mmmmm."

"Says here big money for combat-hardened veterans."

Joe looked up from his glass of beer. He was thin as a rail, with a long face, hollow cheeks, light brown hair, and long yellow teeth like a horse. He often got mad when people said he looked a real hillbilly, though sometimes he thought it funny, and his very bright blue eyes would dart about unpredictably. These eyes now lit at the words about big money his friend had just read.

"Shit, that sounds right for me," Joe said.

"Naw," the barman grinned. "It says combat-hardened, Joe. Man told me you was a cook over there. And all those little scars on your neck and arms that you say was shrapnel, those were caused by pieces of eggshell in hot grease."

The barman poured Joe another draft beer while he said this and gave it to him on the house.

"You know, if I'd been a cook in Nam, I'd a learned something," Joe said, acknowledging the beer. "Way I came back, unless you want to knock off some guy who's buggin' you, I ain't good to you for no other job. Not for long, anyhow. Can't put up with just standing in a place doing something stupid I never wanted to do in the first place."

"You find yourself a nice girl, Joe, and settle down," a wizened man down the bar offered. "She'll take all you can give and knock the stuffin' out of you. You'll quiet down real fast."

"What I need is to make some good money," Joe muttered.

"Right now Youngstown is a great place for that," another man at the bar remarked sardonically.

"There's folks here who've lots of bread," Joe told him.

"Yeah? I wish you'd bring 'em round here some time."

"They ain't my friends. But I know who some of them are," Joe said. "They ain't hurting for money."

"Everyone I know in this town is as piss-poor as I am. Point out your rich friends to me some time, Joe."

"Maybe I will," Joe said cryptically. He finished his beer and left.

He drove his battered Chevy a ways before pulling over onto a waste lot. He left the engine running while he took a pair of Pennsylvania registration plates out of the trunk and fitted them over his Ohio plates. He pressed down on the tops of the plates so that the clips he had welded to the back of these plates fitted tightly. A minute's work. He had taken the second pair of plates from a wrecked Toyota that had been hit by a truck out on 76 near Petersburg. A

THE POINT TEAM

whole family had been wiped out, he'd heard. Pennsylvania people. It was dark enough for him to switch on his lights as he drove along Canfield Road on the southwestern edge of the city. There was still some snow in patches.

He pulled off Canfield Road to the meeting place and looked at his watch by the street light. Ten minutes early. You could always depend on a working stiff being ten minutes early, no matter where you asked him to be. There ready for the whistle to blow. His father had been the same way. A girl had once told him he had a factory mentality or something of that kind. That wasn't because he always got places early that time, but because lying in bed in the morning made him nervous and restless. She had said guilty. Maybe she was right. Making love in the morning was OK with him. It was just lying in bed and doing nothing that got to him. There had not been a day in his mother's life, weekdays or Sundays, when she had not already washed the breakfast things and mopped the kitchen floor by the time the eight o'clock news came on the radio. His father and older brothers would be starting their day's work in the steel mill. He had to leave for high school in ten minutes—to get there fifteen minutes early, of course. He dropped out soon after. He was one of the ones who had not been surprised or upset by the rigors and regimented way of life in boot camp...

Joe's mind zeroed in on the car that appeared from the other end of the street, slowed, and parked opposite him. Indiana plates. A battleship-gray Trans Am with a red eagle stenciled on the hood. A tall dude with a seersucker suit and a preppy look got out. He carried an airline bag and gestured to the trunk of Nolan's car as he approached.

This was the third time in three months that Joe Nolan had met with this guy, who called himself Charles. Not Charlie or Chuck. Strictly Charles. He wasn't a fag. More an Ivy League sort with a high IQ and an arrogant manner, but not dumb enough to pull shit with Nolan—Joe could see that this Charles was real aware and careful about that

67

sort of thing. He'd had a different car each time, two different Porsches before the Trans Am, all with Indiana plates.

Charles put the airline bag in the trunk of Nolan's Chevy, and they drove back east along Canfield Road into Youngstown.

"I got three sales," Charles said. "Around the State University."

Nolan grunted.

He followed 62 across the Mahoning River. Near the university, Charles pointed out the way. Joe knew Charles had been around earlier in the morning or afternoon, making contacts and sales arrangements. Charles liked to be in and out of town in a single day, before he got noticeable to anyone as a stranger.

"How was it in Miami?" Joe asked.

"Raining."

"I may go down with you next time if you let me know."

"Sure, Joe." Charles glanced at him with interest. "You want to get more involved?"

"You pay me a thousand bucks for one evening's work. I got no complaint about that. But it's only once a month. Maybe I could drive for you in some other local cities—like Cleveland, Akron—or even Columbus. Wherever."

Charles looked at him sharply. "Who says I go to those places? Anyhow, when I sell in a place, I use a local man as a driver and bodyguard. You're my man in Youngstown."

"So what could I do?"

"Do the run from here in the Middle West down to Florida and back. It's a helluva drive to do very often. You take care of that end. I take care of this end of the business."

Joe thought about this. "What would be in it for me?"

"Twenty-five hundred a kilo."

"If I bring five kilos from Miami to Youngstown, I make $12,500?"

"Right," Charles said. "Why not? I got to trust you with almost a quarter-million dollars to buy five keys. You got to be sharp enough not to get ripped off for the bread at that end. You won't have trouble with our suppliers— we're chicken-feed to them, and they're not going to mess up their reputations for us. It's just that a lot of guys can't stay cool with a quarter-million in a brown paper bag. They don't have the nerve for it. You do."

Joe pulled the Chevy over where Charles indicated. "You'd trust me?" he asked.

"Me? Sure. But it wouldn't be just me. It'd be me and a lot of mean dudes with networks all over the world. If you tried to take off with the money, they'd probably flush you by cutting up your family here. One by one. These people aren't macho mob guys. They come after the women and kids, too."

Joe Nolan was silent.

He knocked out the lights and switched off the engine. They sat in the dark, waiting.

"Think about it," Charles said after a while.

As if Joe wasn't.

A car pulled up behind them. Its lights were extinguished. Charles got out, opened a rear door, got in the back seat and closed the door after him. The fellow from the car got in beside Joe and handed back an envelope to Charles. Joe listened to Charles flick through the money in the back seat.

"Give him one of the green bags," Charles told Joe.

Joe got out and opened the trunk. He unzipped the airline bag. There were two smaller plastic green bags and one larger yellow bag inside. One green bag. He hefted it in his hand. Half a kilo.

Another place down the road the second sale, of the other half-kilo, went smoothly too.

They had the kilo left to sell. For fifty or fifty-five thousand. At least someone in Youngstown had money. Of course, the buyer would cut the coke and sell it for a hundred dollars a gram and more than double his money. Joe Nolan didn't know anyone in Youngstown who could even afford to pay a hundred bucks for a gram. He knew no one. Except unemployed steel workers and their families. That was his trouble, Joe decided—no contacts.

The third buy was to go down on the other side of the State University. Charles remained in the back seat while they waited.

They weren't kept long. A guy in a brand-new Camero pulled over, got out and climbed in beside Joe. He looked Joe over and said hi.

Joe said nothing.

"You got the stuff?" he said to Charles in the back.

"You got the money?" Charles responded.

The guy pulled out a manila envelope from his coat pocket and held it up.

"We got the stuff," Charles said and took the envelope.

If the guy thought Joe Nolan was not watching him, was dumb and just staring ahead out the windshield, the guy was making a mistake. Joe spotted the gun in his right hand even as he was pulling it out of the shoulder holster. As it cleared the lapels of the man's coat, Joe could see it was a revolver—not an automatic. As Charles in the back seat was peering into the envelope, holding wads of newspaper cut into the size of dollar bills, saying, "This isn't . . ." Joe's right hand was whipping across, and his fingers were closing around the gun.

"This is a bust—"

That's all the guy had a chance to say before he had to squeeze the trigger as Joe's hand tried to pull it from his grasp. Nothing happened. He squeezed on the trigger again, hard. This time too, nothing. Joe's fingers were tightly around the chambers so that they could not revolve, thus blocking the action of the gun. He twisted the weapon upward against the Y formed by the man's thumb and forefinger and broke his grip on the gun handle. Instead of trying to point the gun, Joe slapped him over the forehead with the heavy metal.

With his left hand, he switched on the ignition and pushed the gear into drive.

"Drug Enforcement Agency," the half-stunned man beside him shouted. "You're under arrest."

Then he realized the car was in motion and jumped Joe before it could gather speed.

Nolan now held the revolver, a .357 Magnum, by its handle and brought the barrel down in a savage chop across the man's face. The guy kept coming at him, and Joe pistol-whipped him to a daze as he steered with his left hand and picked up speed on the dark empty street.

Two pairs of headlights blinked on behind him almost simultaneously, and moments later he heard their sirens. Joe drove without lights and pressed the accelerator hard to the floor.

The agent, holding his bleeding face in his hands, was thrown back against the door as the car hung a sharp turn into a small street on the left. Joe kept up his speed and wove in and out of the almost-deserted streets. He pulled up to the curb and listened. The two sirens were far away and growing fainter.

Joe leaned across and opened the front door against which the agent was leaning. The man fell out on the sidewalk and crawled away.

After a few blocks, Joe pulled up again and removed the Pennsylvania plates clipped over his Ohio ones. Then he turned on his headlights and drove slowly and legally across town to Canfield Road, turned into the street where Charles' Trans Am was parked, and got paid his thousand bucks in tens and twenties.

Joe clutched the notes in his hand. "If we'd been busted, how many years would they have sent us up for?"

"Hard to say," Charles answered. "They're not consistent. We could have got anything from five to twenty-five."

"I risked five years for a thousand dollars? That's two hundred dollars a year. I hope you do better than that."

"Sure I do. But I take bigger risks than I've ever asked you to. So far. You want the bread, you got to take chances."

"OK."

"We'll talk," Charles said.

"Sure."

Joe threw the .357 Magnum and the Pennsylvania plates in the Mahoning River, then headed back to the neighborhood bar. His friend had gone but had left the newspaper folded at one end of the counter. The "employment offered" column of the classified ads was short, and he soon found the ad his friend had mentioned. Big money for combat-hardened vets. A box number. It couldn't be any worse than what he was thinking about now.

Chapter 7

HARVEY Waller's friends said he was never the same again after being with the Marines in Vietnam. Even the ones who had sat next to him in class in high school and played basketball in the yard with him hour after hour claimed he came back real different—they maybe couldn't spell it out for you in what way he was different, but *different*. Some even said that now he was *strange*. What none of them knew was that Harvey Waller was a great deal stranger and more different than anyone who knew him in Flemington, New Jersey, could imagine.

Harvey had gotten the freeze-out treatment when he got home from Nam, just like all the other veterans who had to add to the disillusionment they picked up in Asia the further disillusionment that awaited them at home. Baby-killer. Genocide. Fascist. People said these things who couldn't find their way from a diner to a post office anywhere but in their hometown of Flemington—people who'd never been anywhere in their lives and hardly knew what was happening in front of their noses, let alone the real facts of what happened in Vietnam.

The real facts were clear in Harvey's mind, but he found

THE POINT TEAM

it hard—impossible—to explain them to people who had never experienced that reality. People laughed at him when he claimed that the Russians controlled the American press and TV—he didn't mean controlled, he meant manipulated. But they were already laughing too loud. He didn't believe Rather and Jennings were secret communists, Russian moles put there to subvert American opinion. He *did* believe that Rather and Jennings were unsuspecting victims of Russian propaganda and subtle machinations. He saw Vietnam not as an American military defeat but as a Soviet victory in psychological warfare. The U.S. Marines had not been defeated by the Cong and North Vietnamese—it was the American public at home who had been defeated by being duped by the Russians into believing they were participating in something wrong.

Most people were tired of the whole damn thing. They wanted to forget about it. Get on with the "me" generation and jogging and giving up cigarettes. The last thing they wanted to do was analyze the experiences of someone they regarded as a killer of women and children, even if they had gone to high school and played basketball with him.

It was everywhere. Penetrating every level of society. Espionage. Soviet agents buying secrets on how to make computers, Xerox machines, Coca-Cola, bombs... Americans being conned wholesale as they tried to abide by their principles and behave "decently" with a foe who was implacable and unscrupulous. The Soviets believed that anything which advanced their cause was acceptable—they claimed that a lie which helped communism thus became the truth. Most Americans could not really believe such people existed and intended to wipe them out. But some Americans did...

Harvey Waller met the first of them at a picnic on the Jersey Shore near Cape May. He had made some statements about his beliefs during the afternoon, casual comments, and was invited to a meeting the following week by the boyfriend of a Flemington girl who was along on the picnic. Harvey was amazed. Here were people who thought like he did, knew more than he did, and were prepared to do something about it. The possibility of doing something instead of only complaining had not really occurred to Harvey before. It took time for him to gain their trust and confidence, but when he did, he found his whole life changed. Money was no problem anymore. Some members of the group were very well-heeled and contributed generously to what were called the "active members." This was not a spectator sport. No one sat on the sidelines. Every member had his own special skills and responsibilities. Some were information gatherers, others were financial backers. Still others were known as producers—they made all arrangements and smoothed the way for operatives. And finally the operatives performed the effective action decided upon in an open discussion. The group deliberately had no name, no leaders and no written policies. They referred to themselves only as patriotic and concerned citizens.

Harvey's skills were those of a Marine with heavy combat experience in Vietnam. When he was accepted by the group as being fully trustworthy, he was put on PAD—preventive action detail. He was paid three hundred a week in cash, tax free, to be ready to move out at any time. A second phone was put in his mother's house in Flemington, and he was given a new Buick Regal. The members of the group were the only ones who had his special phone number, and the phone had an answering machine so that he could call home from elsewhere and hear any messages left for him. All went well for more than two years.

"Goddammit, Harvey, we got the FBI and the NSA, not to mention the New Jersey State Police, all on our case and you won't ease off!"

Waller looked at the man with the contempt he always

felt for those who showed fear in the absence of physical danger. He himself had been scared shitless a number of times, but there was always a gook at the business end of a mortar or some other helluva good reason visible to all for a man to be frightened. This little creep was worrying about his reputation or his vice-presidency at the bank or whatever if it ever came out he was associated with a far-right paramilitary group—and the description paramilitary was a joke here, since only Harvey and one or two others were worth anything. The others couldn't fight their way out of a paper bag. Including this little nothing who was whining at him now to take it easy.

"Ease off, you say?" Harvey bellowed at him. "You're one of the biggest alarm-raisers about the Soviets and how we gotta stop 'em. Now you're worried in case someone pisses on your front lawn."

"Harvey, hear me out. The original concept of our activities in the field was to collect incontrovertible evidence and present it to the FBI in order to force them into action. Somewhere along the line, something went wrong, and now we end up with the FBI trying to find out who we are. We were supposed to be working together!"

"We tried," Harvey said. "They wouldn't take action. They promised to involve this agency and that person and take things to the highest levels, but they did damn all. Since Hoover died, the FBI has lost its go. I think they may be penetrated."

"I've no doubt of that, Harvey! Every branch of government is rotten with fellow travelers and Soviet informers. Why should the FBI be an exception? But the point of the matter now is that they're hot on our trail, and we all agreed to ease up our operations until the heat dies down. All except you, Harvey. You're going to get us all crucified because you're too damn stupid and stubborn to lie low till they call the hunt off."

"And you're just trying to protect your ass," Waller shot back. "Which is a real come-down for a superpatriot who one day is willing to die for his country and the next is willing to let the fucking Russians take over rather than risk his job or something. Remember what you used to say? Better dead than Red! Seems to me like you and the others have gone back on what you used to say. You guys were all big talk and flag-waving till you had your bluff called. Then your chicken-shit knees began to knock together."

"Harvey, I got into this to help our government, not to form a vigilante group."

"You got into this because you saw communists manipulating our society on every level. You backed me when I took action where no one else would. You were one of my big supporters."

"I still am, Harvey."

"Bullshit!" Waller exploded. "You're a calm-sea sailor. Now that the going is getting rough, you're backing away from me."

"It's not just me, Harvey. Everyone wants you to tone down things till we see where we're..."

Harvey stubbed him with an index finger in the solar plexus and stopped his talk. "How do I know the commies haven't gotten to you?" Harvey moved his unshaven jowls closer to the nervous little man. "Maybe you've sold out to the Reds, eh?"

"Me, Harvey?" A nervous laugh. "You know me, I'd die first."

"Maybe you're going to have to."

Harvey did not know quite what he meant by that. It was just a vague threat. And it was taken as such.

After this conversation the others stayed away from him. They stopped notifying him of their meetings—he suspected they no longer had any. No one phoned. No money was sent. No new information. Harvey Waller was left with only his diminishing resources—a small amount of cash and a few targets.

THE POINT TEAM

Aware that the group had used a weekly Trenton paper to run encoded messages as ads in the help wanted section, he bought every issue of the paper and searched for something. Week after week, there was nothing. He was beginning to believe that the group might have become inactive after all, like scared rabbits seeking refuge in burrows. However, there was an ad in this week's paper that promised big money for combat-hardened veterans. He might be able to use something like that if his connections with the group were now broken for good.

He didn't know where to find the other members of the group. He knew them only by their first names. This dawned on him for the first time. They had used him like a servant. They called him, not he them. No doubt they even regarded his financial support as wages, which they now need no longer pay since they had no further need of his services.

Waller strove to put such personal feelings out of his mind in order to concentrate on higher things, such as his patriotic duty.

Ivan's car pulled into the huge parking lot of the shopping mall near Edison, New Jersey. Harvey Waller followed him. This was the third time he had tailed him, and he knew his routine here. Harvey knew the man's real name was Yevgeny Illiyich Konstantinov and that he was a second secretary at the Soviet Mission to the United Nations in Manhattan, but to Harvey all Russians were Ivan. Ivan Ivanovitch. Harvey felt cold fury as he watched the Russian park. Ivan would now get out of the car and walk toward the distant stores, a K Mart, an A&P supermarket and some others. He would thread his way through the parked cars, in no hurry and casually keeping an eye out around him. His contact would be parked somewhere between him and the stores, also keeping watch and invisible in his driver's seat among the hundreds of other parked cars. No doubt he was watching Harvey's car right now since it had followed Ivan's into the parking lot. Harvey kept going, without a glance at the Russian as his car door opened.

He drove toward the stores and then swung about the far edge of the lot so that he was now behind the Russian's contact. He pulled into an empty space but had to leave the car in order to see the Russian walking across the lot quite a distance away.

Ivan was a big man in a heavy coat and old-fashioned hat. His movements were ponderous. Harvey was heavily built, also, but light on his feet. He hunched down behind a Ford LTD and watched over the roofs of the parked cars. The Russian lumbered on toward the stores.

Waller heard a car door open only two rows in front of him, a little to the right. He crowded down further. A man got out and stood for a moment. Then he got back in the dark blue Honda and slammed the door after him.

The Russian had changed direction and was now cutting across the rows of cars toward the Honda, though still moving unhurriedly. He had eleven or twelve rows of cars to traverse. Only a single row separated Harvey from the man who had given the signal. He ran, stooped, till he was directly behind the blue car. Then he crept forward.

The man was not sitting behind the steering wheel but in the seat next to it, taking papers from the glove compartment. The car radio was playing pop rock not very loud, the side window was rolled down all the way and billows of cigarette smoke rose skyward from it.

Waller crept alongside and raised his head to the level of the roof. The Russian was still too far away to be seen because of the other parked cars. Nor could he see Waller. The man in the car sensed or heard someone next to the car and glanced around sharply. Waller slapped his left palm over the man's mouth and pushed his head back against the seat's headrest.

THE POINT TEAM

The man's eyes widened in fear, but he still clutched the papers in his lap rather than release them to defend himself.

Harvey rasped in his ear, "Wimp! Traitor! Commie! Shit-head!"

Waller's right hand came through the car window, clenching an ice pick with the thumb steadied against the upraised steel needle. He held it before the frantic man's eyes as he pressed his hand harder against the man's mouth and his head harder against the seat headrest. Then he began to lower the ice pick slowly, and the trapped victim's eyes followed the glistening point downward.

The man loosed his precious papers and desperately grasped the wrist and arm of the hand that held the ice pick. The nervous fingers hopelessly plucked at the muscular limb that held the weapon. Waller allowed his prey a variation of arm-wrestling, slowly bearing down with one hand against the two that resisted him.

His victim panicked. He put one hand over his chest to protect it from the ice pick now pointing directly at him, and he used the other to try to wrench Waller's hand from his mouth, where its grip held his head clamped against the seat. These struggles were even more futile than those before.

Waller moved the ice pick forward, paused a moment to let it prick the skin on the man's chest, then steadily drove it through.

The man tried to push it away, but already the shaft of the ice pick had penetrated just beneath the curve of the rib cage. Waller pressed in hard all the way and twisted the needle about inside to rupture the vital organs.

The man threshed violently, twisted his head and kicked against the side wall of the car. His teeth chomped down and nearly caught Waller's left hand between them. In spite of the wounded man's struggles, Waller kept the ice pick in place, twisting it about inside the chest cavity.

"Dopey bastard!" he ground out. "You should have fought like that before you bought it. It's too late now."

At last the internal hemorrhaging took effect and the struggles ceased. Waller withdrew the ice pick, looked up to see if the Russian was in sight yet—and when he wasn't, reached in to gather up the papers scattered on the man's lap. There wasn't much blood.

He stuffed the papers in his inside pocket—he'd mail them to the FBI—wiped the ice pick on the man's sleeve, and ran stooped over behind the row of parked cars to the rear of the blue Honda.

A woman was loading groceries from a cart into the rear of a station wagon not too far away. She had three small children and was more concerned with their antics than with Waller. An elderly couple were making for another car, each pushing a loaded cart. No one else was around. Waller eased his head higher. The Russian was almost there! The bulky man in his heavy gray coat and gray hat passed between two cars, crossed the space to the next row, passed through, and looked with a puzzled expression at the blue Honda. Perhaps he was waiting for an all-clear signal . . .

The Russian's right hand dived into his overcoat pocket; he looked about him carefully and walked briskly toward the Honda. He looked inside only a moment, then looked about in a full circle with an expressionless face. He turned about and walked rapidly back the way he had come.

"Ivan is a cool one," Waller muttered, and took a tiny Colt .22 automatic from his pocket. He released the catch and slid a bullet from the ten-round magazine into the firing chamber. Then he went after the Russian.

"Ivan!" he called after him.

He needn't have shouted, for as soon as the Russian heard footsteps behind him he had already begun to turn about. His right hand was still in his coat pocket.

Waller was giving him a sporting chance. The American

traitor had deserved to die the way he had. Waller despised him more than he did the Russian. The Russian was simply doing for his country what Waller was willing to do for America. Fight for her tooth and nail... The Russian had a more than even chance. Waller's little automatic was deadly at close range, but only a few yards and the Russian's heavy coat would make a lot of difference—especially if, as Waller expected, that right hand emerged from the overcoat pocket holding a 9-mm Makarov automatic, which despite its heavier caliber had two shots less than his own gun. Or these agents sometimes carried the 9-mm Stechkin, which could be switched on full automatic. His own Colt and a Makarov, in spite of being called automatic, were only semiautomatic, meaning the trigger had to be pulled separately for each shot, no matter how rapid the rate of fire. The Stechkin on full automatic could blow out all twenty of its 9-mm projectiles in one steady stream with a single press of the trigger. The Russian pulled his right hand from his overcoat pocket.

It was not holding a gun. The thick fingers were clutching a short, thick cardboard tube, only a few inches long, with metal ends and a key ring near the top. The Russian pulled the key ring loose, lifted a metal lever, and threw the tube at Waller.

Harvey had no time to shoot. When he saw the lever lifted, he knew he had about four and a half seconds. Since the mini-grenade was an offensive grenade, it had the shock-killing and stunning effects without the lethal metal fragments, and so the thrower did not have to take cover. The blast of TNT flakes did all the work. Harvey threw himself on the asphalt and rolled under the nearest car.

The projectile exploded just before it hit the ground, causing the cars on each side of it to buck and rear like frightened horses. The blast shattered windshields and car windows all about and caused people all over the parking lot to look in amazement in that direction. There was no smoke. No fire. They went back to their immediate concerns.

Harvey Waller's head lay in a pool of blood beneath the oil-caked transmission of a car. He moved slowly—first his arms, then his legs, his neck, then his back. He looked at the pool of blood on the ground next to him and rolled from beneath the car. He reached for a door handle and pulled himself upright. No one coming. Good. He looked in a sideview mirror. Only a bloody nose. He grinned and wiped it. But he had no idea how long he had been unconscious. Minutes? An hour? He remembered everything.

Steadying himself against the side of the car, avoiding the tiny shards of the broken safety glass of the side windows, he craned his neck over the roofs of the parked cars. He had been out for only less than a minute! The Russian was still making his way across the huge parking lot toward his car.

Waller checked to make sure the papers were still in his inside pocket and searched for moments before he found the little Colt next to a burst tire. Keeping down so he wouldn't be seen, he ran back toward his own car.

He had a fit of dizziness just before he reached it and sank to his knees. Then, just as suddenly, his head cleared and he got to his feet again. He made it to the car, got in and started the engine. His vision was a little strange, and he figured he was suffering from a mild concussion. The bad nosebleed had probably made him a little light-headed. But now he had to think.

The Russian would probably head back for Manhattan and the safety of his consulate. But Ivan would be edgy, watching for tails and for more attacks. And Ivan was a professional, Harvey granted him that. Couldn't deny it, since Ivan had beaten him to the draw. Ivan's only mistake was he hadn't waited to finish him off.

Harvey Waller made for the nearest exit and pushed out into the traffic. His driving was a little erratic at first, almost as if his car had very loose steering. He headed for the turnpike and kept his speed down. Already a few miles north on the turnpike, traveling in the slow lane and beginning to wonder if he had made a mistake, Harvey spotted the Russian in the center lane. He picked up speed a little and let the Russian pass him after a while—and was glad he did so, because Ivan headed for the Holland Tunnel exit rather than staying on for the Lincoln Tunnel to bring him to midtown Manhattan and closer to his consulate. The Holland Tunnel would bring him into downtown Manhattan, not far from the financial district. Harvey wondered for a while who he might be going to see there and whether it was worth following him, but then decided that Ivan was simply changing his usual route after his strike-out in the Jersey parking lot.

The turnpike spur to the Holland Tunnel rose on giant concrete stilts for a couple of miles over the brown salt-marsh grass and beat-up factories of the Jersey Meadowlands. The Pulaski Skyway. Polish name. Harvey had always classified Poles in the same bag as Russians until recently. Now that he knew they hated the Reds too, Harvey was a friend to every Polack in town, he said. Be fitting, he thought, to take care of the Russki right here on the Pulaski Skyway. One for Solidarity. Whoever the hell Pulaski was. Probably a crooked Democrat pol who made a million in kickbacks off this fucking swamp gangplank as well as having it named after him.

Harvey's vision started to pitch and waver again. His car almost struck the retaining wall of the raised roadway. He shook his head violently and took a deep breath and steered into the center lane, away from the wall. Another of these dizzy attacks and he could hit someone. He had to get off the road, out from behind the steering wheel.

The Russian's car was directly in front of him, a green, late-model Dodge Dart. Harvey drove up behind him, close, so there was not more than six feet between the cars. Traffic was light, and he could have passed on either side. The Russian pulled into the slow lane. Harvey dropped back a little. Soon the Russian came up behind a slower-traveling car in the slow lane and braked behind it, since Harvey's Buick was too close behind him in the center lane for him to pull out.

Harvey saw the Russian scrutinizing him over his shoulder. He accelerated and swung to the right so that his right front bumper caught the left rear bumper of the Dodge. Harvey put his foot on the gas and banged into him hard. The Dodge's front end jerked toward the retaining wall of the Skyway, but Ivan swung hard to the left on the steering wheel and managed to avoid contact and stay in his lane with some fishtailing.

It took Waller almost as long to get his car back under control. The Russian's Dodge was now almost on top of the slow car in front of it. Harvey goosed his engine again, this time all the way, and hit the Dodge a fender-crushing blow in the left rear. He followed through on the punch, the Buick's engine power surging and pushing the Dart into the car in front and toward the wall at the same time. The Russian hit both and, with one final push from Harvey, the Dodge flipped, stood on its right front wheel for a moment like a ballet dancer, and was gone over the wall.

The slow car in front veered out into the center lane, and Harvey couldn't avoid sideswiping it. As he passed and fought with his steering wheel to steady the Buick, he saw the car bounce off the retaining wall and do a complete 360-degree spin before coming to a stop in the middle of the roadway. Sure stopped anyone from getting his plate numbers.

Harvey took the next exit off, stopped at a traffic light, and glanced at the newspaper on the seat beside him. He had used up every lead he had gained from the group—killed every fucking traitor and spy he had come across. More even than the group knew about. He really hoped now that the FBI caught up with those cowardly assholes and they had to answer for his deeds. Meanwhile, he might check out that ad in the paper for combat-hardened veterans.

Harvey carefully signaled his turn and drove courteously.

Chapter 8

KATIE Nelson was flirting with the vice-president in charge of the newscast division of the network. She knew he had the hots for her, but had heard he was very cozily married and had never been known to step outside of the bonds of wedlock. Katie enjoyed the feeling that she might be putting some thoughts like this into his head. She didn't care if nothing came of it—he wasn't her type really, but she sure as hell enjoyed seeing him twist and turn in his indecision. And she did everything she could—as long as it required no special effort—to keep the flames high under him, with a glimpse of thigh or breast, a touch of her fingertips, a hug and a little-girl snuggle which made him sit down because of his hard-on.

However, today the VP did not have his usual calf eyes for her—in fact, there was a gleam of amusement in them.

"We finally got back that video camera and sound equipment you lost in Vietnam," he said. "Came back to us via Switzerland."

"How about the tapes?" she asked, not too hopefully.

"Not one, and the camera is empty."

"I thought so."

"I hear you may be taking the equipment on a trip there

again," he said. "Maybe we should have asked them to hold it for you."

Katie's producer came by at that moment, and the VP said to him, "I hear you're sending Katie off to Vietnam again."

The producer said, "Hah! Me sending her? She's going whether I want her to or not! Right, Katie?"

Katie shrugged. "When I suggested a return visit, the Vietnamese okayed it. So did you two."

The producer picked up a photo torn from *The New York Times* that lay on Katie's desk. He read the caption and commented, "Seventy-nine kids of mixed Vietnamese–American parentage and sixty-seven of their relatives allowed to leave Vietnam. Says here it's the largest group ever allowed to leave. You going back to find that kid of yours, Katie?"

Again Katie noticed the amused look come into the once-adoring eyes of the VP.

"I can't think of a better news story," she snapped, "unless Eric were a Rockefeller or a DuPont instead of a Vanderhoven."

The producer backed off. "I agree. I agree. Listen, this is a big story. We don't want to breathe a word about it outside this room, or we'll be beaten to it by someone else. No one's knocking that story. It's just that it's become... well, kind of an obsession with you."

"In what way?" Katie's voice was ice cold.

At this point the VP jumped in. "Well, Katie, you're pretty, and I'm sure you lead a very full romantic life and all, but you're also single, and I suppose you have strong maternal instincts that have been repressed and now this kid, Eric Vanderhoven, needs you, so..."

Katie smiled at him so sweetly that he stopped. She said, "I think I have two nasty little boys here pulling my hair. Remember how you did that when you were little? And look at you now, you're still at it. Grow up, *please*." She saw by the expression on their faces they were

THE POINT TEAM

sufficiently chastised. Now she set about building up their egos again. "But if I *do* return to Vietnam, it'll only be because you two want me to—feel I'm the one who can get the job done. I'll need your help and support, both of you, like I had before. I couldn't manage without that."

"You got it from me," the VP said warmly.

"Me too, kid," the producer answered her.

Katie was looking forward to dinner after the evening newscast. She usually headed out on her assignment in the morning and was back at the studio by three at the latest for editing and timing of her tape. Depending on the evening's newscast, she would often take on a second subject or a rush assignment or fill in for someone who was away. She argued for the favorable placement of her segments and tried to prevent them being cut to mere seconds by the editors. By the time she dressed and made up for the newscast, did her piece or pieces on the show and came down from the high anxiety after it was done, she was normally exhausted. This evening was different.

She had run some old tapes from the files on the man who was taking her to dinner. They had footage of Michael Campbell as a colonel in the Green Berets in Saigon, back from relieving a beleaguered column in the north, a film of him in a Montagnard village someplace in the Central Highlands, and two minutes of exciting action as he and a unit were dropped by helicopter under enemy fire in the rice fields of the Mekong Delta. The lean, battered colonel was photogenic and quite affable with the reporters on each of the occasions, explaining the purpose of what he was doing in straightforward terms.

All in all, Katie decided she could handle this handsome warrior and get him to do her bidding. The Four Seasons had been his suggestion for dinner. She would not have thought a professional soldier or mercenary or whatever Campbell was these days would have chosen such a glamour hole as the Four Seasons—she would have expected a steak house or even a burger and fries on a checkered tablecloth at a macho bar. The nickname Mad Mike she found less appealing. She was definitely of the opinion that a man named Michael would be more useful to her than one called Mad Mike. But men were silly. He'd probably once drunk a gallon of beer without taking a breath and earned that nickname forevermore. His buddies would be calling him Mad Mike when he was ninety with no teeth and in a wheelchair.

She was late. Of course. She was familiar with how the very ordinary entrance of the Four Seasons on 52nd Street suddenly blossomed into art, marble and flowers inside, and she ascended the grand staircase. A page led her past the Grill Room through a glass-and-marble walkway that overlooked the lobby of the Seagram Building and led to the Pool Room—an enormous square room with a ceiling several stories high. The windows ran from floor to ceiling and everything else was paneled in dark wood, and in the center of the room water babbled in a pool surrounded by trees. The tall, spare man she had seen in the TV footage sat alone at a table, not looking a day older or softer than he had in those rice fields in the Delta.

She joined him in a dry martini, and they took stock of each other.

"Who knows of this operation at the network besides yourself?" he asked.

"You're not much for small talk, are you?" she parried.

"Not when I've more important things to discuss. Let's get them out of the way so we can enjoy our food and conversation without worrying about what's coming next."

She smiled. "All right. They know I've been invited back to Vietnam of course, since they had to approve the trip, and they know—a few people, my vice-president and producer and a few people higher up—who Eric is, a Vanderhoven. They'll keep quiet about that in case the *Times* or another network steals it from us. None of them know about you. They think it's just a good story as is."

THE POINT TEAM

"Without Tarzan swinging out of the jungle and snatching the kid?"

"They might have second thoughts about that," she said.

"That's how it's going to be, for all intents and purposes. You realize that?"

She nodded.

He persisted. "No second thoughts?"

"I never have them." She laughed. "If I did, I wouldn't last in this business."

"I'll be frank with you, Miss Nelson, when I say my chief concern in dealing with you is that whether the mission is a failure or success, you win either way, since you get your media coverage of the event."

"No, you're wrong, Colonel."

"I'm retired, Miss Nelson. Call me Mike."

"If you call me Katie. Mike, sure I can use a segment of you being grabbed by the Vietnamese and being hauled off in a cage. Except that's not what people want to see. They'll want to see Eric rescued from a communist slave camp and brought back to America to inherit billions. So far as I'm concerned, I don't even want you or any of your bloodthirsty friends to show your faces for one second in the coverage."

"Good," he said. "We think alike on that. Another thing you must understand. When we move in to evacuate Eric, you and your crew become part of my team for that period. Which means you obey my orders, do not question my judgment and will be shot if you endanger our safety by disobeying orders. I want you to consider that carefully."

"No problem," Katie said easily. "Why should I disagree with what you want to do? Good Lord, I was never even in the Girl Scouts. I wouldn't know how to tie a knot."

Campbell was alerted by her too-easy acceptance of his conditions and semihumorous dismissal of them. He knew any further talk on this subject with her would be wasted.

He had stated his position clearly, and she had agreed to it. He would hold her to it.

She had a pâté of salmon and crabmeat as an appetizer, and he, crisped shrimp filled with mustard fruits. As the main course she ate quail with deep-fried grapes, and he, sautéed calf's liver. They washed these down with two bottles of Pouilly Fumé and finished with the restaurant's famous chocolate cake. Katie noticed a definite softening in his attitude toward her as the meal progressed.

"I'm kind of surprised," she said, "to find that someone like you, with a reputation as a hard-boiled soldier of fortune, has any use for fine food and wine."

"It's when you go without something for long periods of time that you develop an appreciation for it. If our plans work out, I expect I'll be living on rice and bits of dried meat in the jungle not so long from now. The thought of that is enough to make me savor every bite of good food while I can."

She nodded her head vigorously. "The food in Vietnam is awful. If Burger King opened in Ho Chi Minh City today, there's be riots. Tell me, does this—what I mean to say is that I expected to find you a sadistic bully." She paused, a bit confused, both by him and the wine. "You're not. And I lied when I said I thought you'd be a bully, because I reviewed some tapes of you on file when you were in Vietnam during the war. How can you kill people like you do and not turn into an animal?"

"That's putting it straightforwardly." He smiled and squeezed her hand to show her he was not annoyed. "A lot of people who have never seen combat think that a soldier goes out and murders soldiers on the opposite side. Cold-blooded murder sometimes happens, but it's a lot rarer than the armchair philosophers realize. Most of the fighting happens on a kill-or-be-killed basis. There's no time to think, or if you try, that split second you hesitated could cost you your life. So you have to do your thinking before you go. When you're on the battlefield, it's too late to start having doubts. I make sure I'm on the right side going in—on what I believe is the right side anyway. Obviously things happen to change a man's mind—but even then, his first duty to himself is to get out alive."

He continued, "So far as this mission is concerned, I think it's worth rescuing the son of an American father who is being persecuted because that is what he is. Any totalitarian government that takes away the liberty of individuals is worth fighting. I'm not going to kill anyone who doesn't try to stop me. I'll respect their lives. But what you've got to realize is that communists these days are very free with bullets. They've given up on the gentler forms of persuasion, since no one is fool enough anymore to hand over everything to them out of free choice. If I come across any of these types, I can only hope mine will be the finger first upon the trigger."

She told him about the mothers she had seen separated from their babies in the compound outside Ho Chi Minh City. "That's why I don't feel I'm doing something bad against them after they've invited me back—I'm sure they've asked me only because they expect to make use of me."

"Vanderhoven told me you've made inquiries about Eric."

"They told me where he is," she said. "I have a map for you with the exact location of the reeducation camp. Somebody at the Pentagon confirmed the camp's existence there from a satellite reconnaissance photo taken for Mr. Vanderhoven. The Vietnamese have given me permission to meet Eric and perhaps even photograph him."

"I wonder why."

"Mr. Vanderhoven thinks it's to goad him," Katie said. "He thinks that the Hanoi government wants American money—so-called reparations they claim Nixon promised them—before they'll release any prisoners they still may have and most of these American children. They release small numbers of children every now and then as bait, or allow some information on MIAs to leak out to keep interest warm. Eric Vanderhoven has become just another pawn in their game."

After they left the Four Seasons, they stopped off at P.J. Clark's on Third Avenue for a nightcap.

"I live just around the corner on Second Avenue," Katie said. "Why not come around and see the view from my window? I'm very proud to be living on the thirty-second floor up among the clouds and skyscrapers—which is quite something for a girl from a place as flat as Nebraska."

Mike found she had not exaggerated the view from the giant plate glass windows of her apartment. This night, long streaks of low-lying clouds trailed in front of the floodlit spire of the Empire State Building like overdone stage effects. Katie joined him at the window and leaned her long supple body against his. Nothing needed to be said.

Campbell felt her warm, firm thighs against his. The food, wine, view, and comfort of her luxury apartment made for a big change from his usual simple life in the trailer in Arizona. Tina would be mad as hell if she saw him now. Yet he would not exchange her and his trailer for this big-city aerie and sexy TV lady. Not that he was going to turn down Katie, either...

He ran his hands gently over her body and kissed her full on the mouth, darting his tongue between her eager lips. He felt her body relax into his, and he ran his lips over the smooth skin of her neck. His manhood was stiff with urgency, and her lower belly tremored in response to the pressure of his giant probe.

They looked deep in each other's eyes. Again, nothing needed to be said. Afterward they would have love play, fondling, and dalliance—right now their animal longing was too strong, had to be eased. They walked quickly hand in hand to her bedroom, peeled off their clothes, and gazed avidly at each other in naked, open lust.

Campbell touched her, and she drew a sharp breath. They lay beside one another on top of the bed and embraced. Then she slid beneath him, parted her legs, and raised her knees in submission to his throbbing member.

He thrust his full length into her warm, moist, welcoming depths.

They could not be sure in the gathering dusk which village it was. Lt. Tranh Duc Pho and his fifteen-man unit had been on patrol since shortly after dawn, except for a three-hour break in the hottest part of the day. The lieutenant liked to keep the morale of his men up by frequent stays in mountain and foothill villages. Army rations and no women were bad for the nerves. They had been lucky to find this village. And he had the means to celebrate. They had taken three bottles of Japanese Suntory whisky from a smuggler that morning. One bottle for him, two for the men. They would sleep it off tomorrow.

"Montagnard?" he asked one of his men.

"Can't tell in this light."

"We're down off the mountains far enough so they could be Vietnamese," another said in a cautionary tone.

"Yes," the lieutenant said sarcastically, "but what kind of Vietnamese?"

All the men listening knew what he was referring to. With a Montagnard or other hill tribe village, they could behave almost as they pleased. The Montagnards were regarded as confederates of the Americans, antiprogressive in the Leninist sense and plain damn hard to control in the everyday administration of the new peasants' and workers' paradise. The hill tribesmen could not complain about the behavior of loyal communist forces. There was no one to listen to them. A Vietnamese village was different. They would have party cadres, and a complaint from them would go straight to the highest military command. Soldiers behaved like angels when party cadres were about.

But there were Vietnamese and Vietnamese. The lieutenant suspected that these villagers might be dispossessed peasants from another area or translocated city people who had moved up into the foothills for pernicious independence and seclusion from party influence. The existence of such backward communities was well-known if not often discussed openly, and soldiers in such a place need not be on their best behavior.

Lt. Tranh Duc Pho pointed. "Let's go in."

The men spread out, with at least five yards between each man, their AK47s hanging casually on shoulder straps. They strolled into the village in a familiar nonthreatening way, although their weapons were switched to full automatic and ready to fire.

"They're Vietnamese," the word came back.

The lieutenant knew there would be courtesies to be observed. He would visit the house of the village leader and pass verbal pleasantries with the elders while his men found out if there were any party cadres present, how the village earned its livelihood, if there were pretty women. His unit knew the routine.

In the village leader's house, seven elders were gathered. Lt. Tranh Duc Pho occupied the place of honor and insisted that they taste some of his Japanese whisky. He poured some in a bowl and they passed it from hand to hand after careful sips. The lieutenant almost smiled at the deep politeness to a stranger which prevented them from screwing up their faces and spitting the fiery liquor out.

"No, get me my American glasses." The lieutenant was very proud of the two clear, heavy bar tumblers he had been given by a superior officer. "Those pottery bowls hold bacteria and spread disease," he lectured the elders.

They were too polite to ask him what bacteria were.

Tranh Duc Pho set about drinking the whisky, filling up half a tumbler at a time and adding a little water from a second tumbler. The elders glanced nervously at him and at one another as the effects of his huge swallows of alcohol became obvious.

THE POINT TEAM

Two of his men entered the house. One spoke. "These people are smugglers. Parasites. The women are preparing us food."

The elders were silent, waiting for the officer's reaction.

"Get me a woman," he said in a slightly slurred voice. "I'll be along after I've eaten."

"No! No! No!" a chorus of the elders shouted.

The soldiers ignored them. The one who spoke before addressed the lieutenant. "What about us?"

Tranh Duc Pho leered at him. "Hold the prettiest one for me, untouched. Then help yourselves."

"No! No! No!" the elders kept shouting.

One not quite as decrepit as the others leapt to his feet. "We won't allow you!"

The lieutenant gestured to him to be seated, and when the man had squatted down, the officer spoke in an undertone to one of the men. The soldier left the house, but was back in a couple of minutes with a military-green canvas sack. The soldier untied and loosened the rope strung through the top of the bag and handed it to the officer. Tranh Duc Pho reached in and scooped out a handful of what looked like dried peach halves. He dumped them on the table before him and scooped handful after handful out of the bag so that they ran off the pile on the table and lay scattered around the floor.

The village elders looked impassively at the dried human ears.

The lieutenant held up one for their inspection. "They're like pebbles from a riverbed. They look better when wet."

He dropped the ear into the tumbler of water. True enough, it immediately looked fresh and newly severed.

The officer looked about him and asked in a drunkenly sentimental voice, "Do you think that if they could, the owners of these ears would listen to me now?"

None of the elders made a reply.

The lieutenant held out the whisky bottle and poured a little into one ear lying at his feet. He shouted at it, "Can

you hear me now?" He pointed to another ear, this one facing downward on the floor. "He's still not listening."
Tranh Duc Pho ordered the two soldiers. "Food. Women."
They left grinning.
The elders made no sound.

Chapter 9

AT fifty-four, Andre Verdoux was over the hill. Mike Campbell wasn't serious about hiring him for the mission when he arranged anonymously to meet Verdoux in response to the latter's reply to his ad. But he did give the Frenchman a clue. He arranged to meet him for lunch at Lutece.

"I knew it had to be you, Mike," Verdoux greeted him in the little front room of the Manhattan restaurant, "when you arranged to meet me here."

"What the hell are you doing reading small-town Maine newspapers?" Campbell said, shaking his hand. "I thought you never left the city except aboard the Concorde for Paris."

"I'm looking for an old trawler to convert. I thought I might see one for sale in local New England papers. You know how your eye drifts out of curiosity. I saw your ad."

"I hope nobody who shouldn't got too curious," Campbell said. "I've got some replies I don't like the look of, so I'm not contacting them."

Verdoux ordered a kir and raised his glass to Campbell. "Your health. So it's a genuine mission?"

"Forget it, Andre, you're not coming. This meeting's just for old time's sake."

"Of course. By that you mean you need to discuss it with me—what do you say, pick my brains? Yes? Well, let's discuss it and perhaps I can help. Maybe you won't be able to manage without me."

Mike shook his head. "Andre, you're past doing this one. I think our table is ready."

They were led to the garden section of the restaurant, a glass-roofed area with pink stucco walls covered with white latticework. There were paving stones beneath their feet, wicker chairs about the tables and big plants in brass pots. Verdoux immediately got into a heavy conversation in French with their captain, and Mike indicated to him that he should order for both of them.

Verdoux tested the bottle of Bâtard-Montrachet and nodded to the sommelier. He said to Campbell, "Ah, you think I'm past my prime, don't you? I've never enjoyed women, cognac, and haute cuisine more in all my life— why not soldiering, too? Young men don't know how to appreciate what's given them. You have to wait till my stage in life to really know how to live!"

Mike told him everything that had happened so far on the project.

"I don't like this ad in the newspapers," Verdoux commented. "You will collect all kinds of questionable types—including myself, of course!"

"There was nothing else I could do. I've seen eighteen applicants so far and have hired only two. The first was Joe Nolan, an ex–Green Beret now in Youngstown, Ohio. He's really still a kid—a bit of a floater, never settled down after the war. Yet he knows what he's doing as a fighting man, although he'll always need someone with common sense to keep an eye on him. The other was an ex-Marine in Flemington, New Jersey. His name is Harvey Waller. Strange individual—bit of a fanatic, I suppose—

THE POINT TEAM

but I can handle him. I'd certainly rely on him in a fire fight, but he may not be too tightly wrapped headwise."

"You always were good at figuring a man out," Verdoux said. "Did you tell them where you were going and why?"

"No," Campbell replied. "I let everyone infer it was Southeast Asia, of course—I had to—but beyond that I allowed them to believe we might be after MIAs."

"Good. This is a touchy subject now, particularly since Washington is making no progress on these issues. You have to assume that at least one of the men you spoke to is an informant."

"Sure. I just hope it's neither of the two I hired."

"It's strange to know I'll be going back there again," Verdoux mused.

"Andre, you won't."

"When I first went to Vietnam," Verdoux continued as if he had not heard Campbell, "I had hoped to get into the plantation business there as an agent or something after I got out of the French army. The reality of what I found there was a little different from what I had been led to believe at home in France. Our glorious colonies were growing tired of us. Then our defeat by the Viet Minh at Dien Bien Phu. We could not believe what was happening to us. I stayed in the army. For the debacle in Algeria." He shook his head sorrowfully and sipped his wine, but his sad expression instantly evaporated when they were served their appetizers of snails in butter and herbs, each in its own little porcelain dish. Andre talked about snails for a while and the pros and cons of serving them with or without their shells and gradually veered off into his days as a merc in the Congo.

"Another disaster!" he summed it up for Mike. "Is this why you don't want me along with you? Because I'm unlucky?"

"Certainly, Andre. I blame you personally for all France's losses in Indochina and Africa."

Verdoux's crab stew with a pastry top arrived, along with Campbell's Basque-style roast chicken. More talk from the Frenchman about the quality of the food. Then Angola. Mike and Andre had served alongside each other in that part of Africa as mercs on Holden Roberto's—the losing—side. Taking advantage of America's paralysis after its disaster in Vietnam, Russia sent Cuban troops into the newly independent Portuguese colony to side with the left wing in a civil war. The CIA gave some halfhearted aid to Roberto's side, but the Cubans proved to be the deciding factor in the war.

"Remember Turner?" Andre asked, tasting the first glass of a new bottle of wine.

Mike knew he was meant to be softened up by all these reminiscences of their being comrades-in-arms, softened up enough to agree to take Andre along on his mission to Vietnam. At first he had regarded it as being simply out of the question—the man was fifty-four—and he was along only for the pleasure of Andre's company. Then Mike found he badly needed to discuss his project with a mature, seasoned soldier, which Andre certainly was. Mike now discovered with wry amusement that perhaps his mind was not *completely* closed to taking Andre along. It was still highly unlikely. But not out of the question.

"Turner was a crazy bastard," Mike said. "First time I ever rode with him in his Land Rover, we were going into FAPLA territory and we could have been ambushed at any minute. We spotted this African by the roadside—probably one of their spies on his way to our territory. I thought Turner would have him executed on the spot. Instead, he asked him if the road was mined from this point on.

"'No,' the African replied, 'I know for a fact it is not.'

"We grew suspicious of the positive way he answered us. So Turner tied him to the iron grille in front of the Land Rover.

"He told him, 'If you see a mine in the roadway, raise your right hand.'

"We'd only gone a few hundred yards when the man waved us to a stop at a small bridge. He claimed he couldn't remember where exactly the mines were, but we could go no farther than this bridge. Turner shot him in the head with his pistol and turned back."

"Turner was a mad dog," Andre contributed. "He became an animal—and we French do not think much of the English, but we do not expect an Englishman to become a hyena. Finally, of course, he turned on his own men and killed them when he could not beat the Cubans and FAPLA. I remember he had a row with one English merc—I forget about what—and he would have shot him were it not for the merc pulling the safety pin from a fragmentation grenade and holding it out before him. If Turner had shot him, his hand would have released the pressure trigger and everyone there would have been cut by the metal fragments. Next day I think Turner had something else to distract him, and he forgot about the incident. He was a maniac."

They had both heard each other tell these stories before. It was like they were ritually displaying the tokens of their previous friendship to establish their standing with each other now. They were still friends from way back. But were they still on an equal footing as fellow mercs? Andre fought to dispel this question from Mike's mind. He had no doubt he was as good as he had ever been.

What neither of them mentioned was the incident which had cemented their friendship. Campbell and Verdoux were at the back of an open Land Rover manning an M60 machine gun as they went from observation post to observation post. An Angolan drove the vehicle, and three others mounted guard at front and sides with their FN automatic rifles. It was only another routine patrol. However, day by day these patrols grew more chancy as the FAPLA columns advanced. All that was holding them back now were the destroyed bridges which had to be rebuilt and mined roads which had to be made passable for their Russian-built tanks. Once the tanks got through, there could be no holding back the FAPLA leftists with their Cuban officers.

For a while the Land Rover bounced across open rangelands devoid of livestock and wild game—all shot by troops of both sides either from hunger or for fun. They reached a narrow asphalt road that had once led to a group of Portuguese farms and that was free of mines since it had no strategic importance. Long brown grass stood motionless in the afternoon heat on either side of the road. Campbell adjusted his machine gun and swiveled it on its mount, while Verdoux rechecked the ammunition feed belts. Both men's activity revealed their uneasiness in these surroundings, without their being aware of what they were doing. The Angolans peered into the long grass nervously, and the driver picked up speed.

The Angolan beside the driver saw him first, opened fire with his rifle and missed him. After that, it was too late. He was a tall, skinny black man, in green fatigues, who had suddenly stood up in the chest-high grass near the edge of the road a hundred yards ahead of them. Campbell swung the machine gun around to bear on him, but never got a bullet shot. The man already had the RPG2 launch tube on his right shoulder, his right hand on the forward pistol grip and his finger on the trigger. For an instant he sighted along the top of the tube at the Land Rover, then released the free-flight missile. The Soviet-made antitank missile hit the front of the vehicle with a violent thump.

The driver and the man next to him were killed instantly in the fiery impact. The four other occupants of the Land Rover were thrown onto the road. AK47 rifle fire raked the air above Campbell's head, and he saw little black spurts of tar knocked out of the road surface by bullets ricocheting off it. He rolled for cover behind the burning wreck of the Land Rover, which lay on its side still holding two charred corpses and sending a mournful column of black smoke up into the motionless air of the blue sky.

THE POINT TEAM

Andre Verdoux came rolling in a split second after him, pursued by a hail of gunfire that spattered off the steel of the disabled vehicle. The two other Angolans were not so lucky. One was almost cut in two by the hail of fire and curled into a twisted knot by the edge of the road. The second man lay on his back in the middle of the road, either dead or unconscious as a result of being thrown from the vehicle. Automatic fire ripped into his prone body and bounced it along the road with his arms waving in a grotesque imitation of life.

Mike stopped Andre from unstrapping his FN rifle from his back. He pointed to the long grass on the western side of the road, pulled two British L2A1 hand grenades from his belt and handed one to Verdoux. The Frenchman nodded that he was ready. Together, they pulled the safety pins and, momentarily rising from behind the cover of the burning Land Rover, threw their projectiles at the enemy and ducked down again. The grenades had a 4.3-second fuse, and the thin sheet steel case of each contained a coil of notched wire that broke into many lethal fragments on explosion.

As the charges blew almost simultaneously, the two ran and disappeared into the high grass. They stumbled through the growth, bent almost double for a while. Then the grass showed signs of thinning out the farther they got from the road.

"Let's lie low and see what happens," Mike gasped to Verdoux, restraining him by the arm.

They unstrapped their Belgian FN 7.62-mm automatic rifles. They had plenty of spare twenty-round magazines. Mike fitted the tubular bayonet over the flash suppressor at the tip of the barrel. Sounds of the FAPLA soldiers' voices drifted toward them. Campbell and Verdoux did not risk peering over the top of the grass to see what was going on. They could guess. The voices were quieter now as the men spread out and beat through the grass, searching for them. The Angolans kept in touch with one another in subdued

Portuguese larded with words from their own African languages. Only one voice was loud, instructing the men to move this way and that, in Spanish, not Portuguese.

"Goddamn Cubans," Mike muttered.

"They'll come at us in a line," Verdoux whispered. "If we can slip through that line and stay behind them, they'll never find us."

Mike nodded his agreement. He knew the chances of this happening were not good, since it sounded as if they were being searched for by a full platoon of twenty-four men. What neither had bargained for was that the Cuban officer could not keep the Angolans in a Northern Hemisphere-style straight search line. These Africans knew more about finding their quarry in their own landscape than military training could improve on. They ignored the shouts of the Cuban and performed their own private circling motions, each man working independently of the others. Campbell and Verdoux recognized they were in deep trouble at the approach and retreat and new approach of searchers crashing through the grass near where they lay.

A man rustled through the grass, and they could tell by the ever closer crunch of his boots on the dry stalks that he was going to walk right into them. Mike waved Andre back to cover him and knelt in waiting for the soldier. The FAPLA trooper did not see Mike until he was only a couple of feet away, whereupon Campbell drove the bayonet into his midriff. The Angolan gasped and crumpled. His AK47 did not go off.

"We'll stay here," Mike rasped to Andre, after waiting to make sure none of his fellow troopers had noticed the demise of the FAPLA soldier.

The searchers were all about them now, calling to one another, laughing loudly to give themselves courage and making plenty of noise as they advanced in the hope that whatever evil lay hidden in the long grass would flee before them. Mike and Andre waited.

THE POINT TEAM

Soon another soldier stumbled on them. This one was more alert than the previous one and would have returned their fire if he had not been distracted for a moment by the sight of the corpse of his comrade Mike had bayoneted. The dead man was not a pretty sight.

Verdoux took the Angolan with a burst of fire. Now that their position was revealed, they ran again, keeping stooped beneath the top of the high grasses. They could hear the Cuban screaming at the Africans behind them. They hid in a dense stand of grass and listened as the din of voices quieted and the search got under way again.

Gradually, the FAPLA troops neared them again in their apparently random search through the tall grass. This time, Campbell did not give the man a chance to discover them. When they heard him coming, they got ready to run. Then Campbell blasted him through the stalks of grass, and the trooper died without knowing what had hit him.

More panic. Shouting. Maneuvering. The hunt resumed. Campbell and Verdoux lay low in their new hiding place, having agreed on which direction to run on their discovery. They noticed that the Angolans were now less enthusiastic and, judging by their voices, moving about in small groups rather than singly. Verdoux smiled with satisfaction at Campbell. This was what they wanted. Although they were trapped in this area of tall grass, they were far from being taken. The sun was getting lower in the western sky, and there were no more than two hours of daylight left.

Finally they were approached by a group. From the voices, they reckoned there were six or seven. Verdoux and Campbell could afford no mistakes. Mike gestured he would sweep from center to right. Verdoux nodded. Both realized they could not leave anyone standing after they had emptied their twenty-round magazines. A single man could take out both of them while they reloaded.

Again, Mike did not wait till they were in full sight. He cut from center to right with full automatic fire and then cut a full swathe from right to left. Verdoux performed a mirror image of Mike's action. His bullets sawed through the grass and the figures it concealed till he ran out of ammo. Momentary silence settled, broken by a nearby groan and then the Cuban officer's shouting in Spanish. Mike and Andre reloaded as they crept away from the scene of carnage.

The Angolans gathered about their fallen comrades for a time and seemed unwilling to resume the search once again. None of them wanted the misfortune of being the ones to discover the mercs. They set grass afire along the edge of the road, but it burned slowly since there was no wind to make the flames travel. Soon the brief equatorial dusk would fall, then the darkness of night.

Mike and Andre considered attacking them. Before they could decide on tactics, the Angolans and their Cuban officer moved off down the road on foot. No doubt they had vehicles not far away.

As darkness fell, the two mercs set out for their base camp, about a hundred miles away. A detour to one of the forward observation posts could end in disaster if the post had been abandoned or overrun. They had a little water each, but no food. After following the road a little way, they branched off on a dirt trail in the direction they needed to go. It was during this walk that the friendship between the two men grew. They trudged all night by the light of the huge stars and talked to keep themselves warm and awake. They had been walking more than seven hours before being picked up before dawn by a market truck in safe territory. Not long after that, they had another long talk and decided to get the hell out of Angola while they could. They were among the last white mercenaries on Roberto's side to escape over the border to Kinshasa in Zaire. Those left behind died in battle, were executed or still rotted in nameless jails in Angola's communist state.

The Lutèce house specialty of chilled raspberry soufflé was served to them, and they followed it with coffee,

Armagnac and a replete feeling that all was well with the world, or almost.

"I really would have gone into business in Indochina if it hadn't been for the defeat of the French army at Dien Bien Phu," Andre Verdoux mused. "That's why I picked up a good working knowledge of Laotian and Cambodian as well as Vietnamese. I can manage to communicate in a number of the Montagnard languages, too, although these tend to change every few miles you go. That sort of knowledge could come in handy in your mission, Mike."

"Possibly," Campbell grudgingly conceded.

"You know a bit of Vietnamese, I suppose," the Frenchman said condescendingly. "Special Forces lingo you picked up in the field?"

"That's about it, I suppose."

"A lot of people there speak good French," Andre went on. "I'd hate to try to make my way with only a little Vietnamese and a lot of English."

"We don't expect we'll be chatting with that many folks, Andre. You imagine I'll be stopping people to ask them the way?"

"I know a lot about their customs, too," Verdoux added.

"I doubt we'll be attending any folk dance festivals," Mike said shortly.

"These two you've hired, you think they could help on this level?" The Frenchman answered his own question by shaking his head vigorously. "They're triggermen. Gunslingers."

"You're pretty fast with a gun yourself, Andre."

"Oh no, my friend, I am old and slow according to you. This mission would be too much for me."

Campbell sipped on his coffee and said nothing.

"Where do you go from here?" Verdoux persisted. "To interview more of these lunatics who will answer your stupid newspaper advertisement?"

"You answered it," Mike pointed out.

THE POINT TEAM

Verdoux raised his hands in a Gallic shrug. "I am a stupid lunatic."

"Why do you really want to go?" Mike asked seriously. "It's important."

"I know you think I am retired, Mike, and what I told you about looking for a trawler to convert is the truth. Of course you assumed I wanted to convert it into a houseboat and tie it to a jetty in Florida. Let's say I have other plans. Also, you should know I've been arranging some arms deals and training programs for some of the people I once fought against in Africa. These days it turns out to be my highest recommendation to them—the slaughter this white devil once wrought upon them. Now the same people want to buy my advice on how they can best do it to their neighboring tribe."

"I had heard talk along those lines about you," Mike said.

"You've hired two and you need three more men. What are your plans?"

"I'm seeing two candidates on Long Island this evening. Then I drive up to Vermont tomorrow to see an Australian."

"I'll go with you," Andre volunteered. "We'll share the driving."

"That would be great. Only this does not amount to a commitment on my part to you coming on the mission."

"*D'accord*. Agreed, *mon vieux*."

They both knew that Mike Campbell had lost the battle on this one.

Verdoux beamed and ordered more Armagnac.

Chapter 10

OUTSIDE Rawsonville, on the edge of the Green Mountains of Vermont, Bob Murphy pulled his jeep beneath the sign that read TAVERN, whose glow was lost in the early afternoon sunshine. The inside of the tavern was dark and cavernous, and several customers along the bar shifted and blinked like disturbed bats at the blinding light that shot in for a moment as Bob came through the door.

The barman reached for a bottle of Chivas twelve-year-old scotch when he saw him come in, and poured a treble measure over ice.

"Your wife sell you yet?" he asked with a grin.

Bob held up his drink. "Your luck, chum." He finished it in a single swallow and banged the glass back on the bar for a refill. "I been bought and sold so many times, I'll hardly notice it one more time."

"Caused a lot of talk about here, your wife's ad in that newspaper did," a gaunt elderly man up the bar said in a broad New England accent. There was a mixture of censoriousness and envy in his voice.

"Fuck 'em," Bob grunted.

His accent was as broadly Australian as the other man's was Vermont. Bob himself admitted that his accent had much diminished in the years he had spent overseas from his homeland—he liked to claim that when he first arrived in Britain, his accent was so thick people did not realize he was speaking English to them. Most people did not even recognize the word "Australian" when it was pronounced by him as "Strine."

If Bob Murphy's down-under accent had mellowed, very little else about him had. He was short and stocky, with shoulders way too broad for his body, arms too long for his frame and huge, gnarled red hands with which he liked to snap empty beer bottles clearly in two and lay the halves before him as a way of signifying he was ready for another. His face matched his hands. Beneath an unruly mop of straw-yellow hair, a couple of days' growth of yellow beard was scattered like wheat stubble on the red expanse of his jaws. His lips were thick and sensual, and his nose showed signs of having been broken and rebroken. In contrast, his eyes were brown, soft, and mild. When his language was obscene and his gestures coarse, his eyes gave him away to women. They saw his soul in them, the beauty beneath the beast. Other men explained his success with women by claiming his dick was a foot long and thick as a baseball bat. They did not believe him when he claimed he had never been unfaithful to his wife.

"What ad?" another man down the bar asked.

"You haven't seen the ad for Bob?" the barman asked. "In the paper two weeks ago?"

"If I had, I wouldn't be asking, would I?" the man said irritably. "What are they talking about, Bob?"

"I have the paper here," the barman said.

He handed his customer the local paper already folded over at the right page. From the well-thumbed condition of the newspaper, this topic had obviously been a conversation piece for some time in the establishment.

" 'Husband for sale,' " the man read laboriously. " 'A willing mate but mostly absent skiing, hunting or fishing. Answers to the name Bob. Contact Mrs. Eunice Murphy—'

Damn, she even put your phone number right here in the paper."

"Eunice thought it was funny when she did it," Bob explained calmly. "She had to have the number changed. Know why? Most of the callers didn't want to buy me, they wanted to come round and take care of her loneliness. Lot of weird people in this part of the world."

"They'd be people up from New York City, not local men," the elderly New Englander said with solemn certainty. "This whole part of the state has been spoiled by outsiders."

"Thanks," Bob said with a grin.

"I didn't include you," the man said humorlessly. "Though there's not all would agree with me there."

"Give him a drink," Bob told the barman. "I like an honest man."

"I don't want your drink," the elderly man said querulously. "I've been independent all my life. No one has ever given me so much as a piece of thread without being paid for it. I'll pay for what I drink here myself, in spite of your kind offer. Just as I did before you arrived and will after you've gone."

"Cancel that drink," Bob said to the barman.

The dourness of the old New Englander cast the tavern into a silent gloom. Bob thought about his wife, Eunice. People who knew them were divided in their opinions of the relationship. Some of Eunice's friends who had been to Bennington with her in their student days regarded Bob in the same way as if Eunice had married a pipe-playing shepherd clad in a goatskin—exotic to be seen with but definitely something you did not bring indoors.

Other women, mostly those who felt strongly attracted to the Australian, said that Eunice had been lucky in getting this hulk of a man to bed her and stick around. After all, even though Eunice was very rich, no matter how much one cared for her, one had to admit she was very ugly. Bob was no beauty, either. And he was good to

THE POINT TEAM

her. Certainly, she had a sparkle in her eye and a flush in her cheek after three years of marriage that none of the rest of them could claim. They could see the advantage of being married to an animal—excitement! And the brute was faithful to her... in spite of their efforts!

Eunice had surprised Bob once by explaining her awareness of their situation in other people's eyes. Eunice generally felt it was bad form to make such intimate communications, having been brought up in a family where women were expected to talk without moving their jaws. A lawyer at a party had been making cracks about Bob to his face. Bob wouldn't acknowledge the challenge for his own private reasons, of which Eunice was aware. She knew that if someone was aggressive to him, Bob saw no reason why he should limit his response to words even if the attack had been only verbal. In his book, when he fought he chose his own weapons, or he chose not to fight. Eunice saw Bob considering how he might take the lawyer apart physically, and she shook her head at him. He smiled back, and she was reassured. Then the lawyer's wife remarked in a loud voice that she did not know how Eunice could put up with a husband who didn't work and spent his time chasing deer, geese and fish. Eunice responded, sharp as a blade, that she'd prefer her husband to spend his time chasing fish and game than chasing other women. The lawyer went deadly pale, and his wife looked crushed. They left the party shortly afterward and were divorced six months later. Eunice must have taken that as an example of the dangers of expressing a strong personal opinion, for Bob had not heard one from her since. Perhaps the newspaper ad was the nearest that she came to one. And no doubt that had been at the goading of some of her Bennington friends.

Bob told nobody about the other ad in the paper. He would never have seen it if it hadn't been on the same page as his wife's ad offering him for sale. He didn't care about the big money, it was the phrase "combat-hardened veterans" that appealed to him. He was bored. In the winter he skiied, in the spring he fished—except for the Easter week, which he always spent with Eunice's family on Bermuda. In the summer he liked to take some fishing trips into northern Ontario, and they always spent the July Fourth holidays with her family at Newport, from where he did some open-water sailing. Fall was the busiest time of year for him, out before dawn every day of the hunting season. Then they always spent Christmas Day with his family on their traditional holiday picnic at the beach; from Australia they would spend a couple of weeks in one or more of the South Sea Islands. Then it was back to Vermont for the skiing.

After three years of this, Bob felt himself getting into a rut. Screwing someone else's wife was not his idea of a change. He was very happy with Eunice. He needed something to make his adrenaline flow, to make his hair stand on end, to make his knees knock and a cold sweat form on his forehead. Other people had those sensations all the time—even driving with him in his jeep! There were days when Bob felt he was made of lead. Dammit, he was a man of action who hated whiners and complainers. He would do something about it. Liven up his life. He had replied to the ad, received a phone call yesterday and arranged to meet him here today.

The phone call had been brief and mysterious.

"Mike's my name," the caller said. "You said in your letter you had been with the Aussie army in Nam."

"Right," Bob said. "Two tours of duty. And before that I was on loan to the Malaysian government as a jungle warfare expert. Hell, I wasn't no expert when I went there, but I sure was when I got out."

"And then you put Nam on top of that?"

"I had a ball," Bob chortled.

"How would you feel about going in again?"

Bob's chortle was cut short. "Is this what that ad's for?"

THE POINT TEAM

There was a lot of uncertainty in the voice, and Mike decided, against his better judgment, to put it to him over the phone.

Mike said, "Will it be worth my while driving up there to see you?"

There was a long silence.

"Yes."

"You sure?" Mike asked.

"Come on up."

"Where can we meet tomorrow afternoon?"

That had been about all. Bob laughed gleefully within himself as he sat stony-faced at the bar. He was so damn gung-ho, he had practically agreed to volunteer over the phone without even seeing who he was going with or getting any details. Eunice would take this hard. He sighed. And all because of her silly newspaper ad...

The barman polished some glasses with a white cloth and whistled to dispel the gloomy silence. It might be an hour before some of these daily customers said another word, but it wasn't usual for the Australian to be this quiet. However, the barman knew his job and did not intrude on Bob's thoughts if that was the way he wanted it.

The place was shook up by the arrival of three young men who looked barely of legal drinking age. They sat at a table, knew the bartender by his first name, and ordered a round of boilermakers. After their third round, they had gotten no quieter.

"Gonna go up on the old logging trail past Andrews' place and git ourselves one of those bears that's been seen there," one said boastfully to the bartender.

"Yeah, I hear a couple of big ones have been seen around there," the barman replied. "Five foot high, they say he was. Damn, that's big for a black bear."

The young man pointed up at a bearskin on the wall, complete with head and claws. "How big you think that one was?"

"Woulda been close to five feet," the barman said. "More drinks, boys?"

"No."

"We gotta go. We gotta shoot straight."

"Man, you can't even see straight. You gotta better chance of hitting those bears with your car than you do with your gun."

They went on kidding each other as they got up from the table and headed for the door.

The barman called after them, "Watch it, boys. This ain't hunting season. If they see you up on them hills with rifles—"

One of the three turned around and opened his jacket to reveal a heavy revolver stuck in his belt. "We don't have rifles." He patted the pistol handle. "We're gonna use these."

Another boasted, "We're gonna give the bears a fighting chance. Let 'em take a run at us, draw on 'em and shoot 'em down."

"You hope," the bartender said.

They laughed and went out through the door.

Bob Murphy stirred himself for the first time in half an hour. A mischievous smile spread across his face as he got to his feet.

"I'll be back in an hour," he said. "I'm expecting to meet someone here named Mike. Be sure he waits, and his drinks are on me."

Bob turned back for a moment and put a twenty-dollar bill on the bar. He looked across the room and said, "I want to rent that for a while."

The Rawsonville boys couldn't take their car up the unpaved logging road, but that was all right with them since they needed a little time to let their heads clear before tangling with bears. The climb up would straighten them out. Also, some dude in a four-wheel drive had passed them on the road, and they could tell by the dust which hadn't yet fully settled that he had gone up the logging road. Probably some fairy from the city on his way to pick wildflowers. But they couldn't be certain. He'd be long gone by the time they climbed to where the bears were being seen.

The road twisted around outcrops of naked rock and wound its way up the side of the mountain among stands of pine. Areas were free of timber where the soil was too thin for a tree's root to take hold, and here and there grew patches of the berry bushes that bears liked to feast on. It was too early in the year for berries, but the boys were townies and did not realize that. Their hands hovered over their pistols every time they came to a place they thought suitable for the animals, and they were so busy eyeing the bushes on each side for a sudden attack that they stumbled and sometimes fell in the dried-up gashes rivulets of water had cut in the road.

"You know they say a charging bear runs faster than a racehorse."

"Yeah, man, grizzlies are meaner than black bears, but grizzlies don't climb trees. Them black mothers'd run up a tree right after you. You got nowhere to go when they decide to kick ass."

"You should play dead. Lie face down and don't move. Even if they paw you."

"Talk loud. That's what we should do is talk loud. It frightens the fuckers, and you can hear 'em crashing through trees as they run away and get a shot at 'em."

"But don't whistle. You know why? 'Cause human whistling is like the sounds bears make when they got the hots for each other. You might get a big mamma bear come out of the sticks and put it to you."

That really broke them up.

They climbed on a way, their confidence building. None of them had gotten around to raising false alarms yet. They still believed that any moment now—maybe around the

THE POINT TEAM

next big rock or behind that bush—a bear might jump out on the roadway and challenge them.

"Hey!" One of them stopped and pointed to patches of chest-high bushes along a ridge. "I saw something move."

The others waited and watched.

"It was probably a bird."

"Or a squirrel."

"Maybe just wolves."

"Sure. Nothing to worry about."

They had only taken a couple of steps when one shouted, "Goddamn! It's bear! Look at the black fur! A fucking big bear."

"I saw it," the second confirmed.

The third hadn't seen it, but all the same he took his pistol from his belt, a .357 Colt MK III Lawman with a four-inch barrel. The other two had .357 Smith & Wesson M28 Highway Patrolman models, one with a four-inch and the other with a six-inch barrel. They packed a lot of stopping power and were none too worried as they spread out of each others' way and advanced on the bushes concealing the bear.

"He's got to break left or right. If he tries to go back over the top of the ridge, we got him sitting out in the open."

"Instead of going to either side, he can come right at us."

"Yeah. Gotta think of that."

"Mothers are faster than racehorses."

"Soon as you see him, blow the fucker away."

They advanced carefully, three abreast.

All three of them saw an area of black fur and then, to resolve all their doubts, they saw the bear's head and its bulging eyes glistening as it watched them. They started shooting. The bushes waved about as the bear threshed among them.

"I think we hit him!"

"Let's finish him off!"

They ran forward.

Zip! A bullet whizzed between two of them, followed by a gunshot. They stopped.

"What the fuck was that?"

"Come on, man. Must have been an insect flying by."

"That was a shot."

"From where the bear was."

Two more bullets whined passed them. Then to their horror, they clearly saw in the bushes a black bear with a revolver in its hand taking aim at them again!

They ran.

"You're really going to bring that imbecile along?" Andre Verdoux said to Mike Campbell under his breath.

Mike nodded and relaxed in the leather upholstered easy chair.

"He dresses up in a bearskin and shoots at hunters!" the Frenchman expostulated. "And you're going to bring him into Vietnam!"

"Yes."

"He insults us at dinner before his charming wife—who is no beauty, but she is sincere—"

"He didn't insult us," Mike explained. "He was joking."

Bob Murphy had persuaded them to stay overnight with him in order to meet an English acquaintance who had fought in Malaysia with him. Bob thought he would be the right man for the job. Verdoux had argued against this, out of Bob's hearing.

"Andre, you were the one who was against me seeing unknowns who answered ads. Now you don't want me to see someone with a personal recommendation."

The Frenchman snorted. "I would not call a recommendation from this Australian as something to take seriously."

"Perhaps not. But let's take a look. If you'd seen those two creeps I had to interview on Long Island yesterday, you'd know why I want to wrap this thing up any way I can. I'm sure one of them was a cop. When he saw I wasn't going to hire him, he thought about trying to bust me on the spot. I've seen enough of these guys. Besides, I don't feel like a five-hour drive back to New York this evening."

They had been surprised at the severe grandeur of Bob's residence. Somehow the restrained, traditional New England architecture and furnishings did not reflect Bob's personality. They understood when they met Eunice, whom they both liked. Needless to say, not a word was breathed to her concerning the forthcoming mission.

"What do you do, Mr. Campbell?" Eunice asked at the dinner table.

"I'm retired from the army," Mike replied.

"They're bird-watchers," Bob told his wife.

"Really?" She looked at them with interest. "I'm sure you'd prefer to be called ornithologists. Did you spot anything interesting today?"

Mike was not sure how to field this question. "Well, I live in Arizona. Desert birds are my specialty. I guess everything up here is new to me."

She turned to Andre. "And you, Mr. Verdoux. How does the avian wildlife here compare with that in France?"

Andre shot a look of hatred in Bob's direction before answering her. "Very different, I can assure you."

"Did you see a robin?" she asked.

"Ah yes, of course. With the red breast, no?" Andre said vaguely.

"What do you think of our American robin compared to the French robin?" she asked brightly. "Ours is huge in comparison, isn't it?"

"Yes, indeed. Big. Much bigger. Everything in America is much bigger." With cold fury Andre looked down the table at Bob, who was leering at him openly. Andre asked Bob, "What is that you call your Australian kingfisher?"

"Laughing jackass," Bob answered.

"Exactly." The Frenchman folded his napkin before him with satisfaction.

Chapter 11

"Van Ho Ven, get up!"

Eric Vanderhoven received a light kick on the thigh as he slept on a pile of rice straw, half covered with more of the same.

The next kick was a bit harder, so he opened his eyes and sat up.

"I'll wake the others," he said and struggled to his feet.

"This evening, after your work, we will discuss the burdens placed upon small countries by the great colonialist powers," the party cadre told him. "I want you to make a statement in front of the others."

"I'll remember to mention Russia as the biggest present-day colonial power," Eric said enthusiastically.

"Why? Why?" the cadre shouted. Then the cadaverously thin man in his thirties wrung his hands and lowered his voice so as not to wake the others. "Don't do this, Van Ho Ven. They will keep you here when I report it. I don't want you here. I want you to go away. You have been warned over and over. If you make this accusation of Russia, you will make me look like a failure. When I report it, they will punish you."

"Then don't report it," Eric suggested calmly. "Tell them I'm reeducated."

"I would if you could hold your tongue," the cadre said desperately.

"Let me see the papers you are putting through recommending our return to Ho Chi Minh City, and I'll keep quiet. So long as you don't ask my opinion at one of your dumb meetings."

The cadre thought for a moment, obviously tempted. Finally he shook his head regretfully. "No. The other cadres would know, and at least one of them would inform on me. I could be thrown out of the party."

"And have to go back to working again," Eric said sarcastically.

"Yes, indeed," the cadre answered with great feeling, "that could happen."

Eric pointed a finger at the cadre. "You do a deal with me on getting us out of this reeducation camp, and I'll keep my part of the bargain. But so long as I have to slop shit all day, I'm not keeping my mouth shut and there's fuck-all anyone can do about it except shoot me."

"They will," the cadre promised. "Now you are still a child, but when you turn sixteen, if you are then saying the things you say now, they will shoot you."

"I'll never see the age of sixteen in this goddamn piss-hole of a country. That's three years away," Eric said with a thirteen-year-old's awe of such a vast tract of time. "I'll be dead by then or gone out of Vietnam."

"You keep this up and you'll still be working here in this camp," the cadre muttered darkly. "I'll be the one who is dead or gone from Vietnam."

The skinny man exited through the door of bamboo canes. The walls of the hut were constructed of bamboo canes also, and the roof was thatched rice straw. The floor was bare earth beneath a covering of straw. Eric smiled to himself after the man was gone. He could see the gray streaks of dawn spreading in the east. There would be a struggle of wills at the ideology meeting tonight after work about whether he would be asked to speak. Eric guessed he might be, if only the cadre and the Amerasian kids were present. If other cadres or local peasants came to the meeting, Eric knew he would not be asked.

Eric's threat of becoming a blot on a bureaucrat's otherwise perfect record was his sole power. There could be no failure permitted in this new workers' paradise—and thus if Eric, a child of thirteen, could not be reeducated, it was because the cadre's approach to him was incorrect. The least hint of "incorrectness" in a cadre would be a calamity to his immediate progress within the party and could prove to be a taint difficult to lose in the future. Eric Vanderhoven was the kind of problem a party worker did not solve, but one whose responsibility he tried to shift elsewhere as soon as possible.

Eric woke up the eleven other Amerasian boys in the hut, using the cadre's light kick on the thigh followed by a somewhat harder one. Then he went outside and lit a fire, went to the well with two wooden buckets on a yoke across his shoulders, heaved a black cast iron pot upon the fire and partly filled it with water. When the water was boiling, he poured rice into it.

The other eleven youths, all twelve or thirteen years old, appeared in ones and twos. The first had a songbird he had killed the previous night with a stick. He poured some boiling water from the pot on it to make it easier to pluck. Others were foraging for edible herbs. One boy had some shredded pork left over from the cadres' dinner the night before. Another had a mouse that he had smothered with a shirt in the hut during the night. He disemboweled and skinned it and added its piteously small carcass to that of the tiny plucked and cleaned bird. They fried the meat in a skillet, deboned it, and chopped it into exceedingly fine morsels. They stir-fried the edible plants and chopped those up also. When the rice was cooked and drained, they mixed the meat and vegetables into it and then divided the whole into twelve equal portions. By the time they had wolfed the food with their fingers from wooden bowls, the sun stood clear of the eastern horizon and had burnt some of the mist from above the jungle trees.

The twelve Amerasian boys headed for the rice fields with the other workers. They kept apart from the others on the way in order to talk English among themselves. When Eric had first arrived at the camp, three of the Amerasian youths did not know a word of English. In only a few months they now had built up a limited vocabulary—what they could say, they said colloquially and naturally. The other boys, who had a basic knowledge of English, improved their skills rapidly under the strict standards and unforgiving attitude of Eric Vanderhoven.

"The cadres said yesterday they know we talk English out here," one boy told Eric.

"So let them come out to the rice fields and see for themselves," Eric said unconcernedly. "You'll never find a party member anywhere near where there's hard work to be done. It's the one place we don't have to listen to their crap."

"Yeah, but the informers tell them everything," the boy argued.

"The other people here are the same as us. Their word counts for nothing. Relax. We're Americans. We talk English." He raised his voice to a shout. "Fuck the commies."

Several of the workers looked over at him and quickly averted their heads. They did not understand what he said, but the tone of his voice had been clear, and he had spoken in English.

"You'll be reported," the boy said fearfully.

"Let me take care of that," Eric reassured him. "Quit worrying all the time. I'm looking out for us all."

Eric had this kind of talk—building up the morale and courage of the nervous—several times a day. Mitch and Red had been sent to the reeducation camp with him.

Although the other nine Amerasian boys had been strangers to him, he had become their unopposed leader within hours of his arrival at the camp.

As another boy approached, Eric realized that this morning he was having to deal with two extremes—the fearful and now the reckless.

"Pete. I've been thinking about Pete," the boy said. "They never caught him. Right now I bet he's walking the streets of Danang. He just walked out of here."

Eric sighed. "You suggesting we head south down the road and walk a few hundred miles to Ho Chi Minh City?"

"I am," the boy said steadfastly.

Eric pointed at the steaming, thick jungle bordering the rice fields. "If I walk anywhere, I'd prefer to take my chances in that direction, across Laos, into Thailand and *real* freedom."

"Over the mountains?" the nervous boy said aghast.

The reckless one said, "You go, I'll go with you. Right now."

"You think I haven't thought about all this before?" Eric said irritably. "Look, why do you think they don't bother to put guards on this reeducation camp? Simple. We don't have to run anywhere. If we want to get out of here all that bad, all we've got to do is become reeducated. Learn some of Ho Chi Minh's poems and quote a bit of Lenin, smile at the cadres, and we'd be out of here in a couple of weeks—after we've got the rice planted."

The others laughed at the accuracy of this observation. There were two rice harvests a year, and although work was continuous throughout the seasons, it was especially heavy during planting and harvesting. During these periods, no one was released from the camp, no matter how reeducated they had become.

Eric went on, "They don't care if we run off into the jungle. If the snakes or animals don't get us, if we don't die of fever, if the hill tribesmen don't cut us in pieces, if we don't lose our way... hey, you know at least one of those things is going to happen to us. If we could get a few rifles and ammunition, it would be different. We could steal enough rice here to see us through and cook it before we left."

Eric was unaware that he had started out putting down this escape route and had ended up kind of half-planning to use it.

Each of the youths was assigned a bundle of sprouted rice plants.

Eric commented in Vietnamese to the man who handed them out. "We shouldn't have to bother with this. The Americans have discovered you can plant the rice directly in the fields and it grows like any other grain crop. That's the way they do it in the States."

The man handing over the seedlings gave him a frightened smile and said nothing, but another adult spoke angrily. "The Americans are wasteful. They spatter rice seed all over and then have to thin the plants because they are growing too thickly. Vietnamese make every grain of rice count. That is our way."

Eric did not know what to reply to this, so he scowled and walked away.

The Vietnamese sentenced to the reeducation camp avoided the Amerasian youths in off-work hours for different reasons according to their backgrounds. The Viets disliked them because they were not pure Viets, just like they disliked the hill tribesmen and those of Chinese ethnic background. The ethnic Chinese, who had thrived as merchants under the various regimes prior to communism, had a double suspicion to live under—their bourgeois tendencies and possible sympathies with Vietnam's new enemy, communist China. The last thing they wished for was association with an outcast group like Amerasians.

On top of these conflicts lay the mutual dislike for each other of city and country people thrown together in the camp. City people sent to labor in the countryside looked

THE POINT TEAM

down on their tasks as demeaning to them and fit only for brutal, stupid peasants. The peasants sent to the camp were familiar with the work, hardened to it, easily made their quotas, and looked down on the smart-talking city people who did not know even the most basic rules of survival and self-sufficiency—they often joked that people from the cities thought rice grew on trees. Further, they identified communism and its communal farms, land seizures, forced labor and compulsory moves away from traditional villages and their ancestors' graves as being the work of city people. Amerasian youths were one of the few groups upon which they could vent their frustration and anger.

However, at work no one could be an outcast since that would affect the work production of all, and their food and treatment depended on their production in the fields. They had all heard stories of times when there had been trouble and soldiers were brought in. Some of the dissidents were killed, all were beaten continually even after they had stopped their protests, and many claimed that after having been supposedly released from the camp, they all disappeared. Although no one knew how true these stories were, no one wanted to test them.

The workers waded into the brown waters dammed in the rice fields.

"Hell, we got the lower fields to work today," Eric grumbled. "I bet we get assigned to plant in a whirlpool."

He was not far wrong. The upper fields were easier to work in because the depth of the water was rarely above the boys' knees. The water levels were deeper in the lower fields, and to reduce the level to permit work, water was released through sluice gates. The country people moved rapidly in to take the best positions in the fields—places with the easiest working conditions. The twelve youths were ordered to plant their rice seedlings where the muddy water was deepest and a current tugged at their legs as the water swept toward the sluices. The water came up to the chests of two of the youths who were pint-sized, and they had to struggle to maintain their footing on the slippery mud bottom.

"We'll have to wait for the water to go down," Eric yelled to them. "Come over here till it gets shallow enough."

They waded back from their assigned area.

"At least we can't get flukes when we have to work in these damn currents," Eric cheered up the others.

Two of the boys had been attacked by flukes, tiny invisible creatures that swam in the still water and entered the human bloodstream through the skin. The flukes caused abscesses and burst vessels in the gut, where they laid their eggs. All the boys had been already infected by malaria from mosquito bites, but none had a very serious infection, and the pills they were given kept them able to work. One boy had died in their first month at the camp. The party medical worker had not been able to figure out what was wrong with him, and no doctor was available.

The youths followed Eric out of the deeper, fast-moving water whose currents became swifter as more sluice gates were opened to speed up the lowering of the water level.

"Where's Harry?" one boy asked.

Harry was one of the smallest of the youths. He spoke not a word of English and had only a Vietnamese name when Eric arrived. Now Harry was Harry, because that was what Eric and therefore all the others called him.

They turned around to look, and at that instant saw Harry come to the surface where the brown water was swirling toward a sluice gate. Eric dropped his seedlings and splashed across a shallow area toward the deeper channel. He dived in, swam about trying to locate Harry, who had disappeared again beneath the surface. One of the boys pointed, and Eric saw a glimpse of Harry's shirt ten feet away in the murky water.

Eric half-ran with the current, half-swam under water, till he bumped into Harry and clutched at his clothes. He felt Harry's hands grasp and cling to him, and he turned and made his way against the flow of water back to the shallows as the panic-stricken smaller boy held onto him with the crazed energy of a giant wood tick.

Eric threw Harry face down on a mud embankment and knelt hard with both knees on the small of his back. A couple of quarts of water were forced out of Harry's mouth. When Eric released him, he began to vomit, taking huge, gasping intakes of air between convulsive spewings-up of water.

"Who's got my seedlings?" Eric asked.

No one had.

They spotted them floating half-submerged a little distance away, and three of the boys ran to fetch them. One of the peasants who functioned as a kind of overseer brought a huge double armful of rice shoots and dumped them on the embankment beside Harry. He left without a word. This extra work was punishment for what had happened— the seedlings had to be planted along with their regular allotments. Eric said nothing, because the peasant was respected by the other workers since he had proved he was not an informer. This did not mean he liked big-city Amerasians.

A bony, wizened old man joined the youths and helped them plant their extra seedlings, after motioning to Harry to stay where he was resting on the embankment. The old man reminded Eric of the gaunt monks he used to see begging outside the temples before the communists took over. He thought this man might be a monk and, not knowing what else to say to him, he asked him if he was.

The old man laughed and did not pause in his work as he answered, "Have you ever seen a monk plant rice? You think I learned to work like this in a monastery?"

Eric could see that this man by himself could plant more rice seedlings per hour than all twelve of them put together, so he shut up.

The old man continued, "You know, people weren't always so bad here in Vietnam as they are now. Today they have seen so many terrible things, they have become hardened. Before the Second World War, I remember, it was the French who were our masters, then the Japanese, back came the French again, then the Diem family in Saigon, and when they were gone Marshal Ky, the Viet Cong, and the Americans. Now it is the communists. We country people do not care who is in power if only they would leave us alone. But they never do. The worst of all are the communists. I am a wise old man. I do not shout my opinions for all to hear. I smile and say, yes, comrade. Until they moved me from my ancestral land. That I will not take . . ." He suddenly straightened up from his work, and his eyes blazed in his wrinkled face. "No. They cannot do that to me. When I leave this place, I will go back there again, even though they have forbidden it."

"Is that why you are here in this camp?" Eric asked.

"Yes. For being on my own land. Next time, they will have to spill my blood on the soil where my ancestors are buried before they can move me."

He stooped again at his work, and Eric worked alongside him, aware that his movements were slow and clumsy in comparison to the old man's. After a while, the old man showed him a certain way to hold the shoot and move his hands which involved less effort on his part. The man watched Eric for a while as he got the hang of it.

"That's good," the old man said, and looked about at the efforts of the other eleven boys. He smiled. "You must teach them what I have shown you."

"I will," Eric promised.

"I am sixty-eight," the man said. "I've had my life, and I am ready now to accept death. I've seen a lot of things—amazingly good and very evil. I don't think I want to stay around here much longer. It's you young people I feel sorry for."

"Don't," Eric told him. "We won't be staying here much longer, either."

The old man gave him a penetrating look and then returned to planting rice shoots in the mud beneath the water.

Chapter 12

LARRY Richards was thin, small, fast. His hair lay short and lifeless on his small head, and his face had a sort of yearning look that women much larger than him found irresistible. Men were more apt to notice the weasel expression in his face. Larry had been called a little rat more than once. He didn't mind.

Hannigan's Bar was across the street. Larry Richards sat behind the wheel of his car and waited patiently. This place was a gold mine for Provos. As soon as the Paddies came to this side of the pond, they lost all caution. As well they might, Richards thought to himself. Most Americans, even when they abhorred the violence, were on the side of the glorious rebels. British intelligence, on friendly territory with Washington when dealing with most other issues, was only now for the first time getting back against the IRA gunrunners and fund-raisers. However, problems still persisted on the individual level. FBI agents with Irish names—and also many without—could not be trusted to make a reasonable effort or even to cooperate as fully as they might on something else. The city police in New York, Boston, Philadelphia, and Chicago were worse.

Richards, a Londoner, was a freelance agent. He went

where pay was highest. Theoretically. Because in real life you worked for one power center, and if you stepped out of line, they fucked you good and proper. All of which brought Peregrine Addendale to his mind. Addendale, the one at the British consulate who dealt with Richards, was something out of a John LeCarré novel. He was elegant, understated, Stonyhurst and Oxford. Richards' background was the drab northern London suburb of Finsbury Park and the fairly new Sussex University.

Peregrine Addendale had style. He had insisted that Larry do this job with the gun issued to him, an Enfield revolver No. 2 Mk 1. This was a variation of the gun issued to the British army in 1932! Larry supposed he was fortunate Addendale hadn't insisted he drive a vintage car. And he was to leave the gun on the scene... This old British Empire revolver was to be a signature to tell the Provos they were not safe on this side of the Atlantic, either. As far as Larry was concerned, this was Oxford amateur theatricals.

The Provisional IRA did not use Hannigan's Bar as a meeting place, as far as Larry Richards could tell. The neighborhood bar in Woodside, Queens, was just a casual waterhole for any of the lads who happened to be in this New York City borough. The subway here was elevated on steel girders, and trains clattered almost directly above where his car was parked. It was less than half an hour's run into Manhattan.

Richards once again riffled through the wad of photos, front and side shots of hard-faced men and a few women. He stopped when he came to Don Morgan's mug shot and stared with hatred at the calm visage which looked out at him from the photo. Morgan had been sentenced *in absentia* to fifty-five years in jail in a Belfast court for the killing of one British parachute regiment soldier and the wounding of three others. Morgan had placed a radio-controlled bomb at the side of a narrow country road and detonated it from his hiding place as the patrol of four soldiers passed the bomb in their Land Rover. From what Richards had heard, two of the three soldiers who survived were so mutilated it would have been a greater mercy had they been killed outright. Morgan had been arrested and confessed to the crime under interrogation. While on his way to a court hearing, his prison wagon was struck by a heavy truck and Morgan was rescued at gunpoint.

Morgan had dropped out of sight for more than two years when Larry Richards saw him one afternoon leaving a bar on Third Avenue and traced him to an address in Kearney, New Jersey. At first Peregrine Addendale, then new at his job, had refused to believe Morgan had reappeared on this side of the Atlantic and further insisted that everything had to be done in a lawful manner to apprehend him. Richards placed Morgan in the Jersey location and asked Addendale to call in the Feds. As Addendale somewhat shamefacedly put it later, the FBI, the Marshals Service and the Bureau of Alcohol, Tobacco and Firearms all turned down his request because the British had never listed Morgan in their computers. After four hours on the stakeout with no action, Richards phoned Addendale to ask what was happening. They agreed to call the New Jersey State Police or Kearney police only as a last resort, and, on Richards' suggestion, Addendale tried Immigration first. Two inspectors came and left empty-handed. Morgan himself left the place ten minutes after they had gone. Addendale started to learn at that point he was no longer in Buckinghamshire. That had been five months ago.

Now Richards had Morgan spotted again. He came several mornings a week to Hannigan's and spent an hour or so there. Richards decided not to risk following him, since his informant had said this could easily spook Morgan. Addendale hadn't held back this time. It had been a straightforward "Get rid of Morgan." Then he was handed an antique weapon! Actually, there was nothing wrong with the Enfield revolver. It had been standard British army issue throughout the Second World War and continued in service till replaced by the Browning HP35. In spite of its being a bit cumbersome in comparison to modern weapons, it was reliable because its double action was built to stand up to the wear and tear of military use.

Morgan came out of the bar with two other men. Larry Richards recognized one of them. He flipped through the photos rapidly—he knew the position of the photo vaguely—and checked out the mug shots of a fair-haired man. Willie Stevens. Murder. Possession of high explosives and firearms. No information as to why he was on the loose. Peregrine Addendale had probably never heard of him and would expect Richards to capture him with a butterfly net. Fuck that. If Morgan walked down the street with Stevens, Richards would call it a day. Come back some other time. He wasn't going to take those two on—and he had no idea who the third man was—with a fucking King George VI all's-well-with-the-world Enfield revolver. After all, Larry Richards said aloud, he was not down from Oxford.

Morgan stood for a while talking with the two men, then shook hands with each and headed off down the sidewalk by himself. He turned into a street of residential homes and disappeared from Richards' view. Larry Richards started the car's engine, slipped it into gear and drove across the intersection and into the street. He saw Morgan five hundred yards farther along, drove past him and pulled into a space at a fire hydrant. He pulled on a pair of leather gloves, took out the .38 Enfield, twirled the chambers and replaced it in his side pocket.

He knew Morgan would register his presence in the parked car. A man on the run notices details in a way that would be paranoia in someone not being hunted. Richards wanted Morgan to be aware of him—he wanted to see a flicker of fear in the man's face, wanted to see him run for his life and then recognize it was too late, that retribution had overtaken him, that death was here. Such a ceremony was far more satisfying than simply creeping up behind someone and shooting him in the back. The end result was the same in both cases, but the first method was that of a craftsman who enjoyed his skills.

The Provisional IRA man strolled by the car with only the most casual of glances inside. Richards was not fooled. If he had made a move, Morgan would have thrown himself out of the line of fire in a split second. Richards climbed out of the car and closed the door quietly behind him, and the sinister click of the lock being pressed shut rather than the door being thoughtlessly slammed caused a perceptible stiffening of Morgan's body, but he did not turn around. Richards walked on the sidewalk after him, and for a moment the sound of their footsteps, slightly out of sync, was all that could be heard on the quiet street.

Richards held the .38 beneath his coat. Morgan's hands swung beside him as he walked. If he reached for a weapon, Richards would blast him to kingdom come before he could free it. He did not want to move too far from his car, hired as always under a false name, but he wanted to see some reaction from his victim before he wasted him.

A car came down the street from behind Richards. Morgan quickly turned and began to cross in front of it. The driver had to brake to a stop to avoid him. But Morgan wasn't looking at the car, he was looking straight at Richards, and his eyes dropped to where Richards was holding the revolver beneath his coat. Morgan knew.

"What the hell's with you, fella?" the driver of the car shouted to Morgan. "Get the fuck outa my way."

"Shut up, you thick-headed fool," the Provo responded in a sharp, almost Scottish accent.

The driver jumped out of the car. He had the build of a football player and was in his early twenties. He walked up to Morgan, still standing in front of the car. Morgan swung out in a sudden uppercut and decked the driver across the hood of his car. Car doors opened, and two other big bruisers leaped out to join the fray.

THE POINT TEAM

Richards smiled and decided that the Provo was unarmed. Well, this was not going to get him out of the trap. As Morgan faced off against the two, holding up his fists and moving on his feet like a trained boxer, Richards raised the Enfield, sighted quickly down the barrel and squeezed the trigger.

Morgan was knocked off his feet by the impact of the bullet, and the two men about to fight him looked down in puzzlement at his body on the road. They were standing next to the running engine and didn't hear the shot or see Richards walk away back up the street to his car.

Bob Murphy had called him the previous night and said he wanted him to meet two men, an American and a Frenchman, with a proposition that might interest him. Richards would drop off the hired car at La Guardia Airport, hopefully vanishing without a trace there if someone saw the car, then catch a taxi from there to Republic Airport in Farmingdale and fly his Cherokee Six 300 up to Bennington, Vermont.

He got in the car, made a U-turn and tossed the Enfield revolver out the window as he sped away.

Campbell, Verdoux and Murphy spent the morning skeet shooting on Murphy's private range. The Australian outshot the others easily, so the close competition was between Campbell and Verdoux. When Andre beat Mike narrowly, it was silently recorded by Verdoux as another factor that qualified him for the mission—something that showed he still had a good eye and reflexes, something to demonstrate he was not yet over the hill. Mike pretended not to be aware of this.

Mike knew that Andre was up to something. He had driven into Bennington first thing that morning. Mike suspected he had gone to make calls on a public phone, and when he took off alone again after lunch, he was sure of it.

"Larry Richards will be in sometime during the afternoon," Bob Murphy told them. "He had an appointment he couldn't break this morning, so why not let's all relax until we get his call from the airport. I guarantee he'll fit your team, Mike, and be raring to go."

"You seem pretty sure of him, Bob," Campbell commented noncommittally.

"I served with him in Malaysia," Bob said. "When you chase commies in the jungle with someone, you know real soon whether you can depend on him as a partner or not."

"I know what you mean," Mike agreed.

"After that, Larry was with the SAS in Ulster for a couple of years. I would think whatever he mightn't have learned in Malaysia, he picked up on there. A bit of postgraduate study, you might say."

"Larry Richards was never in Vietnam," Mike said, "and I hadn't intended taking anyone along who hadn't already been there."

"That's for you to decide," Bob conceded, "but I've seen combat in both places—Vietnam and Malaysia—and it doesn't make a hell of a lot of difference in which one you happen to be if you're lugging a thirty-five-pound backpack and your equipment and you're knee-deep in swamp water crawling with snakes, with mosquitoes big as hummingbirds—"

"All right, all right," Mike laughed, "I'll keep an open mind."

When the call came from the local airport, Bob left to pick up Larry Richards. Andre Verdoux had said nothing much for a while. Mike guessed he did not approve of Bob Murphy, but was saying nothing because opposition from him now might endanger his own place on the team.

Mike teased him. "If you don't think much of this Aussie, wait until you see the other two I've recruited. This is going to be a real rat pack, Andre."

The Frenchman gruntled moodily.

When Bob Murphy brought the Englishman, Mike took

THE POINT TEAM

the newcomer to one side without delay. What he did not need were contributions from Andre and Bob, negative or positive.

"Well, you seem like you've seen a bit of action," Mike started in a friendly tone.

He told him very little about the mission, that it would be worth a hundred thousand dollars to him, and that it would be a very high-risk operation.

"Why do you want to go?"

"For the hell of it," Larry answered.

"Not the money?"

Richards shook his head. "I'd make that much money in a day flying in coke from the Caribbean. No, I want to do some soldiering again. And if that's the way I meet my Maker, so be it."

"Where do you go from Bennington?"

"I live in Rome, New York, not far from Utica. Less than an hour from here by air."

"You got a wife and kids?"

"Back in England somewhere," Larry said. "I'm forty-two and I got a girl friend less than half my age. So I'll be no irreplaceable loss to anyone except myself."

"Looks like you're on the team, then."

They shook hands and rejoined the others.

After a quick look at Campbell, Verdoux took up the offensive. "Lawrence Richards is a familiar name in some circles. I don't suppose you'd be the same one who works for Canadian intelligence in surveillance of French-speaking Quebecois on this side of the border?"

Richards smiled nonchalantly. "All you Frenchies imagine the Anglo-Saxons are out to get you."

"I hear our host"—Verdoux gestured to the Australian—"was along on some of your assignments."

Bob remained silent.

"It seems also"—Verdoux was enjoying himself—"that you haven't completely severed ties with your mother country, Mr. Richards, in spite of becoming an American citizen. I hear that you provided protection of some sort during Her Majesty's recent visit to California, that you have been involved in funneling arms to Belize via the Bahamas, that you once were involved with Libyan transactions but they no longer deal with you, that the Provisional Irish Republican Army has a price of ten thousand dollars on your head... I'm sure there are other things I've forgotten to mention. Bob Murphy doesn't seem to be involved in anything but spying on the French Canadians.'' Andre paused for effect. "I got all this today with two telephone calls. Imagine what I could come up with if I had time."

Mike Campbell swiveled his eyes around to Larry Richards. "Any reason I should trust you to come on this mission?"

Richards dismissed Verdoux with a contemptuous wave. "Certainly Frenchie here is right. I'm a field operative, and since I'm a successful one I happen to be well-known. Only those who never achieve their objectives manage to stay undercover. But, Mike—you wonder, am I a security risk to you? According to Frenchie here, the Canadian and British governments trust me to do work for them—I'm not acknowledging that I do. If they can trust me, why can't you? The Canadians and British have nothing to gain from me selling them information about you, and you yourself, Mike, say that Washington is on to you, which is why you're recruiting in the lonely hearts columns or whatever. I bet that's where you found Frenchie."

Verdoux exchanged an amused look with Campbell and said nothing.

Richards went on, "Take you, for example, Mike. Mad Mike Campbell. How many phone calls do I have to make to give you a lurid bio? None at all. You're the last person on earth, Mad Mike, to query me on my résumé."

"I said you were on the team, Larry. Now shut up."

Richards clammed up. He and Verdoux exchanged malevolent glances.

THE POINT TEAM

"All right, you men," Mike said in tones of this-is-the-colonel-speaking, "get this and get it straight. We go into training in five days' time. You will be informed of your mobilization area twenty-four hours in advance. You will be given a phone number to call if you want to drop out between now and then, but once in training you're stuck for the duration of the mission. I repeat. Once in, no outs. No communications. No nothing. You've gone. Clear? Now, I'm a nice guy and I don't want to have to see you suffer, so I'm telling you now to start running. If you can run ten miles without throwing up by five days' time, training won't go so hard with you. Because you'll be running twice that distance in ten days' time. This is not going to be a golf-cart war, so if any of you old-timers can't hack it, do us all a favor and quit now. Any questions?"

"Where do we go for training?" Bob asked.

"Location G."

That was the end of the question period.

As they drove back to New York, Andre asked Mike, "Where is Location G?"

"Sounds good, doesn't it?"

"You mean I'm going to have to take them jogging around Central Park reservoir?"

Mike laughed. "I think I'll be able to come up with something better than that. After all, I've got five days. What are you angling for, Andre? Second-in-command?"

"I should think so, considering I'm the only other sane person besides you on this mission. Not forgetting, of course, that you're Mad Mike."

Chapter 13

THE two southerners, both from the Mekong Delta, were awed by their visitor. Their agency was not one of the favored ones in the Ho Chi Minh City bureaucracy, as evidenced by the upturned wooden crates they used as desks and the single light bulb that provided illumination in that sectioned-off area of the warehouse. The younger of the two southerners still hoped to use influence to get transferred out of the Commission for International Media Goodwill. The fact was this government bureau had nothing to do; the international media were not allowed into Vietnam and goodwill was the last thing anyone was expected to show them. The older man, the commissioner, knew that for better or worse this was where he would have to either sink or swim in the new freedom of the communist state.

The visitor, totally unexpected, was reputed to have been one of General Giap's most important intelligence administrators during the war of liberation against the American imperialists and their puppets. In many ways he looked like Mahatma Gandhi—thin, ageless, ascetic, wire spectacles, but with a shock of virile, Asiatic black hair instead of a bald pate.

THE POINT TEAM

Both the southerners knew this Hanoi visitor was much more dangerous than a party functionary they could flatter, fawn before and perhaps even bribe. This man was an idealist. Useful in times of war but a nuisance during peace. Many of his kind had already been jailed by the new leadership—but they could not touch the legends. With Ho Chi Minh safely in his grave, they had deposed Giap out of necessity but let the other heroes stand.

The younger of the two southerners had obviously decided not to utter a word under any circumstances during this meeting. There were worse survival ploys, the older of the two acknowledged to himself, but he was obviously not to be allowed to take refuge in blessed silence.

"You have granted a license for the return of this American woman Nelson and her television crew?"

"Only after clearing it through the appropriate channels. The Commission of—"

"Yes, I know," the man from Hanoi said. "But yours is the signature permitting this woman to enter the country."

The southerner paused. "I recognize I have undertaken a heavy responsibility and that I am ill-fitted to do so. Any advice from an illustrious person such as you would be very welcome."

"May we dispense with the courtesies?"

"You are too kind in your offer," the southerner responded, becoming even more formal and rigid than before.

The man from Hanoi twisted his old dry hard mouth and pointed a bony finger. "Your name is on the permit for this woman and her crew."

"A formality. That is all. I sign the papers. You people in Hanoi give the orders." All his formality was gone; he might have been bargaining in the market. "You know as well as I do that I didn't make this decision. I don't have the power to! She's not here yet! Let's cancel it! That's what I'll do! Cancel it! Null! Void!"

"You don't have the power to cancel it," the man from Hanoi said, like someone making a seemingly innocuous chess move that somehow seems vital to an unseen deadly attack.

"Both of you speak English very well." This was a statement of fact from the man from Hanoi. "You both will be held responsible for the success to communism of this imperialist woman. She can be guided to see the positive aspects of our society. That was done on her first visit here, with which you were not involved. Have you seen the videotapes of her American special?"

"Yes."

"What did you think?"

The southerner did not hesitate. He had heard the correct responses a hundred times. "She showed little understanding of our socialist way of life, but also no animosity. She did not show unfavorable footage or make vindictive commentary. While she showed nothing new for an audience here or in another communist country, she did show imperialists that we are human beings who cherish the right to work and real freedom in terms that their corrupted minds could understand."

"Word perfect," the man from Hanoi commented drily. "On her second visit we have a slightly different purpose in mind. Listen carefully to what I have to say." He told them quickly about Eric Vanderhoven's theft of the TV equipment and of his subsequent discovery and dispatch to a reeducation camp. He said nothing of the tapes made of Russian ships. "The interesting thing is that neither she nor we associated this youth with the robber baron of that name in America, although it was on record that his father had married a Vietnamese woman. We only realized it when the grandfather tried to have him released first by threats from Washington and, when those failed, by diplomatic maneuvers through the Swiss. We have said nothing and waited for this to be publicized in America. They kept it quiet. Now this woman Nelson comes here to film this youth in the reeducation camp in order to cause a cheap sensation in America and make a lot of money for her employers. Do you understand?"

"Yes."

'We will permit her to do this. Why, I will discuss in a minute. It is important that she does not learn this, that she thinks she is gaining access to the camp through stealth. Her guides will find themselves outwitted by her tricks. The cadres at the camp should know, but no one else there, particularly not the boy himself. Understood?"

"Yes."

"Why are we doing this? You should know, in order to control things properly. We must have access to world markets, and American dollars, not Russian rubles, are the means of exchange. When the Americans see the grandson of a man with a billion dollars stooping at work in one of our rice fields, they will pay anything to rescue him. Rich people are sacred in America, like cows in India—people get upset when they imagine they are being mistreated. Do you understand?"

"No."

"Americans are very strange people," the man from Hanoi counseled him. "You have seen them with your own eyes while they were here. They are in a hurry. They want impossible things. But we have learned one thing from our Buddhist ancestors—those who cannot wait never win."

"We can wait."

'We have waited long enough," the man from Hanoi contradicted him. "We have allowed a trickle of children out of the country and stories of American prisoners. This will focus the problem. And, as you know, Americans solve problems with money."

"My responsibility will be to see that she gets to make the film without us seeming to permit it, that the boy is well treated from now—"

"No! The little mongrel must not be pampered."

"I'll do my very best."

"I hope so," the man from Hanoi said, "especially since you were the one to sign the Nelson woman's entry permit."

"Sit down, Mr. Campbell." William Vanderhoven gestured to a chair by his desk. "Bear with me for a few minutes while I attempt to untangle some knots in my business day."

New York Stock Exchange results floated from right to left across one CRT display to the right of his desk. On a second CRT, certain stock readings were being frozen in place momentarily, interrupted by graphs, shown again and finally replaced with new ones, for which the process was repeated.

Vanderhoven picked up one of the phones and punched some numbers. "John, what the devil are you trying to tell me?" He listened for a while, then said, "Run that past me again." After watching the material once more on the CRT, he said, "It's worth a try. See what you can do."

A pretty woman in her early thirties stood in his open office doorway waiting for him to finish. "You see the performance of Pequod Data?" she asked.

"Jumping up and down like a yo-yo."

"We could make a lot of money with a straddle.... Even *I* could do that."

Vanderhoven looked at the pretty girl. "Go ahead, then, take two hundred and play with it."

"Me? Oh, I couldn't." She giggled and fled.

"Emily," Vanderhoven called after her, but she didn't come back.

Campbell assumed that the two hundred the old man told her to take amounted to two hundred thousand dollars and that Emily had lost her nerve at the prospect, temporarily anyway. Or she might be aware that had she lost some of the money, the old man's countenance might not be so sunny and her prospects in the business grow very dim.

THE POINT TEAM

A lean man in his fifties poked his head in the door. "We're doing good, Mr. V."

"Give me a number."

The man gave him a number and disappeared.

"You better talk while you have the chance, Campbell."

Mike looked at two buttons lit on the phones and a third blinking. "I'm here to talk about Location G."

"What?"

He had the old man's attention. "That island you own on the South Carolina coast between Charleston and Georgetown. I'll need it all next week."

"You got it," Vanderhoven said. "It's not that far north of Parris Island, where the Marines train. I assume you have something similar in mind."

"I have. I'd also like to use your Gulfstream Commander Jetprop to drop us off and pick us up."

"You're limited to seven passengers and fourteen hundred pounds of baggage," Vanderhoven said.

"That will do fine."

"Anything else of mine you got your eye on?"

Mike grinned. "I'll let you know."

Vanderhoven waved his arms about him. "Think you'd like this kind of life, Campbell?"

"Can't be certain, but I doubt it."

"You can have a lot of fun doing what I do, even an old guy like me. I wield a lot of power over a lot of people."

"I'm more interested in gaining power over myself," Mike said seriously. "Seeing what I as an individual am capable of firsthand. I guess I don't get a charge out of doing things through other people."

"Some people call me ruthless, Campbell, but I'm not sure I could pull the trigger to give someone a bellyful of lead."

"I think you would, sir, if you thought he was on the point of doing the same thing to you."

"Maybe. Maybe. I don't know," Vanderhoven mumbled.

Mike did not mention that judging from what he had

THE POINT TEAM

heard of Vanderhoven, getting a bellyful of lead would be a quick death compared with the mortal wounds he had administered in the financial world. He had once been known to boast that not a year had passed in his business life without a failed rival taking a walk out a high window.

"All set with Katie Nelson and her TV people?" Vanderhoven inquired.

"No problems."

"I told you before, she's got nothing in writing from me. I don't give a damn how you treat her."

"I'll cooperate with her fully so long as everything's on the level," Mike said.

"That's your business, Campbell. Look, I deal with percentages here. What are your chances of success? Give me a number."

"Why? Are you opening a betting operation on us?"

"I'm investing two million in you," Vanderhoven replied. "What are my chances of seeing that kid in this office?"

"Not great."

"That's what I figured." Vanderhoven waved his hands about the screens and equipment. "You think Eric will like all this computer stuff? Sure. Any kid would."

Chapter 14

MIKE Campbell took an early morning flight from New York to Atlanta and changed there for the connecting flight to Mobile, Alabama. Cuthbert Colquitt was expecting him in Mobile, and Mike hoped to finish his business there quickly, catch a flight to New Orleans and another from there to Phoenix. This would give him a couple of days with Tina before heading for training on Vanderhoven's island. Andre Verdoux, now ensconced as second-in-command, was handling everything from New York, where they would mobilize before going into training.

Mike had dealt with Cuthbert Colquitt many times before, and there could be no doubt in the arms dealer's mind why a well-known merc such as Campbell was paying him a visit. A dependable source of arms was essential to any military operation, mercenary or otherwise, yet at the same time it represented one of its greatest security risks. It was through arms dealers that word often leaked about upcoming mercenary operations. On this point Mike was certain: Cuthbert Colquitt was silent as the grave.

If Mike could, he would delay the pickup of their arms till the last possible moment. For overseas operations, he

THE POINT TEAM

liked his crew to arrive in the area without carrying incriminating evidence on them. After arriving they would have a chance to review the local situation before taking delivery of their arms supply. Possession of military-grade weapons by soldiers of fortune seized by government authorities was usually equivalent to automatic guilt on the part of the mercenaries. If the team was not holding explosives or guns, little more than vague charges of conspiracy could be leveled against them, which at the worst might result in their being deported. However, once a merc picked up a gun, he was in water way over his head.

Despite the popular concept of a merc team arriving in the dead of night in inflatable rafts with camouflage nets and blackened faces, laden with rockets and small artillery, Campbell usually arranged for his crew to enter a country in business suits or as tourists and to travel by scheduled flight or whatever was normal. He was convinced that this was by far the most inconspicuous mode of entry into a heavily populated area. Entering into remote or isolated regions obviously posed different problems.

The pickup of weapons created a point of vulnerability for the team. Availability of the latest technology was no problem, even in relatively primitive parts of the world. The latest arms designs were available anywhere in the free world to those with the cash to pay for them. Through Cuthbert Colquitt in Mobile, Alabama, Mike could order just about anything for delivery just about anywhere outside China, Russia and most other communist countries. Easy as telegraphing flowers on Mother's Day.

From the Mobile Aerospace, he took a taxi out to the edge of town. The office and warehouse of Colquitt Armaments, Inc., were in an industrial park with clusters of azaleas in several shades of red, orderly flower beds and busy lawn sprinklers. Inside the plate glass double doors a truly exotic creature, whose long graceful legs sprang from a narrow skirt, was adjusting an eyelash before a pocket mirror.

"Where's Mary Lou?" Mike asked.

"Gawn. She had a fight with Cuthbert, I guess. I'm Sue Ann."

As a newer model of weapon with added features renders another model obsolete, Mike guessed Sue Ann had been added to Cuthbert Colquitt's arsenal. However, as Mike soon saw, Cuthbert himself remained unchanged. He launched his huge bulk out of his desk chair to greet Mike, shook his hand with his great paw and beamed with loose red jowls and square white teeth clamped on a cigar.

Colquitt removed the cigar with his left fist and said, "You workin' for them Yankee carpetbaggers again, Mike, down here to rob us poor simple Confederate folk?"

"The day I rob you, Cuthbert, is the day I decide to run for governor of Alabama."

"We've had worse than you running this state, Mike. Meaner, bigger, thicker-skinned. Could bite into live 'gators, some of 'em. But you ain't come all this way to talk about local doings. Sit you down here now and have a glass of good bourbon to ease your troubles."

Colquitt poured out generous measures for both of them. Campbell guessed that somehow this was neither the first nor even the second drink Cuthbert had had this morning. He was just bursting out all over in good-ol'-boy joviality.

"You have any problem with Thailand?" Mike asked after they had exchanged some pleasantries.

"Hell no, boy, them Thais is just like cousins to me. I do business in Bangkok easy as I do in Montgomery, Alabama. A little easier, in fact."

"Great. So we'll need six M16s—"

"Mike, if you're going where I think you might be going, you'll have to carry all your ammo with you. You can't pick up those 5.56-mm shells anymore like you could in the old days when you needed fresh ammunition."

"I thought a lot of the communist militias still use captured M16s and stuff we left behind."

"Up until a couple of years ago," Colquitt said, "but not so much anymore. They've replaced most of the old weapons with new Kalashnikovs, and as you know, the Russians make those bullets 7.62- by 39-mm so they don't fit no Western guns."

"So we should carry AK47s?" Campbell asked.

"Sure. I can get you six of the latest model, the AKM—though folks still call it the AK47. It's a lightened and slightly modified version with a stamped-steel receiver, a ribbed receiver cover and a cyclic rate reducer that is incorporated into the trigger mechanism. The bayonet is different—it won't fit on the old AK47. It's the sort you can use as a wirecutter against its scabbard."

"This new model still have the cleaning rod mounted beneath the barrel?" Campbell asked.

"Sure thing. Just like a damn old musket."

"Handy thing, though," Mike said. "Give me six of the AKMs. With night scopes."

"You got 'em, boy. How about some nice Uzis as well?"

"The Uzi is a nice gun, Cuthbert, and we need a submachine gun. But you're talking about almost eight pounds in weight for each gun, and we're on foot—not touring the scenery in a personnel carrier. What about an Ingram?"

"The M10 model is a bit over six pounds, and I can give it to you in .45- or 9-mm parabellum. The M11 weighs only three and a half pounds and takes 9-mm shorts in a 16- or 32-round box magazine. You can't beat the M11 for lightness and reliability. Only thing is, you're giving away a lot in effective range when you compare it to a Uzi."

"Yeah, I know," Mike said. "The Uzi is about two hundred meters, while the M11 is only fifty."

"The Ingram M10 is seventy-five meters."

"No, I'll take the M11. Give me six of them, with sound and flash suppressors."

Cuthbert whistled appreciatively. "I can just see all them dead commies lying all over the place already."

Mike guessed that Cuthbert Colquitt had never in his life shot at anything bigger than a jackrabbit, but when it came to accurately describing the capabilities of weapons, he knew no one better at it than this Southerner. They continued to discuss in detail all Mike's requirements, comparing weapons and equipment. He could see Cuthbert was impressed that so far Mike had never asked the price of anything. Mike intended to bargain only after he had got a satisfactory array of hardware together. When they had covered all his conventional needs, Cuthbert heaved himself out of his chair.

"Come on, Mike. I want you to see some things I got in my warehouse."

Campbell feigned reluctance, developing a resistance to Colquitt's steamroller salesmanship. "I don't know, Cuthbert. I've seen very good stuff in Sweden and Belgium recently. I don't think you could match it."

Colquitt looked hurt. "Foreign junk! These here goods I'm going to show you is fabulous made-in-USA stuff, all-American. Come on, Mike, bring your bourbon and take a look. Maybe you want to stop off on the way and attack China with the shit I got in my showroom. You'd win."

The Gulfstream Commander Jetprop took the team to the airport outside Charleston, where a limo picked them up and conveyed them to a seventy-foot yacht top-heavy with a flying bridge, two decks, sun canopies, a ton of chrome, glistening clear varnish, and dazzling white paint. The "captain" of this elegant craft saluted them as they came aboard. He had a lot of gold braid on his peaked hat and starched white shirt.

THE POINT TEAM

"He looks more like an out-of-work actor than a seafaring man," Bob Murphy muttered to Mike Campbell.

"We don't have to go to sea with him, just in among the islands."

Two immaculately uniformed stewards stowed their baggage, seated them at café tables on the aft deck and adjusted umbrellas to keep the sun off their faces. They were served drinks.

"Looks like this is going to be a real mean bitch of a mission," Murphy said happily, relaxing back in his deck chair and rattling the ice cubes in his glass as a signal to the steward to refill it.

Mike noticed that Joe Nolan from Youngstown, Ohio, and Harvey Waller from Flemington, New Jersey, were much more ill at ease in all this ostentatious luxury. Both glowered at the captain and the stewards. Nolan went out of his way to stamp out his cigarette ends on the gleaming deck boards. And neither of them did anything to hide their antagonism toward what Waller called "the foreigners" on the team, the Australian, Englishman and Frenchman. They were careful, however, not to cross swords with Campbell.

Andre Verdoux, in his turn, was behaving in a somewhat superior manner to his four teammates. No one could doubt his attitude was meant to suggest that this mission was Mike's and his, and that the rest were merely porters and water bearers.

Murphy seemed unaware of all these alliances and animosities, chattering on in a loud voice above the ship's engines as they made their way across the water. Richards said very little to anyone.

The splendid vessel, with the captain clutching its walnut wheel as if he were rounding the Horn in a gale, made its placid way over the calm waters along the Intracoastal Waterway between James Island and the mainland. Farther north, they passed inside the shelter of Sullivans Island, the Isle of Palms, Dewees Island... At last they came to a small island, perhaps a mile long and half that in width, that seemed little more than a glorified sandbar. A wooden dock stretched out from the landward side of the island, which was salt marsh near the water and covered with bushes and low trees in the middle. Beyond the trees, high dunes hid the ocean from view. They could hear the waves breaking on the beach.

"Mr. Vanderhoven's cottage is this way, sir," the driver of the first dune buggy come to meet them told Campbell and Murphy.

The others, except for Verdoux who stayed to supervise the baggage, piled into the second dune buggy. Vanderhoven's "cottage" turned out to be a huge, two-story stone house built in imitation of some old European style and sheltered in a hollow with dunes to one side and pine trees around the others. Because a big meal had been prepared for them, Campbell had not the heart to refuse it.

He warned his men as they sat at the dining table, "We've come here to lose flab, not gain twenty pounds. After this meal, this house is out of bounds. We have six mattresses in the attic above what were once stables. That's where we'll live. So, gentlemen, eat, drink and be merry, for tomorrow we train."

"I want you bastards to run, run, run," Campbell bellowed at them as he kept up the pace on the hard sand along the ocean's edge. "You may be able to shoot, fuck and sing, but you goddamn cripples can't run worth a shit."

As long as Campbell himself did whatever he demanded of the others, none were in a position to complain without admitting that they couldn't take it. They muttered among themselves for the first few days and began referring to Campbell as Mad Mike with emphasis on the first word, but no one dared rebel. They ran and ran and ran. Up and down the wet hard sand of the beach. Through the soft deep sand farther back that drained a man's energy and burned the bottoms of his bare feet. They ran up the sides of giant dunes where the sand gave way beneath their feet almost as fast as they could climb, with the result it was almost like running in place. From dawn to dusk, with breaks of an hour at a time, they ran around the island, up and down it, across it...

"Solely as a matter of intellectual curiosity, Mike," Andre Verdoux asked on the third day, "why are you doing this to us? We are all reasonably fit, and we hope to fight our way to and from our mission goal, not run like hell. Why?"

"You see the way everyone, including yourself, Andre, was giving everyone else the business on the way here on the plane and in the boat?" Mike asked. "I said to myself, to hell with this, I got a bunch of civilians here, this is not a fighting team. What I need is soldiers—guys with disciplined minds as well as physically fit bodies. After a couple more days of this, everyone will have forgotten all their petty little bitcheries from the civilian world. Or some of them anyway."

"It's hard, Mike. Damn hard."

"I told you that you were too old, Andre."

The Frenchman scowled and never questioned Mike's running program again.

Apart from heaving smooth rocks approximately the same shape and weight as hand grenades into a circle marked on the beach, they fired some rusty old rifles retrieved from the house at Driftwood. Mike had thought Vanderhoven's rifles would be in better condition and had brought along two target practice nose-marker versions of the high-explosive antitank (HEAT) 75N Energa rifle grenade. They fired these inert practice grenades with ballistite rounds. The grenade had a reusable marker which left a colored chalk mark on the target after each shot. However, the rifles were in such bad condition, they never could get down to some serious competitive shooting among themselves.

THE POINT TEAM

On the fourth morning, two South Carolina State Police helicopters landed on the beach, one in front of and one behind the six running men. A voice over a loudspeaker commanded them to surrender, as heavily armed state policemen in riot helmets jumped from the choppers onto the beach. They surrounded the six barefoot men dressed only in boxer's shorts.

"We got this here search warrant." The sergeant waved it in Mike's face. "We heard from Washington you're training a private army down here."

"You're looking at them."

"We kinda expected at least forty or fifty men," the sergeant said. "Aside from Mr. Vanderhoven's staff, there's no one else on the island?"

"Except for you people."

Mike heard him radio from the chopper, apparently sending back two boatloads of reinforcements.

"We're gonna take a look around," the sergeant said menacingly to Campbell.

In a while they came back with the two HEAT rifle grenades. Campbell took them apart to show that they were duds, but the sergeant took them anyway—"as evidence," he said.

Mike commented to Verdoux as they left, "You notice they didn't touch a damn thing of Vanderhoven's?"

"You were expecting them, Mike?" Andre asked and answered himself, "Which is why we had no proper weapons."

Campbell said shortly, "If we let Washington stop us, they will. If we don't, they won't."

Chapter 15

THEY interrupted the long plane ride from New York to Bangkok with a day in Tokyo and six hours in Hong Kong. The oppressive heat and incredible traffic jams on the way to their Bangkok hotel from the airport, combined with their exhaustion, rendered them semicomatose. However, the memories of R&Rs spent in this Thai city during the Vietnam war were awakened at the sight of particular things—ornate Buddhist temples, neon signs for go-go bars, crowded streets and, most of all, the graceful ivory-skinned women of extraordinary beauty.

"You giving us some time here to get acclimatized?" Bop Murphy asked Campbell in the hotel lobby.

"Is that what you call what you were doing in Tokyo and Hong Kong?" Mike countered.

"Come on, Mike," Bob said. "Larry Richards has never been here before. I want to show him the sights."

"We have a couple of days," Mike admitted with a grin. "You better pack whatever you can in, because we've all got some lean times ahead."

Campbell was surprised at how well Verdoux spoke Thai. Although many of the people here spoke some form of rudimentary English, particularly the ones who had something for sale, the ability to speak their language opened up a different world for the Frenchman. The Thais were flattered that a Westerner had learned their difficult tongue, curious about him—which was not so welcome—and anxious to please.

"What do you think has changed most since you were last here?" Andre asked Mike.

"It's almost ten years. I guess the place seems even more crowded than it was before."

"Would you believe that since then the population has doubled to more than five million?" Andre went on. "I heard one American describe the city as 'downtown Thailand.'"

That evening Mike and Andre wandered over to Patpong Road, the honky-tonk section. The area was crawling with Japanese, American, and European tourists, with relatively few American servicemen to be seen.

"They run sex tours from Tokyo these days—a few days away from the wife and kids," Andre said.

Mike indicated a flashing neon sign ahead. "I remember this place from the old days."

An American flag hung below the neon sign which flashed RANCH in the dusk.

"We used to call it the Raunch," Mike said. "You want a beer?"

In the dark interior a dozen bar girls, unusually modestly dressed, were serving heaping bowls of vegetables, rice, and fruit to four monks in saffron robes with shaved eyebrows and heads.

The madam approached them quickly and spoke in English, "You boys come back in a while, yes? We get blessing now for fifteen years open today." She lowered her voice to a conspiratorial whisper. "The girls take off their clothes and we put up naughty pictures on wall again. OK? We were afraid maybe monks change their minds and stop being monks. You come back in a little while," she repeated as she expertly pushed them back into the street.

Andre smiled after she had gone. "At least we're old enough to see the humor in the situation."

"*You* may be," Mike said.

Bar girls accosted them in the street, many in cutaway camouflage fatigues. Others were clad in tight silk dresses that rippled tautly as they moved. Tourist buses disgorged scores of Japanese businessmen who all plunged into a single bar at the same time, grabbing whatever was there while the place next door was empty.

"Remember how a lot of Americans would come down here to fight?" Verdoux asked. "I often wondered if some of them ever got laid."

"Frenchie, you got a lot of things on your mind."

Verdoux did not like Campbell to call him by this name, although he accepted it from the others. He realized his mistake had been in criticizing Americans in any form to Campbell. Campbell himself said what he wanted about Americans, and he never objected when other Americans, such as Nolan or Waller, said negative things—but when anyone not an American, even an old friend like Andre, said something the least uncomplimentary about America or Americans, they got to know real fast that Campbell's ear was not sympathetic.

They hit a few places along the way. Mike secretly wished he were back in the trailer camp looking forward to seeing Tina. But he was in Bangkok, not Arizona. And he had to admit that some of the sensual creatures here in their slinky outfits were enough to distract the mind of any man.

Though Mike looked over all the slick city girls, he found himself selecting a cute girl who obviously had been a peasant working in the fields until recently. She had an earthy quality that appealed. Like all the other women, she was small, she had black hair and large brown eyes, her skin was smooth and hairless and her clothes revealed almost as much as they hid. She had two important differences from the city girls—her hands were strong, sure and capable—not useless fluttering appendages—and when she spoke her smattering of English she looked Mike in the eye and expected some response. The other bar girls said what they were expected to say and looked anyplace about the bar except at the man they were with.

Andre Verdoux had got the most sophisticated-looking woman in the bar to talk French to, so he was happy. Mike thought to himself that if Americans liked to fight in places like this, Frenchmen seem to enjoy talking French more than having sex. He wished he had thought of this earlier. He and the peasant girl, whose name, surprisingly, was Veronique, slipped away. Mike assumed her real name was some Thai word of seven syllables. They went to a cheap hotel with rooms by the hour not far away. Mike paid for six hours and told her that any hours he did not use up, she could use the room. He had spread old man Vanderhoven's money generously around the crew so they could have a good time. Now he might as well spend some on himself.

The room was fairly crummy, but clean. Some people were partying in the room next door to Western rock music on a tape deck. Farther away, a flute was playing a melancholy air. As usual, the din of traffic and horn-blowing in the street rose and fell like waves on a beach.

"Sukhothai girls give the best blow jobs," Veronique said.

Mike remembered hearing that joke before about the town north of Bangkok. She probably made it to English-speaking customers half a dozen times a day. He was wondering if she also had jokes in Japanese when he felt her warm, soft lips enclose the head of his cock. He had no idea if girls from Sukhothai really were the best, but at least this one was right up there.

Next morning the police came to the hotel. Mike showed them everyone's passport and there was much talking among the police in Thai, which they assumed reasonably enough none of these foreigners understood.

Andre took Mike off to one side and said quietly, "It seems we weren't supposed to have been allowed off our plane, except someone at the passport control goofed. They're trying to make up their minds whether they have the authority to arrest us."

Mike approached the police officer who seemed to be in charge. "Is something out of order?"

"No, sir. This is just a routine check. Do not worry."

There was more rapid talk among them in Thai, along with some less than friendly glances. Mike began to feel a little desperate. The embarrassment would be hard to face down if his team were arrested in a Bangkok hotel and deported before the mission even got under way.

"We'll be leaving Thailand the day after tomorrow," Mike said to the cop.

This had an immediate cheering effect. "What? You go?" Then suspiciously, "Where to?"

"Singapore."

"Day after tomorrow to Singapore. Very good. Let me see your plane tickets."

"We plan to go overland."

"Not so good," the police officer said, not so believing now.

Mike pretended to misunderstand. "Why not? I know there are troubled areas, but we'll be traveling by day."

The police officer waved a hand to silence him. He collected their six passports from the other officers.

Mike asked Andre surreptitiously, "Does he expect a bribe?"

"I don't think so. Don't try unless he at least hints at it."

The officer handed the passports to Mike. "Forty-eight hours."

"We'll be gone," Mike answered him.

After they left, Campbell switched on the radio to loud, atonal Thai music. He told the others, "You've got to assume our rooms are bugged. From now on, if you have

THE POINT TEAM

to talk on confidential mission matters, go outside, or if you must do it indoors, keep that radio loud. Better not to talk about such things at all. Washington is going to be pissed they didn't make fools of us. Stay away from all Americans today. Have yourselves a good time, but report in here to me before eleven tonight. We've got to keep tabs on each other from now on.''

Campbell motioned for Verdoux to stay as the others left his hotel room. He turned off the radio and they went down into the noisy crowded street.

"We go early tomorrow?" Andre asked.

"Yes. You think the others guessed it was tomorrow, not the day after?"

"If they are using their minds, they did. But they're so busy fucking their brains out, perhaps they did not register what they didn't want to hear."

"I'm sure all of us are under some sort of surveillance," Campbell said as they threaded their way through the crowds. "It must be child's play around here. If the cops believed we're not leaving till the day after tomorrow and if Washington is relying on local forces to do their bidding, maybe we can get clean away tomorrow morning."

"A big maybe," Andre said pessimistically.

"I agree. I think the CIA will try to hit us when we move out."

"Sounds logical," Andre agreed. "Or at the weapons drop. Where do we pick them up?"

"Just this side of the Laos border. We go by road. I didn't mean to originally because it's a journey of more than three hundred miles from here to the border with Laos. I had a plane chartered for tomorrow morning under an assumed name. Obviously we're not going to show up for that. If they're anywhere, they'll be at the airport waiting for us."

"Do you have a driver?"

"We're on our way to see him now," Campbell said. "I

want you along to speak Thai and maybe to cause a diversion in case we're followed."

They caught a taxi on one of the less-congested thoroughfares. "Klong Toey," Campbell told the driver, who looked at them oddly in his rearview mirror.

"I don't go in," the driver said when he came to the edge of the shantytown.

Mike paid him off, and he and Andre walked down one of the refuse-strewn lanes that wound through the one-room huts. These shacks, constructed of every conceivable material from palm fronds to plastic sheets, were built next to each other. Through the open doorways, they caught glimpses of the crowded life within—women cooking, children playing. Others carried containers of water—there seemed to be no plumbing.

On one lane they came upon eight or nine men with the emaciated bodies and glazed eyes of opium or heroin addicts. The men confronted them and spoke angrily in Thai.

Verdoux translated for Mike. "They say they want money or they will kill us."

Mike said, "Tell them we've come to meet Nart Yodmani."

When Verdoux mentioned this name, they fell back. None of them were threatening anymore.

Mike held up a U.S. ten-dollar bill. "Andre, get that one to take us to Nart."

As they followed the addict through the extensive slum, both men continued to check behind them for a tail, although they recognized it was hopeless. Anyone who wanted to know where they were going had only to ask the addicts.

"Who is this Nart Yodmani?" Andre asked.

"An associate of Cuthbert Colquitt. Cuthbert said to contact him if we needed local help in a hurry while in Bangkok. For some reason he lives in the middle of this slum himself, while he has six or seven sons who own big houses in the suburbs."

Sweat ran down their faces and inside their shirts as they followed the addict over the uneven, dusty lanes through the never-ending vista of hovels. The addict held up his hand and said something.

"He says to wait here," Andre translated.

After a last anxious look at the ten-dollar bill still in Mike's hand, the Thai loped off around a turn. He was gone for about ten minutes. Then they saw him walk back with a huge Thai, muscular and grossly overweight as a Sumo wrestler, and a small nervous man with a thin face, a mustache, and a machine pistol in his right hand. The addict snatched the ten dollars from Mike and seemed in a hurry to depart.

"I am Nart Poonsiriwongse, the third son," the blubbery giant announced in American-accented English.

Mike told him who he was and that he wanted to see his father. The son did not respond much one way or the other. In a little while Mike saw why. A tall, thin man with a nervous tic in his left eye came up to them and introduced himself in English as Nart Yodmani. Campbell saw he was not going to come any closer than this to Nart's hideaway, so he got down to business.

"I want you to hire three vans as nearly identical in appearance as possible. You must hire them legally—I can't afford police trouble on some minor issue. That's for eight tomorrow morning."

Nart nodded.

Mike continued, "The day after tomorrow I need you to collect our belongings at our hotel, pay the bill and hold our baggage for us. We go tomorrow without taking anything with us, since we will be watched."

Nart nodded again.

Mike went on, "We're being watched by the Bangkok police, probably Thai government intelligence and definitely the CIA. Though I have to admit I haven't been able to spot any tails."

Nart glanced at his son, who said, "Their taxi had no tail when it arrived in Klong Toey."

Nart turned to Campbell. "We have been following you."

Mike paused a moment to consider this. "The CIA hired you?"

Nart evaded the question. "I do much work for the United States. But they pay bad. You pay more?"

"Sure."

"Where you go tomorrow? Laos? Cambodia?"

Mike hesitated a fraction of a second. "Laos."

"Ten thousand U.S. dollars, we take care of everything."

"Surveillance, hotel, three vans and drivers?"

"Everything."

"OK," Mike agreed. It was daylight robbery, but it was Vanderhoven's money, so all it amounted to was one rogue thieving from another.

Nart pointed at his mountainous son. "Poonsiriwongse will drive you back to the city center. He will collect all the money in advance."

Hard looks were exchanged as the team ate breakfast in Campbell's hotel room at seven the next morning.

"You mean we're going in on an hour's notice?" Richards complained above the sound of the loud radio.

"We have to leave all our things behind?" Nolan bitched.

"You'll be wearing camouflage fatigues and the boots you broke in last week in South Carolina," Mike said. "You can bring cigarettes, whatever, but no transistor radios or tapes or dope or booze. You can bring ID if you want. If they take you alive, they won't believe it anyway."

"Who's *they*, Mike?" Bob Murphy inquired.

"We cross Laos into Vietnam—so there's going to be a lot of 'they.' Take your pick."

"We after MIAs?" Waller asked.

"More or less," Mike said, deliberately vague.

Richards got to his feet. "Are we on some crazy job to assassinate Viet leaders?"

"No," Mike said evenly.

Richards subsided into his chair. "I'm relieved to hear that."

"Let's get moving," Campbell said. "No phone calls. No talking to anyone outside the team. Remember the rooms are probably bugged. Take what you can get in your pockets. No bags. Got it? Dismiss."

The men wore looks of mixed feelings on their faces as they left the room. The way Campbell talked, he was the colonel and they were soldiers again. That was what they had come for, but all of them were a bit angry at having the mission dropped on them like this with less than an hour's notice.

Poonsiriwongse was on time. At eight exactly he arrived outside the hotel in a brown Volkswagen van with heavily tinted windows. Campbell and his team of five climbed in and the van pulled out into the heavy traffic.

"Everything set?" Mike inquired.

"All OK," the Thai said with a big smile.

After driving for ten minutes, they pulled into a gas station and into the big garage at the back of it. An identical brown van was waiting inside it with a heavy-set driver and four or five Thais inside. Mike waved for them to go, and the brown van pulled out of the garage.

"Anyone following us won't have time in this traffic to figure out what the hell's going on. They're headed down the peninsula toward Malaysia, right?"

"They'll go south as far as Ban Na Kha and spend the night there before turning back," Poonsiriwongse said. "It's two hundred and fifty miles or more there—they will be lucky to make it in one day on that road."

As they picked up speed leaving the eastern part of the city, another brown Volkswagen van came out of nowhere and sped alongside their own. The Thai driver gave Poonsiriwongse a cheerful wave, and they proceeded to race and weave in and out of the thundering, brightly painted trucks that were themselves involved in races of their own.

The huge Thai laughed at their apprehension. "Out here there is no police to worry about. The one who is fastest and has most courage rules the road."

"It helps too if you have a ten-ton truck," Mike observed wryly.

"The other van will take the main road north to Vientiane. We branch off to the east a few miles from here. Again we have created confusion, I think."

They had passed through a rice-growing region and were now in higher ground where corn and other plants grew. The two vans continued to interweave in and out of traffic in this upland section. It was considerably more than a few miles before the hills began to drop down into low-lying, waterlogged rice fields again, and the second van departed on the road to the north. Men, women and children stooped to their tasks in the fields, usually knee-deep in water. Women carried burdens by the roadside, and children watched over enormous water buffalo wallowing in the river mud or sat on their broad backs as they waddled along pathways. Men fished with nets and visited fish traps in canoes. Ducks paddled in convoys, and long-legged water birds rose flapping with huge wings from clumps of reeds.

Poonsiriwongse pointed to mountains to the south. "The Dongrak range. Beyond that is Cambodia. There are a hundred thousand refugees in that area alone, but you won't see any of the camps this far inland. The Vietnamese army is trying to seal this border between Thailand and Cambodia, but it will be impossible for them to do so. The communists wrecked Cambodia, and even they now need Thai goods. Stupid men." He drew his finger across his throat to show his solution to the problem of their existence.

"Do they smuggle opium around here?" Larry Richards asked.

THE POINT TEAM

"No. That comes from the north, and most of it comes into Thailand from Burma. We allow the Americans to come in here to help us stop the growers. Do you know what happens? The hill tribesmen agree to destroy their poppies and plant tea or plums or peaches instead. Yet when they try to sell their tea, the merchants in Bangkok don't want it, and when they try to sell plum wine, the government will not give them a distiller's license. So they have to go back to the opium poppy. They make only about 2000 baht—less than a hundred dollars for a kilo of raw opium, so they're not the big-money men in the business. That only starts after the drugs leave Asia."

"You sound like you know the business fairly good, Poon," Joe Nolan said.

Poon—as they had taken to calling him—gave Nolan a big smile and said nothing.

They drove on in the hot sun, Poon refusing all offers to spell him at the wheel. They stopped at an inn for a meal of fish, beans and rice and drank excellent Thai beer while they waited for Poon to wake from his siesta. When they were on the road again, the heat and beer made the others sleepy, except for Mike, who was growing increasingly edgy. He had refused to tell Poon their final destination—only that it was a small village on the bank of the Mekong river beyond the sizable town of Ubon Ratchathani. Poon insisted that the police would be watching for them at that town, so they would have to skirt it by back roads.

"Poon, your father as good as admitted to me that the CIA is paying you to watch us," Mike said. "Where does that leave us with you?"

"The CIA is not paying me," Poon said indignantly. "They paid my father, and he in turn paid some of his sons to watch you. Then you paid him, and so he paid the rest of his sons to get you away from our brothers. We will see which is the smartest set of brothers."

"The CIA field agent is not going to understand this. He will think your father cheated him."

"Why should he? He was unlucky to get the stupid sons, and you got the smart ones."

"Are your other brothers really stupid?"

Poon laughed loudly. "They think they are smarter than me."

Campbell found none of this very reassuring, but he readily accepted Poon's explanation of his role. Mercs on a mission normally do not expect to attract to their aid the more stable and less venturesome elements in society. They ask few questions and hear a lot of lies.

Darkness was falling as they neared Ubon Ratchathani and veered south of the town. The border with Laos was an hour away. After driving for a while on what were little more than water buffalo paths, Poon announced that because of the failing light they would have to go back onto the road again.

"We're well past the town," he said. "It will be safe here till we get to the river."

He picked up speed on the surfaced road and was about to switch on the headlights when he saw a line of flickering lights ahead.

"Keep your heads down," Poon yelled to the others and accelerated. "They won't see us till the last moment."

Mike sat upright beside the driver, staring through the windshield and trying to figure out what the lights were. As they neared, he saw. A line of oil barrels stretched across the road, with an open-flame lamp on top of each. In the wavering light behind the barrels, he saw police or soldiers with rifles standing guard. Mike saw them peer into the darkness as they heard the van's engine approaching but could not see the vehicle. Two of the men unstrapped their rifles from their shoulders, but the rest seemed less concerned.

Then Mike saw fear across those faces in the lamplight as they suddenly realized that the unlighted vehicle was bearing down on them at high speed out of the night. He braced himself against the dashboard as the Volkswagen van hit two of the barrels and scattered the armed men.

Poon flicked on the headlights for a second to get a glimpse of the road ahead. It lay empty, and the van sped on into the total darkness, with a few metallic scrapings as bullets ricocheted off its sides.

"Police!" Poon said with disdain. "If they had been soldiers, they would have been waiting with a machine gun on this side of the roadblock in case someone broke through."

"It seems that maybe your brothers are not so dumb after all," Mike said.

Poon shrugged. "How do you know that roadblock was meant for you?"

"If it wasn't, the next one will be, after those guys get on their radio," Mike replied. "What will you do after you drop us off?"

"I'll pull the van off the road behind some trees, sleep there tonight and tomorrow return to Bangkok by daylight. If they stop me to ask questions, I'll tell them where I dropped you. By then you will be in Laos. You must cross over tonight, or they will catch you on the Thai side tomorrow."

"We'll cross if we can," Mike said.

"You just have to wade across," Poon exclaimed. "We won't have the rains for another month. The Mekong is at its lowest. Which village do you wish to go to?"

Mike told him, and they lapsed into silence as the van sped along the pitch-black country road. The headlights were on now, making them an easy target.

"Here it is," Poon said, slowing to a halt among a collection of thatched bamboo huts, many of them on stilts on the riverbank, all without a sign of life in the beams of the van's headlights.

All six climbed out of the van and stretched their limbs. Poon sat behind the wheel and watched what they would do. Mike decided he would rouse someone in the nearest hut and then get Poon to leave, but meanwhile they needed the lights of the van to see by.

"Michael Campbell!"

An American voice came out of the darkness. They whirled about to see three Westerners in white shirts and khaki pants approach them.

"Glad to see you, Mr. Campbell," one of them said.

They looked the polite sort who would have shook hands all around if they each hadn't been holding a Colt Cobra revolver.

"My name is Parker, assistant military attaché at the embassy. Phillips and Wiley are on staff, too."

Parker and the two others loosely slapped them down for weapons. When they found none, Parker made a point of putting his pistol in his belt. The others did also.

"Mind if we look in the van?"

Parker, followed by the two, opened the side door and peered into the van. He then climbed in. Wiley got in, too, while Phillips stood outside.

Mike called in to them, "You won't find anything there."

Campbell caught Poon's eye. The big man very deliberately put the VW van's stick shift in gear. Mike got the message. He winked to Poon, turned quickly, and pushed Phillips off-balance through the open side door. Simultaneously Poon took his foot off the clutch, and the van shot away with the three CIA men inside.

Chapter 16

As soon as the van roared off into the night, the village that had seemed deserted until then suddenly came to life. Verdoux spoke in a loud voice, and half a dozen different voices responded to him at the same time as oil lamps were lit and figures climbed down the ladders of the thatched huts on stilts.

"They say we must go now," Verdoux told them. "We must take our weapons now. They will lead us across the river and bring us to the place where the Laotian mercs have been waiting for us a couple of days."

"Tell them we're ready to move out," Mike said.

Almost twenty men and boys accompanied them by the light of the oil lamps to the middle of a bean field. The boys scraped away the earth from a ten-by-ten-foot area and revealed heavy timber boards. The boards roofed a pit lined with plastic sheeting to keep moisture out. Mike jumped down and made a quick inventory of what was there.

Mike climbed back out and called Verdoux to one side as the others lifted the equipment out of the pit. "Andre, we don't have time to check the stuff on this side of the river. Those three CIA men must have stopped Poon by now. They'll be back here any minute with scores of armed police. How deep is the river at our crossing? Do we use a boat?"

Andre questioned a man in Thai and told Mike, "We wade across. He says the water will be waist high, no higher than our chests, at most. They want us to hurry."

Mike handed him two hundred dollars in ten-dollar bills. "Give one to everybody here now, as a gift. Careful how you do it, I don't want their pride offended. They've been well paid by Colquitt's agent here and so have the Laotians across the river who are waiting for us."

Mike saw no sign of offense being taken in the eager way they each grabbed a bill from Verdoux.

One by one the oil lamps were quenched, and they all stood still for a moment in the bean field beneath a sky of huge stars. Mike listened to the sound of the others breathing. Far away there was a strange animal cry.

Then they set out in single file, one of the villagers leading, then the six mercs loaded with their gear, finally four village men with extra ammunition and grenades as a gift for the Laotians. They crossed the road to one side of the village and descended the riverbank into water a little above their ankles. Staying close behind each other in order for each man not to lose the man in front of him, they walked across the sand and gravel banks just beneath the water's surface. All that could be heard in the darkness now was the gurgles of the water and the splashing of their feet. From time to time they could see the stars reflected in smooth patches of water.

None of the men had to be told how the human voice carries across water. Not a word was spoken. They realized the enormous width of the river, even if they could not see it, by the length of time they walked through the shallows. Then very quickly the water came up to their knees, then halfway up their thighs, and they could feel the greater force of the current sweeping downstream against their legs.

THE POINT TEAM

The villager leading them slowed his pace as he negotiated the main channel. Even if the river was at its lowest point toward the end of the dry season, the man still showed a healthy respect for it, taking his time to find good footing and searching with his feet for the sand bars he knew to be there.

They felt the cool, flowing water at waist level and kept their weapons, grenades and ammo above it, knowing that at any time they might step into a deeper hole in the riverbed or lose their footing on slippery gravel and soak or even lose their load. After a long time they grew aware of the water level dropping slowly as they climbed out on the Laos side of the channel. Now more serious obstacles than slippery stones began to present themselves in their minds. Could they trust these villagers? For all they knew, they might be communists or in league with them. Were there river patrols at night on this section? Probably. The CIA knew where to find them in spite of their maneuvers. Would the Laotians? Had the Laotians heard they were coming? Were they, right at that moment, lying on the opposite bank watching them through night scopes? They were defenseless now, standing in open water a little more than a foot deep, their guns and ammo still wrapped in waterproof plastic sheaths. What the hell had they come here for? It was all a terrible mistake. They would go home. Call it all off. Never again.

Of course none of the six wanted any of the others to know of his rising panic and second thoughts, so each of them looked mean as hell—though no one could see their faces in the dark—and they sloshed determinedly on through the water. Each man was damned if he'd be the first to look weak. They guessed the others might be having doubts too, but only Mike sensed that every man jack of them at that particular moment would have jumped at the opportunity to be moving in the opposite direction.

Mike Campbell had bad dreams enough alone with the woman he loved in a trailer in Arizona—he did not need to make these dreams come true by going back to Nam, the very place that caused them.

Andre Verdoux was enjoying sex, food and wine with a greater appreciation and finesse in his mid-fifties than he ever had in his life before. He would not have thought this possible, but it was so. And here he was, in a single irrational act, throwing the good life away—this was worse than a teenager running off to join the Foreign Legion!

Joe Nolan could have gone to Houston, like a lot of his buddies had done. He didn't much care for the sound of life in Texas—folks not having much use for cowboys in his part of Ohio—but shit, it had to be better than fucking Laos and Nam. He didn't even have the excuse of being ignorant. He had been here before. Probably he'd have been better off hit with that coke bust.

Larry Richards had to think about the loony Irish wanting to cut out his English liver and daft French-Canadians who would dismember his body with a smile—but they seemed almost like old friends now that he was out here in Asia again, where he had sworn a hundred times he would never set foot again. Not after Malaysia. He didn't even know this lot, the Laotians, Viets and whatnots. The others had the advantage on him there. They knew what to expect. But he really doubted if it could be rougher than Malaysia.

Harvey Waller's high school friends might have recognized the Harvey he was now—unsure, hesitant, fearful...not the Red-baiting, two-fisted Harvey who had come back crazy from Vietnam. The way the others had dumped him when the FBI got on their case had been a great blow to Harvey—despite all their patriotic talk, they had crumpled before the first blow had been struck against them. He was alone now—marching by himself into commie hell. These others on the team knew nothing and would care less about his great purpose.

Bob Murphy had to agree with his wife's estimate of him—he was a fool. Self-indulgent. Out of touch with his true feelings. In need of professional mental help. Selfish. A psychopath. Uncaring for her or for anyone but himself. He must not forget his childish sense of humor. His total lack of appreciation of all the things she had done for him. How she had sacrificed her life to pander to his thoughtless pranks, a woman like her who could have picked and chosen among the most eligible and wealthy bachelors of good family in the whole of New England. She was right! She was definitely right, Bob Murphy decided, two-thirds of the way across the Mekong river into Laos. He felt a sudden surge of emotion for his wife and wished sincerely he had spent more time in her company.

They heard wind in the leaves above them, and grass rustled against their legs as they blindly followed the villager along a narrow path on the Laotian bank. After they had walked for twenty minutes or so, all six of the team wondering how the villager could find his way in this total darkness even if he had spent his whole life in the area, the Thai came to an abrupt stop so that each man bumped into the one in front of him. After some rattling of equipment and quiet curses, they stood motionless where they were for what seemed like at least ten minutes.

A voice called softly from the left, and the villager started moving again with his procession close behind. When they next came to a halt, Mike reached out and touched the side of a hut. The walls were made of a thick weave of dry fronds. He stooped and entered the open door. When all six were inside, the villager lit a hurricane lamp.

Verdoux explained what the man said. "The walls are thick enough so no light can be seen through them, but when we open the hut door we must put the lamp out or cover it with a cloth."

They thanked and said good-bye to the villagers and dutifully covered the lamp as they went out the door.

"Weapons," Mike ordered.

Each man had a Kalashnikov assault rifle, an Ingram

submachine gun and a Colt .45 automatic pistol. Campbell shared out the grenades, ammo and other items. Next, they changed into combat fatigues and ran a check on all their equipment.

"Old Cuthbert Colquitt is OK," Mike said. "We got everything he said we would and seemingly in working order."

"This has got to be a first for any merc mission," Verdoux said wonderingly. "Anybody set eyes on any of these Laotians yet?"

No one had seen them in good light.

"I think we should take turns to stand guard," Murphy suggested.

"No use," Campbell said, gesturing at the frond walls. "One man with one burst of automatic fire could take us all out in a few seconds. You might as well hope for the best and catch some sleep while you can. I know I am."

Mike slept like a log. On waking the next morning with that feeling a man has when he has slept deeply and well, he found it ironic that he had had his best night's sleep in weeks on his first night on enemy soil. He roused the others and opened the hut door. Two other huts stood across from theirs in a small clearing in heavy jungle. Strata of gray mist were floating at different levels above his head beneath the canopy of trees. There was an early morning chill in the air which the sun had not yet risen high enough to get rid of, and birds shrieked loudly everywhere in the forest.

Four of the Laotian guerrillas stood watching him. Mike saw immediately that they were not ethnic Laotians, but Hmong tribesmen. This pleased him. He had worked with the Hmong in Laos during the Vietnam war and knew what dependable fighters and independent people they were. He greeted them in the few words of their language that he knew. They smiled and responded in a Hmong language, dialect or accent totally strange to him. Others came from the other huts, so that there were ten in all—wide faces with prominent cheekbones, clad in dark blue tunics and baggy pants with a tribal-colored sash tied about the waist. None of them could be more than seventeen years old, and two looked no more than fourteen.

Andre Verdoux came out of the hut and greeted them in what Mike recognized as a mixture of Hmong and Laotian. They spoke together for a while.

Mike said, "Ask them why their hair is long. I've never seen Hmong with shoulder-length hair before."

Andre grinned. "I've already asked. They say they have sworn not to cut their hair till they have freed their people—it's a mark among the young men of those who are willing to fight back. This lot were toddlers when you were last here, Mike, but they call themselves 'sky soldiers,' which is what their fathers were known as when they fought for the CIA and Special Forces."

"You guys, bring out the extra grenades and ammo for our friends here," Mike told the others.

Mike formally presented the gifts, using the Hmong words for sky soldiers several times.

Bob Murphy shook his head in an amused way. "Mike, when you said we were going to team up with Laotian mercs, I didn't know you meant a teenage gang."

"You say that only because you don't know the Hmong," Andre interrupted. "Any Hmong teen-ager is worth three Australians."

Bob laughed. "They must be worth a hell of a lot, then, because any Australian soldier is worth ten Frenchmen. We proved that in the Second World War."

"Enough!" Mike commanded. "It happens you both have a good point about these Hmong. They will be good fighters, as Andre says, but they are very young and crazy to think they can take on the Vietnamese troops here in Laos as well as the Laotian army. So Bob is right, too: we've got to realize these kids are probably kamikazes, not survivors. All right now, listen, this is our plan of action.

THE POINT TEAM

We cross Laos well to the north of the town of Saravane and the Plateau des Bolovens. As the crow flies, it is about 120 miles to the Viet border. Inside Vietnam we link up with a Montagnard group who are allies of these Hmong—I suppose they are smugglers. The Hmong will wait at this village for us while we go into Vietnam to our mission target. When we return, these Hmong will accompany us back to the Mekong crossing into Thailand. Any questions?"

"What's the mission target?" Richards asked.

"It's not a political assassination, as I told you before. When it becomes important, we'll discuss it."

Verdoux put in, "The 120 miles to the Vietnam border are across hilly country with lots of forest—I've been over it a few times, as I know Mike has. It could take us five or six days to cross on foot since we have to keep to cover. Also, if we're discovered in the first couple of days, we're done for."

"On foot," Mike qualified.

"I didn't hear you say we would be going any other way," Andre said.

"It's something to keep in mind," Mike said, keeping things vague. "Anybody else got something to say?"

"Let's go," Nolan said.

This was met by cheers and shouts like a football team psyching itself up in the locker room before hitting the field. The young Hmong seemed a bit puzzled and agitated by their behavior.

After a meal of dried eggs from their rations with rice and beans, they split into two units and set out to cross Laos. Campbell, Murphy and Waller, with five Hmong, formed the lead unit. They moved forward in a line, with five yards between each man to prevent them from being all taken out in a single sweep of enemy automatic fire. The second unit followed two hundred meters behind.

One of the Hmong pointed wordlessly at the canopy of trees overhead and smiled. As long as they had this type of jungle vegetation, they could move by day without fear of being spotted from the air. The branchless trunks of the trees rose seemingly a hundred feet in the air, like king-size, crooked telephone poles, each with a small umbrella of leaves on top. The leaves spread out and, competing with each other for maximum sunlight, formed a thick canopy that left everything beneath in perpetual twilight, a thick, wet humid gloom when the sun was high, or, as now, an early-morning chilly damp that few would expect in this equatorial climate.

Campbell glanced in admiration at the way the Hmong moved among the trees, their man at point moving swiftly forward from trunk to trunk, pausing behind the cover of each for a split second to eyeball the terrain ahead, darting forward again with an economy of movement like a deadly hunting, aggressive snake. Teenagers they might be in years, but out here in a jungle combat real-life scenario they were highly knowledgeable men, seasoned with the wisdom of experience. Campbell figured that it had to take at least a couple of years for them to grow hair down to their shoulders. Thus, any Hmong sky trooper with hair this long had survived as an active guerrilla against the Viets and Laotians for a couple of years. Which was no mean achievement.

Bob Murphy and Harvey Waller were moving like real soldiers now. He knew it and they knew it. As a man thrown in deep water quickly remembers how to swim again, they had slipped into an infantryman's wary prowl—aware that he was vulnerable to anything unseen, that his main defense was to strike before being struck. Their heavier, more mature bodies would never again have the almost feline, deadly grace of the young Hmong, but hopefully their more mature minds would more than tip the balance in their favor in day-to-day survival tactics in the jungle.

Campbell himself eased forward in a kind of amble with his neck, arm and leg muscles relaxed, deliberately eliminating the strain of tension. He fell into a loose, nonstop vigilance he knew he would have to maintain for as long as his team was in the field. Like a security video camera, his eyes panned the tree trunks ahead without focusing on individual objects unless one did not fit with its surroundings. His gaze zeroed in with sudden, hard-edged focus on whatever object had sent a visual warning flag to his brain, and his fingers imperceptibly began to close over his AK47 assault rifle, hung on a shoulder sling and resting against his right hip. Then the leaf moving in a beam of sunlight or small animal or whatever it was that had attracted his attention would be recognized as harmless—not a threat—and his gaze would again pan across the trunks and shady recesses of this gloomy cathedral of trees.

The Hmong at point raised his left hand and the unit stopped and sought cover, except for the rearguard Hmong, who retreated till the second unit saw his warning and stopped their advance. Campbell crouched on the ground behind a big trunk, listening and watching intensely for movement.

Calmly crashing through the undergrowth, bored as hell on their daily uneventful patrol, seven Laotian regulars armed with AK47s walked in line from right to left only a hundred yards in front of them.

An advance party for a platoon, Campbell was thinking, and how far away were the others? Not so very far away, he guessed. He would allow the seven soldiers to pass them by and lie low for ten minutes to see if others showed. If no more came by, they would forge ahead and move away from the vicinity of the river as quickly as possible. It made sense that the closer they were to the border with Thailand, the more heavily the area would be patrolled. Once they had moved into the interior of Laos undetected, the Laotian forces would be even less on the lookout for trouble.

The last of the Laotian regulars, the seventh man, stopped while still in sight to light a cigarette. A cloud of blue smoke rose over his head, and he hurried on to join the others. As soon as he had gone, the five Hmong in Campbell's unit jumped from cover and took after him—along with Harvey Waller, who deliberately avoided looking in Mike's direction as he bolted into action. Bob Murphy started to move out too but responded to Campbell's wave to back off. Campbell could not stop Waller or the Hmong without a risk of exposing their presence to the Laotians. Instead, he ran back and signaled to the second unit to hold their positions.

The five Hmong in the second unit vacillated for a moment before they finally decided to obey Campbell's command.

Mike made his decision and told the Australian, "If they get into an extended fire fight and become pinned down, we leave them and move on. If the other Hmong stay, we go on without them. Fuck Waller. He wants to act as an independent agent, he gets treated as one."

"Mike, we can't leave Waller behind," Bob said. "I don't even like the bastard, but he's one of our team."

"Bullshit. He's only one of the team when he's obeying orders. Stay here and cover this position in case more Laotians come. I'm going after Waller and the others."

Mike set off at a trot through the undergrowth. He knew the Hmong would circle about to the left in order to hit the line of seven Laotians at a right angle. He had no chance of stopping them, but felt it would do no harm to check out what was going on since they were taking such a hell of a long time about it. Before he reached them, he heard a long burst of automatic fire and broke into a run.

The seven Laotian regulars lay twisted in grotesque positions on the forest floor. Harvey Waller stood above one body and kicked it. An arm moved. Waller drew his Colt automatic and blew away the side of the man's head with a .45 bullet. The Laotian's brains, fragments of his skull, and streaks of his blood were scattered over Waller's combat boots. He had a silly grin on his face.

THE POINT TEAM

Campbell turned away from him toward the Hmong. It was the only way he could control his anger. Mike knew he might have to kill this American merc if he openly defied him, and Mike knew that he himself would have to blow him away with a .45 slug as cold-bloodedly as Waller had shot the Laotian. Executing one of your men was not the best way to start a mission, but if Waller was going to call him on it, he'd do it.

Mike picked up the radio from one corpse. He received steady calls in Laotian from the wavelength to which the radio was set. The seven men were already missed! He switched to another wavelength and picked up one side of a conversation. The Hmong, picking over the dead Laotians for valuables, all stood and listened. A look of alarm came across one man's face. He pointed to the radio and then pointed back into the trees urgently, indicating that the voices on the airwaves were almost within hearing distance.

Mike beckoned for them to follow him and hurried back to the second unit. All ten Hmong started talking excitedly together.

"Andre," Mike said, "lay it down hard to these bastards that I'm mission commander. If they can't hack military discipline and order, they're on their own. We'll fend for ourselves. If we stay together, they don't make a move without my OK. Make sure they understand I'm not kidding."

While Andre laid down the law to the Hmong, Campbell turned to Waller. "You can find your own way back to Thailand, you stupid fuck. I don't want any jokers on this team who think they're going to be calling the shots."

The others watched Waller for his reaction. He did a slow burn at being humiliated in front of them by Campbell.

Then he said, "I was out of line. Sorry about that. Won't happen again."

Andre came back and said, "They were polite and said they'd do what you say. My guess is what they really think is this. They see themselves baby-sitting a bunch of soft old farts on some loony adventure."

Mike grinned. "It's going to be up to us to show them otherwise. Look, if that seven-man unit was from a platoon of twenty-four, like I think it was, we don't need the other seventeen hunting us down. I wanted to get across Laos without being detected. That was nearly essential. What burns me up is that we blew it in such a dopey, asshole way. Andre, translate this for the Hmong. The rest of the platoon who we heard on the radio know the seven are not responding. They've probably heard the burst of fire, so they'll be on the alert. But they're not convinced yet that something serious is wrong. We got to take them out before they radio back to their company or battalion HQ that they have a penetration by an enemy force."

Andre nodded. "If the whole platoon vanishes without a trace, it may take a couple of days for them to find them and move on it."

"Meanwhile, keep your voices down, because these babies will be coming out of the bushes any moment now."

They did not have long to wait.

Mike's unit had taken the left flank, and Andre's the right. There was not much chance of them hitting each other with cross fire because of the number of heavy tree trunks that would prevent bullets from traveling far. Campbell crawled to a position ahead of the others so he could control the action. He fixed his bayonet on his rifle as he waited and held it up as a signal for the others to do likewise.

Only minutes later they saw the balance of the Laotian platoon moving forward on a combat alert. Every few hundred yards they stopped and tried the radios and shouted for their missing comrades. As they got nearer, Mike had an idea. As the Laotians shouted, Mike looked at the five Hmong in his unit. One smiled and nodded, then shouted back in Laotian. Another joined him. More shouts from the Laotian regulars. Answered by the Hmong.

The effect was instantaneous. The regulars relaxed their cautious advance, letting their rifles hang loose on their slings. The five Hmong, to Mike's horror, rose to their feet and went to meet them. The Laotians could just make out their figures through the trees. Fortunately, none of them sighted through a scope, and the forest gloom helped conceal the loose blue pants which would have immediately given away the Hmong.

The approaching Laotians veered away from Andre's unit and toward Mike's position. With the five Hmong masquerading as the missing seven, there were only three guns to take the seventeen regulars—Mike's, Waller's, Murphy's. These two crawled up to join Mike at his nod, and all three got set to lay down an even wave of fire.

"Hit the mothers!" Mike snarled.

Their AK47s cut into the flesh of the communist troops, doubling them over, knocking them down screaming and clutching their entry wounds, whacking others out cold with an instant mortal blow . . . Three survived the deadly hail of fire. They ran.

Campbell, Waller and Murphy took after them, leaping over the dying victims in their death throes on the forest floor. None of the three had time to change his rifle magazine. Waller held his big Colt in his right hand and his Kalashnikov in his left. The Colt spat flame and barked. One of the fleeing Laotians went down with a massive wound in the back of his neck. He quivered once or twice on the ground and then lay still.

Waller was already throwing lead at Murphy's quarry. He missed with three shots and, with the fourth, ripped a chunk out of the man's right thigh. The regular kept going, clutching his wounded limb, hobbling through the undergrowth. Until he stumbled. Stunned, weakened, shocked, the man remained lying face down on the ground. Bob Murphy ran up and placed his right boot on the Laotian's shoulder to keep him in place. Waller came running also, his Colt pistol still smoking from the shot that had hit the Laotian in the leg. Without pausing, Waller leaned across Murphy and split the injured man's skull with a .45 dead center in the back of his head.

Murphy withdrew his boot from the man's shoulder. "Thanks, Harvey."

The Australian gave the highly excited Waller a carefully appraising look.

The Laotian Campbell chased was wiry and light-footed. He dodged in and out of tree trunks and leaped over roots and fallen branches. Under normal circumstances, Mike would not have bothered to hunt him down—but the whole point of this ambush was to cover up their presence. A single survivor who lived to tell a tale would overturn the whole applecart. They'd have every peasant army and village militia in this part of Laos, along with government and Vietnam troops, out searching for them in a few hours. Mike had to get his man.

The long hours of running on the South Carolina sands were paying off. Although the Laotian regular was faster on his feet than Campbell, the American managed to keep him in sight and gradually gain on him with his superior stamina. The Laotian lost yardage by struggling to remove his backpack. He had already lost or discarded his rifle, and the removal of this approximately thirty-five-pound load from his back would have given him a big advantage over the fully laden Campbell. But a man can't run at full speed and wriggle out of the shoulder straps of a backpack at the same time. When he did get the pack off, it was only to provide a vulnerable area to his American pursuer, now hot upon his heels.

The Laotian looked back over his shoulder in rising panic, and Mike met the glance of his fear-crazed eyes. Campbell repressed a surge of pity for the man, tried to think of him only as the enemy.

With four giant steps, Campbell gained on his prey.

Gripping his Kalashnikov firmly about the buttstock in his right hand, he thrust it forward and drove the tip of the bayonet an inch into the Laotian's back. The man screamed with pain and fright and lost his footing. Mike was upon him in a flash.

Clutching the rifle by the hand guard and buttstock, he used the sophisticated weapon as a primitive spear handle to drive the bayonet deep into the Laotian's chest cavity.

The communist soldier wildly grasped the steel driving into him, severing some of his fingers in the process, and screamed maniacally as his insides were rended by the metal.

Mike pulled the bloody, dripping bayonet out of the man's body, and since he lived and suffered still, drove it in again.

He had to skewer the Laotian repeatedly before he stopped his agonized screaming and twitching. Mike looked at the crimson running off the stainless steel and the cut-open, lifeless rag doll at his feet. He had not forgotten how dirty war could be. It was just that he had been hoping this mission would be different.

Chapter 17

THE Hmong watched in fascination as the Westerners got ready for the day's trek. They themselves slung weapons and ammo over their dark blue clothes in ultracasual fashion. They carried a few first aid items, but, among all ten, probably less than the average American family would take along as a precaution on a picnic to a state park.

Mike's team were all similarly equipped. How each man distributed his load was his own business. Mike washed in a clear mountain stream. He pulled on his heavy canvas fatigues which allowed heat to escape in the daytime and kept it in at night, protected his skin against sharp stones and thorns and biting insects. He wrapped his spare underpants and socks about his calves beneath his pants before pulling on his U.S. Army jungle boots. Next he circled a medical wrap about his chest after checking on its contents: pills for malaria, morphine for pain, uppers for when he needed to keep alert for a long period, scalpel blades, sterile tissues for dressing wounds, elastic bandages and antibiotics in the form of pills, salves and syringe cartridges.

In his shirt pockets he had stores of aspirin, antinausea pills, soap, toothbrush and toothpaste, salt tablets, needles, thread, and scissors, a gun-cleaning kit, and numerous odds and ends. Mike used his trouser pockets for dried figs in wax paper, Lifesavers, raisins, chocolate and so forth. He stashed his C rations and K rations along with his ammo in two dobie bags, one slung across each shoulder. His Ingram miniature submachine gun was slung over his back and held in place by the dobie bags. He strapped on his belt, to which was attached his Colt .45 automatic—the standard M1911A1—a magazine pouch, two canteens and six hand grenades.

On his H-harness he hung an empty Claymore carrier to hold extra AK47 magazines, a rifle grenade, a USMC bowie knife and whatever else he had no room for elsewhere. He carried his Kalashnikov hanging on its sling from his right shoulder.

Mike had given away his machete to one of the Hmong, but the others kept theirs. They took it in turns to carry special equipment such as the two antitank rocket launchers and the rockets.

The first morning the Hmong had kept a distance. Now, on the second morning, all ten watched the preparations as they might the strange behavior of hitherto-unknown creatures.

Mike consulted the map before he moved out. "We have a minimum of a six-day trek to cover the 130 to 150 miles from here to the Viet border. Even if it takes them a few days to find the bodies we hid, twenty-four regular troops don't just disappear off the face of the earth without a big push to find out what happened to them. If we're not careful, we'll find ourselves in the middle of that big push." He waited for Andre to finish translating this for the Hmong, who seemed to find what Mike was saying hilarious. "Unlike our friends here," Mike went on with an edge in his voice, "who seem to have a yen to die in the homeland, I have no intention of having my bones scattered in these hills. Those who think like I do had better listen to what I tell them. We got no room for crazies on this mission." Harvey Waller avoided his eyes. "We got to find something to take us across Laos fast, instead of spending six days at it. We've got to stay on the ground when we get to the Viet border, because of the mountains. Look here on the map. This looks like a major north-south route. It's no more than ten miles away if we follow this river valley. Andre, ask the Hmong what they know of the place."

Andre spoke to them, and they looked at the map. "They say there are a lot of trucks on that route, but no private cars. A truck is what we need anyway, not some damn Russian imitation of a Ford. They also say the river course is the only way to go. However, we will have to watch out for peasants along it—men fishing, women washing clothes, children playing or tending animals."

"Let's move out," Mike commanded.

After about three miles, the forest and its canopy of leaves grew less dense, and they found themselves entering hilly country with dense stands of trees in deep valleys, with hillside fields and occasional villages and with wild, scrubby hilltops. Mike located the river he had selected on the map, and they descended through the trees to its bank. It was a tributary to the Mekong, so they had to follow it upstream till the highway crossed it. The streambed was wide, dry and littered with big boulders. The dry season flow of water was restricted to a narrow channel at its center. They found themselves making excellent time on the unobstructed riverway, although every now and then they had to retreat back into the trees when they spotted people by the water.

The Hmong displayed no urge to kill these ordinary working people, to Mike's relief, although he knew there was no love lost between such lowlanders and the mountain tribesmen. Waller had taken his upbraiding better than Campbell had expected him to, and was on the move like a hardened pro today. Murphy's constant goodwill and shrewd friendliness were a big help to the unit. The Hmong seemed as friendly as the language barrier would permit.

Andre had told Mike he was getting on OK with Nolan

THE POINT TEAM

and Richards, and that the five Hmong with him seemed intent on keeping their part of the arrangement. With a bit of luck, they might now reach the Viet border and avoid another senseless flare-up like the one of the first day. Even if they were communists, Mike felt no better about leaving twenty-four men needlessly dead behind him when all contact with them could so easily have been avoided.

A group of women were at the water up ahead. They could see them soaking clothes, beating them on stones and spreading them in the sun to dry. Mike's unit began its detour through the bankside trees and heavy growth, followed by Andre's after about five hundred meters.

Mike's group was about to cross a path leading down to the river when the Hmong at point raised his left hand in warning. They all froze where they stood—it was too late to dive for cover. On the path, literally only a few feet ahead of the lead man in the unit, two gnarled, weather-beaten peasants ambled toward the water, one with a wooden rake over his shoulder and both smoking awkwardly rolled cigarettes. They passed without seeing the eight heavily armed men watching them in the bushes like cobras rearing to strike.

The man at point did not move, so the others held their position. Right away, the huge bulk and great horns of a water buffalo appeared. Mike was amazed at the silent tread of this leviathan along the path. A wizened old man walked by his head, oblivious of his surroundings.

A girl maybe four or five years old sat atop the hummock of the water buffalo's shoulders and stared with wide brown alarmed eyes at the members of the unit. She said something to the old man, probably her grandfather, and pointed. He looked up at her and then into the bushes at the eight armed men. The old man's eyes glided over the Hmong and settled on the Westerners. For some reason, the water buffalo chose this moment to stop to eat a tender morsel of grass by the pathside.

"Hold your fire," Mike said in a calm level voice.

THE POINT TEAM

Mike met the eyes of the old man, broke the look to glance up at the child, and then stared at the old man again.

The Laotian said nothing. His eyes also expressed that he knew he had no hope of saving her, yet was trying all the same.

"OK, Grandpa," Mike said to him in a kindly voice, raising his rifle barrel in the air, "I'm going to take a chance on you."

With no visible urging, the water buffalo resumed its forward motion and in a few moments was disappearing down the path. The child looked back at them with her beautiful brown eyes.

Mike felt the glances of the Hmong on him, whether in approval or disapproval he did not know. Or care.

"Let's go on," he said quietly.

Murphy gave him a friendly poke in the ribs as they moved out.

They came to the highway in early afternoon and spent twenty minutes observing traffic on it from a heavily wooded area close by. The roadway was surfaced with tarmacadam which heaved in dips and swells because of the poor foundation beneath. The bulk of the traffic was carts drawn by water buffaloes along both shoulders of the road and heavily laden bicycles either ridden or wheeled on its surface. In the twenty minutes they watched, only one truck passed, traveling north.

"If we can bag ourselves a truck like that," Mike said, "every hour we spend driving it, even on a dirt road, will save us a day's trek."

"We should bivouac here tonight," Andre said, "and grab one at dawn tomorrow."

Mike shook his head. "If we capture a truck now and drive for five or six hours, we'll hit the Viet border just as night falls. Even if things go wrong, we'll have the cover of darkness not far away."

THE POINT TEAM

"That's a good point," Andre conceded. "Let me talk to the Hmong." He came back to Mike in a short time. "They say it will not be easy to take a truck. The drivers are heavily rewarded when they resist an attack and likewise heavily punished when they lose a truck. A few shots and a threat won't stop them. They say we must allow them to set up an ambush by blowing a hole in the road."

Mike grinned. "These guys have a real feel for drama. Well, I'll show them the quiet way to do it. Nolan, Richards, you got yourselves an assignment."

Campbell had chosen the two quickest of his team. He went forward with them in the undergrowth and explained their roles to them, which would change according to which direction the truck was traveling. Nolan crept along a tiny brook and then crawled through a four-foot concrete pipe which carried it beneath the road. He would seek cover as close as possible on the northern side of this culvert. Richards and Nolan could only guess at one another's positions on each side of the highway, but as long as they were approximately opposite each other and acted at more or less the same time, things should work out.

They waited almost another half hour before they heard the engine of a truck. When it lumbered into sight, it was such a ramshackle antique that Mike hoped Nolan and Richards would let it pass. Unfortunately, they had no signal to communicate this. Their orders were to bag the first truck. The truck was traveling north at about twenty miles per hour, and Mike saw Richards jump from cover, run alongside the truck for a moment, and then pull himself up on the step beneath the driver's door. Richards shot the man in the face with his Colt and reached in to steer the truck as it wavered and slowed on the highway. Nolan gained entry to the cab from the far side, pulled the driver's body out of the way, slipped beneath the wheel, and braked the truck to a stop. They immediately ran to the back and checked the canvas-covered interior. They waved to the others and climbed in before any of the peasants traveling on the road approached near enough to identify them as Westerners.

Mike and the other three Westerners climbed aboard unobserved, so far as they could tell. Three of the Hmong who were to do the driving waited for Verdoux to translate Campbell's instructions for them.

"About seven kilometers north of here—I doubt if this truck's instruments are working—"

"They might be," Richards interrupted cheerfully. "It's a British Leyland, early sixties' vintage, I suspect."

Mike smiled. "Have them look at the gas gauge, too. Seven kilometers north, they turn east on a minor road that doesn't seem to hit any big towns, but goes all the way to the Viet border." Mike traced the route with his finger before handing the map and money to Andre. "They can buy gas with Thai bahts, and if they won't accept that currency, the Hmong can shoot them. Get the drivers to understand one thing. I don't want anyone to see our round-eye faces between here and the Viet border—and I want to get there before dark."

"Entendu, mon général."

The six mercs and seven Hmong made themselves as comfortable as they could on the bouncing floor of the empty truck, constructed of splintering planks. They took turns at keeping a lookout to the front and rear through rents in the canvas, a duty for which there was no shortage of volunteers, since it was probably more comfortable to stand holding onto the side than sit and absorb spinal shocks through the floor.

Richards was feeling cocky since his capture of the vehicle. He looked out at the impoverished, wild countryside they were passing through and said to Verdoux, "Frenchie, your lot made a proper bollox of this place when you had it as a colony."

Verdoux's blood pressure rose visibly. He said nothing.

"I'm serious," Richards persisted. "Look at the ex-British colonies in this part of the world—Burma, Malaysia, Singapore—they're all still in the free world. Vietnam, Cambodia, Laos... all French and all commie today. Proper fuck-up, I call it."

Verdoux looked as if he were ready to go for a gun or a knife.

Mike diplomatically intervened. "I could tell you guys to shut up. Or since Andre hasn't said anything, I'm going to tell you to keep your mouth closed, Larry, while Andre tells us who lives here. It'll help pass the time if nothing else. Go ahead, Frenchie."

"Don't blame the French!" Andre said, which caused laughter and eased the tension. "The Chinese dominated the whole region for about a thousand years. In the tenth century, the Vietnamese shook them off east of the Annamitique Mountains, while to the west the Khmer people—present-day Cambodians—gained control of what we now know as Cambodia, Laos and Thailand. Even today, Cambodians, Laotians and Thais are all closely related in race and language, and are all completely distinct from the Vietnamese. Which is why they hate them. From about the year 1300 on, the Thais became aggressive. They all fought with each other over the centuries, gaining or losing pieces of territory. The place was such a mess by the nineteenth century, all the French did was walk in and say no more warfare. They managed to keep things reasonably quiet until the Japanese swarmed in during the Second World War, just as they did over the British colonies, too!"

"Let me give you facts about Laos today," Mike said. "At the time the South Vietnamese government in Saigon collapsed in April, 1975, the Laotian monarchy went under. A neutralist coalition government ruled for a short while, but as usual the commies did in their moderate partners and took over. They call themselves the Lao People's Democratic Party and take their orders from

THE POINT TEAM

Hanoi or Moscow. In this country right now there are about fifty thousand Viet regulars. The Laotian government has thirty-six thousand troops. So we and the Hmong and a few other misguided souls are taking on eighty-six thousand full-time trained professional soldiers, not to mention peasant militias and spies and so forth! If we get caught here, we can't expect any help from Washington. The politicians are going about their usual diplomatic bumbling. Know why Washington was so anxious to keep us from coming into Laos? They're thinking of upgrading the U.S. diplomatic mission in Laos' capital, Vientiane, to a full embassy. Our mission might upset their afternoon tea party, where they all stand around in pinstripe suits and white gloves saying, 'Definitely a pleasure to meet you, I'm sure.' They call that a diplomatic breakthrough, while meantime there may be dozens of poor fucks captured more than ten years ago held captive in bamboo cages just because they are GIs. I say screw the ambassador and his garden party."

They passed the time laughing, joking, even dozing. They shared their C and K rations with the Hmong, and at least one always kept a wary eye on the passing countryside. They had no trouble buying gas with the Thai bahts from peasants with fifty-gallon drums operated by foot-pedal pumps along the roadside.

"I bet they are charging us too much," one of the Hmong said to Andre, "because they think we are smugglers. They won't report us because they want to do business with us again. The Laotians are not good communists. They don't understand it."

The truck had been on the road for more than four hours when Bob Murphy shouted a warning, "Roadblock ahead!"

The others jumped to their feet and peered through holes in the canvas cover over the cab. It turned out that roadblock was too strong a word for a soldier standing in the roadway waving a red flag, while his rifle leaned against a fence post fifty yards away. Two other soldiers, both without visible arms, talked with a group of women in a field.

The Hmong drove the truck straight at the soldier in the middle of the road. He got the message fast and threw himself out of its way. Not a shot was fired. They last saw the soldier looking disconsolately after them in a cloud of dust they had raised. The two other soldiers talking to the women had not bothered to turn and look.

Nolan made an obscene gesture with his middle finger back at the lone soldier. Two of the Hmong liked that and practiced the gesture themselves. The others were in good humor at the quick defusing of the potential threat. Except for Campbell. He looked worried and stared moodily out over the tailgate of the truck for some minutes. Then he walked up behind the cab and hammered with his fist on its metal wall. The truck slowed and pulled over. They were on a deserted stretch of road with a crazy tangle of growth on both sides.

Mike jumped down. "You might as well stretch your legs for a few minutes," he called to the others in the back of the truck. He went forward to the driver. He asked in Vietnamese, "How far do you reckon to the border?"

The Hmong understood him and climbed out with the map, glad to exercise his limbs. The other two in the cab lit cigarettes and went back to talk to their friends.

"Maybe an hour," the Hmong said to Andre, who translated.

"You think we should risk staying on the road in the truck?" Mike asked.

Andre interpreted for him. "He says you're right to stop and think about it. I think he's afraid that if he says we shouldn't stay with the truck, you'll say we should to prove you're a braver man than him."

Mike looked up and down the road and weighed the gain against the loss. Stay with the truck, in another hour be done with Laos and into Vietman—meanwhile presenting yourself as a ready, identifiable target that just ran a military checkpoint, assuming those three soldiers had a radio and bothered to use it. Dump the truck, go back to trekking, and add another day, maybe two, to getting out of Laos, plus leaving yourself with low mobility if a general alarm was raised.

Campbell gazed up and down the road, wrestling with his very limited options. He was pleased to see that everyone, including himself, had automatically moved out of the road into the cover of the ditch. A couple of days in the field had brought back gut thinking to the members of the team. Basically he had no choice. Fast transportation was worth almost any risk it involved. They had to keep the truck. There were so few vehicles on this road, there was no great advantage in exchanging this truck for another. He was about to wave everyone back to the truck when he noticed a dark shape out of the corner of his eye.

The chopper swooped down lower over the road, traveling so fast it was upon them before they heard the noise of the engine. The side-door machine gunner stitched a neat row of spurts along the center of the dirt road and through the center of the truck from back to front.

"It's one of our old gunships they've fixed up," Nolan yelled. "The pilot's seen us."

The chopper followed through like a boxer on a haymaker and then swung in a tight circle to come back on their rear and give the side-door gunner a nice view of their backs. They had no cover worth a shit.

"Scatter!" Mike yelled.

Regret flashed across his mind he had decided not to take along the Carl-Gustav M2 shoulder-borne rocket launcher and a couple of rockets because of their weight and cumbersomeness. He had turned down the Redeye heat-seeking guided missile for the same reasons. All he would have had to do with the Redeye was point the missile in the general direction of the chopper, wait till the audio signal informed him that the infrared homing device had locked onto the target, then launch the missile. A booster motor expels the missile from the shoulder-borne tube, the main motor fires after six meters, and the infrared sensor on the missile homes on the heat of the chopper's engine... End of helicopter.

During the seconds that these regrets were running through Campbell's mind, his fingers worked the magazine release on his AK47, freed the magazine from its housing, pulled back the bolt to discard the round in the chamber, loaded a special magazine of ballistite rounds, rapped the bottom of the magazine with his weak hand to ensure that it was properly seated, unhooked the HEAT-RFL-75N Energa rifle grenade from his H-harness, mounted it in his rifle, swung the rifle to his shoulder, took quick aim down the barrel...

The men had scattered in all directions to cut down on their casualties from the machine gunner. Only Campbell still stood in the roadside ditch, looking along his rifle at the helicopter bearing down to one side of him and the machine gunner sending forward a raking seam of fire across the ground a few feet off Mike's right shoulder.

Both the gunner and the pilot saw what Mike was doing and knew they had to move in to take him fast.

Mike took a last aim down the rifle barrel and let loose his one shot into the empty space he figured the chopper would occupy by the time the rifle grenade traveled there. He was blown off his feet by the blast.

The high-explosive antitank grenade had done an aerial job. The others, rifles raised to empty their magazines of small bullets, only 7.62 mm, at the pilot and gunner, or anything they could hit, were blinded by the flash. Then they felt the heat of the explosion on their faces. The sudden blast of hot wind swept by them, bearing deadly jagged pieces of the chopper's metal fuselage. The sound pressed on their eardrums and painfully invaded their brains. Each man found himself standing alone in the smoke and debris, wondering if he was the only one who had survived. Wreckage burned in the middle of the roadside field.

They were startled when, with half-deafened ears, they heard the truck's motor start up.

Campbell stuck his head out the cab door and yelled at them, "The engine's OK! Move your asses! We're getting outta here!"

A Hmong drove the truck at its maximum speed—about thirty-five mph—along the dirt road, and another sat next to him cradling his rifle. They drove with both cab doors partly open, so they could abandon the vehicle fast when next attacked. They knew they would be. On orders from Campbell, all the canvas covering had been stripped from the truck to give the occupants the 360-degree view of the sky they needed to fend against chopper attacks. They could no longer afford the luxury of concealment. Also, they had gained a fast exit over the wooden sides when it came time to abandon ship. No one had any illusions about what a beautiful target they made aboard the truck.

The road had been climbing steadily, and the mountains and hills were higher, the country wilder. The Hmong seemed vague about where exactly they were, and Mike began to worry about coming up to the border crossing unexpectedly. It could not be far away. Perhaps only a couple of kilometers, at most twelve to fifteen. They descended into a broad river valley and could see the road snaking up into the mountains on the other side. The valley bottom was divided into rice fields, with no cover except for an occasional solitary palm. Although the sun was close to setting, people still stooped in the knee-deep water setting rice seedlings in the earth. They looked up as the truck passed them, more to ease the monotony and straighten their backs than out of genuine curiosity.

"Choppers at three o'clock!" Nolan yelled.

Campbell hammered on the roof of the driver's cab and the truck slowed. Three helicopters could now be seen plainly, flying a triangle formation over the road, with the lead helicopter covering the road itself and the two others the land on each side. Campbell and his men leaped from the truck. Their only cover was a mud embankment holding back water in a rice field.

The three choppers disappeared behind a fold in the valley. The men had just about enough time to crouch behind the embankment and raise their weapons before the machines popped out of the horizon and came on them faster than an inexperienced man would have expected.

"Never seen this model before," Nolan muttered.

"Must be a new Russian design," Murphy agreed. "Faster than a bat out of hell, too."

"Hold your fire and lie still!" Campbell yelled as the choppers came nearer, like three monster hornets. "They might not see us!"

The lead machine zapped two rockets at the stationary truck, a left and a right from pods attached amidship. For an instant, the two deadly darts were visible in the air in every detail from their rounded nose back to their stabilizing fins.

The truck disappeared in a huge ball of orange light. The ground shook beneath them from the impact, and the brown water slopped back and forth in the rice field like the wake of a distant boat in a muddy inlet.

The noise and wind of the blast masked those of the choppers passing overhead. Then they could hear the flames lapping the wreckage.

"Hold still!" Campbell commanded. "Keep your head down!"

They could tell by the noise of the engines that the choppers were swinging around for another fly-by.

Verdoux roared Campbell's orders at the Hmong, who obeyed.

Mike eased his eyes above the embankment to gain some idea of the pilots' intentions. He was fairly sure they had not been seen, but he didn't want to be responsible for making his men sitting ducks. A half-kilometer to the west, the three machines hovered, marked by uncertainty. In the rice fields all about, men, women, and children ran in panic, splashing through the water like flightless ducks. The choppers' engines roared, and they picked up speed as they came in on another pass.

"Stay put!" Campbell yelled.

Verdoux repeated the command in Hmong.

This time the choppers zoomed over the fields and machine-gunned the fleeing peasants. The running workers were tumbled like ninepins and sprawled face down, arms outstretched, floating on the water.

One of the pilots must have come to his senses, realized what they were doing and called off the others, because suddenly they all headed back the way they had come, over the far side of the wide valley.

The panic-stricken peasants were still running in all directions. They avoided the area where they could see the truck burning and thus missed discovering Campbell's force.

"We need to move in a bit from the road." Mike pointed to a bank of tall reeds sixty meters away. "We'll take cover there till dark. Follow me and keep your heads down. Our only chance of not being seen is while they are still panicking."

As they moved, for the first time the others saw the bodies of the men, women, and children randomly scattered about the fields.

"Jesus, it's great to be back again," Nolan said bitterly.

They established themselves in the cover of tall reeds. Campbell ordered the men to eat, whether they felt hungry or not.

"Fucking picnic in a bog with dead kids floating about," Murphy growled, which Campbell noted as the Australian's first complaint.

"We move out at dark," Mike explained, "and keep moving till we're clear of Laos."

The sun began to set, and its pink, gold, and orange bars spread rapidly across the sky in the short equatorial dusk. For a moment Mike thought he heard coyotes, but the howls were even more eerie. The sounds made Campbell's hair stand on end as they came closer and seemed to spread about the fields, encircling them. Mike peered out of the reeds into the gathering darkness.

The peasants had returned to collect their dead, and the eerie, nocturnal cries were caused by the grief of women as they recognized the dead faces of loved ones and hugged the wet corpses tightly in their arms.

Chapter 18

THE Hmong had argued quietly but volubly among themselves in the reeds, with much pointing to the various peaks on the far side of the valley. At last some consensus was reached.

"I don't know what they're saying," Verdoux told Campbell. "They've switched dialects on me and they're talking too fast, but it seems like they may remember the mountains ahead."

This turned out to be the case. One of the Hmong spoke to Verdoux and explained that the border checkpoint was five kilometers down the road, at the river crossing. The officially recognized border was the tips of the mountain range, but the Vietnamese had expanded westward into Laos for convenience. The three helicopters that attacked were Vietnamese, not Laotian, according to the Hmong. Viets killed Lao people like that when they could get away with it.

The Hmong said he would lead everyone alongside the road for about a kilometer. Then he would branch out to the northeast from it on one of the many paths across the rice fields. They would have to traverse the area of cultivated fields in total darkness, he said, cross the river and climb through rice fields again on the other side. When they reached rough country at the highest upland extent of the fields, they would wait for the moon. The first quarter would be out for a few hours later in the night. They would travel into the mountains by moonlight.

This sounded like a grueling journey to Mike, but he saw no way to avoid it. Shuffling along on narrow paths in almost total darkness, they constantly whispered to each other in order to maintain contact—like birds make sounds for each other while migrating in the night skies. The river at the bottom of the valley was only ankle deep, and there were fewer rice fields to be negotiated on the far side of the valley. All of them, including the Hmong, were exhausted and high-strung when they settled in rough ground to await the rising of the moon.

Mike ordered them to eat again, to keep their spirits and energy up. Again, this order was greeted with no enthusiasm. They were getting tired of the cold canned goods that made up their C rations and the blandness of the packaged foods that constituted the K rations.

"When we get into the mountains, we'll have a hot meal," Mike promised.

"How about roast Vietnamese commie?" Harvey Waller asked.

"Don't get weird on us, Harvey," Joe Nolan said to him.

They trekked up through a maze of mountain paths in the faint moonlight. Two of the paths were sealed by several strands of barbed wire, and the Hmong turned back.

"Do not climb under when you see this," they told Verdoux. "The wire is to warn their own soldiers of a mine field beyond."

Once, the Hmong became lost and had to retrace their steps downhill past several turnings before they found one that led in the correct direction. They rested for an hour in the darkness between the setting of the quarter moon and the gray breath of dawn. As soon as trunks, rocks, roots and other obstacles became distinguishable in the half-light, they pushed on.

Campbell reckoned that some of the peaks were four thousand feet above sea level and that the pass they were taking through them was close to two thousand feet in altitude. The air was crisp and sharp, smelling of pines and other evergreens that blanketed the slopes.

Verdoux told Mike, "The Hmong say there are lower, easier passes that are too dangerous to take. Except for occasional aerial reconnaissance, we don't have to worry from this point on until we're halfway down the slope on the other side. The Viets prefer to lie in wait down there for smugglers rather than leap about up here like mountain goats."

"Sounds to me like a reasonable decision," Mike commented. "Do we descend the slope? I thought the Montagnard village was high in the mountains."

"Not this ridge, I'm afraid. The village is in the next ridge parallel to this one, so we have to descend this one and climb that."

They reached the highest point of the pass and, all of a sudden, the rugged panorama of Vietnam stretched before their eyes. They all cheered.

Nolan added wryly, "We gotta be crazy—cheering because we're back in Nam. Where the fuck we going anyway, Mike? I'm hardly going to sell the story to *Time* or *Newsweek* from out here."

Ideally, Campbell would have preferred to keep the goal of the mission secret until they had reached their destination in case any of the team were captured. However, he saw that it was unreasonable for him to demand that grown men go farther with him than they had already gone without knowing the true purpose of the mission.

Campbell said there was no need for the Hmong to know, and then told them in detail about their planned rescue of Eric Vanderhoven.

Joe Nolan was aghast. "All this for one shitty rich kid? I don't believe it. More than fifty people dead already. You drag our asses halfway round the world and put our lives on the line for some freak, half-gook kid whose grandpa is a crap-filled billionaire? To hell with this, Mike. It's enough to make anyone a communist. What do you take me for?"

There was a hard glitter in Campbell's eyes, and when he spoke, his voice was so low that Nolan had to lean forward to catch every word.

"Joe, I hired you as a merc, not as a social critic or economic reformer. You agreed to come on this mission for a hundred thousand dollars, aware that you had not been informed of its purpose."

"Sure, Mike, but I thought we were going in after GIs in concentration camps—you know, MIAs."

"Nobody paid us to do that," Campbell said. "If they had, I would have gone. That's not the point. I hired you as a merc to do a job—and here's the point, I'm not going to permit you to back out now."

Nolan looked into the calm gray eyes of Mad Mike Campbell and his indignation evaporated.

"That hundred thou still good?" Joe said jovially, trying not to lose too much face while backing down.

"Sure."

They shook hands.

"Anyone else got anything to say?" Campbell asked. "Now's the time to talk about it, not down there." He pointed to Vietnam. There was silence. Mike went on, "OK, I think we got to grant Joe Nolan that he has a point. We sure as hell seem to be wasting a lot of people in order to save one. And we wouldn't be trying to save the kid if he wasn't an heir to a huge fortune. None of that is under your control. Yet one thing is a matter of honor with you. Your word to me that you would come out here with me as a merc. I didn't pry into your reasons for coming, and you were all desperate to come. Your word to me as a soldier of fortune is worth more than all the supposed social and economic justice that's always just around the corner and never seems to arrive. Now I want you to know that *I* am going down into this garbage leftist country and grabbing that kid and taking him back to America, and what's more, I don't think Washington, Moscow and Hanoi all combined are going to be able to stop me.''

The pine forests protected them from the small single-engine planes that droned up and down the valleys and along the mountain slopes in search of them. They met no ground patrols, somewhat to Campbell's surprise.

"There's too much area for them to cover on foot," Larry Richards opined. "They're avoiding spreading their men too thin and instead are concentrating them in mobile groups, so that when we're spotted by air they can concentrate their troops on the single target area. Bob remembers how we did that against the rebels in Malaysia. A number got away unobserved, but when you do locate them, you can really stick it to them."

"Damned right," Bob concurred. "As Larry says, if one of these aircraft sees us, we'll have a goddamn battalion of Viet army regulars on our heels."

"Andre, warn the Hmong about those planes," Mike said. "Every man freezes till each plane passes over. I don't want anyone to even scratch himself. You think they carry any sophisticated equipment for observation?"

"I doubt it," Joe Nolan volunteered. "Look at those old run-down planes they're using for recon. Some of them look like they were in World War II."

They descended into the steep-walled valley and began to climb up the other side through the thick woods. The sun rose almost directly above them in the cloudless sky, but it was pleasantly cool in the shade of the thick evergreens. The Hmong walked purposefully now, confident of where they were going, and the men climbed silently up the slope on a deep layer of moss and fallen pine needles. They spoke little, weary from their all-night march and all-day trek in mountain terrain.

The reconnaissance planes vanished before noon. They moved north along the crest of the ridge on a well-beaten path, whether human or animal Mike could not say. Their pace had slowed considerably, and Mike wondered if the others had blisters on their feet like he had. As leader of the mission, he had to be above such minor ailments as sore feet, of course, although he was imagining what it would be like to take off his jungle boots and walk on the damp moss in his bare feet.

A sudden movement in the bushes to their right . . . The nearest Hmong whirled about and sent a burst of AK47 automatic fire at chest level into the vegetation. The bushes parted, and a deer with big antlers staggered out, bleeding from four punctures in the chest, and collapsed almost at their feet.

"This guy should have been in Dodge City," Harvey Waller said of the Hmong who shot the deer. "That's the fastest response I've ever seen."

They all agreed, and Andre explained it to the Hmong, who showed he understood by strutting and quick-drawing an imaginary six-shooter with a delighted grin on his face.

"How far to the Montagnard camp from here?" Campbell asked Verdoux.

Verdoux brought back the information. "About ten kilometers. By the way, our colleagues assure us it is safe to light a cooking fire here because the Viets will assume it's a Montagnard fire if they see it, which is improbable. They would also like to show us how to butcher and cook a deer Hmong-style, should we wish to make camp here for the night. They are being very formal and polite about it, so I told them I would try to persuade you."

Mike laughed and sat and began to undo his boots.

They gorged themselves on the rich, gamey venison and easily consumed the entire red meat of the big deer. Having constructed small shelters of tree branches, they spread ground sheets inside and slipped into the oblivion of sleep soon after sundown. The watches were shared at an hour per man, so that everyone got his fair share of rest.

They struck camp at the first light and arrived at the Montagnard village without incident shortly after nine. They stayed behind cover and watched the village for a while. The bamboo and thatch huts were large permanent structures, and the fields of vegetables surrounding it were orderly and well tended. Between forty and fifty huts were scattered in a great circle about a clearing, with others randomly placed in outlying positions.

"What do you think?" Verdoux asked Campbell.

"No one's working in the fields. There's a few men in the village center but no women or children. You notice the chickens running about, but where are the pigs and other more valuable animals? Seems like these folks might be expecting trouble. I think it's time for a straight talk with the Hmong."

"They get evasive and vague on this subject," Andre warned.

"I'll go with you."

The Hmong must have known that they could hold out no longer, and Andre broke the news to Mike. "This is the village, all right. However, none of them have ever been here before. Actually, they are very proud of themselves for having guided us here solely on the verbal description of how to do it from another Hmong. He was the one who was originally supposed to lead the group but backed out at the last moment."

Mike smiled. "Compliment them from me on their navigation. When was the last time one of their tribal group was in this Montagnard village?"

"They told me that a group of smugglers were here about this time last year and transacted good business with the Montagnards. The rainy season followed, and after that the smuggling was abandoned as being too risky."

"So no one has been in touch for twelve months?"

Andre nodded.

"If we didn't need them to guide us to the reeducation camp," Campbell said, "I'd skip the place altogether. Also, we need this as a place to rendezvous with the Hmong on the way back. We have no choice but to find out whether it's secure." Campbell brought his forces back a bit and indicated to Verdoux he was to translate for the Hmong. "So far, no one has seen us Westerners on communist-occupied turf and survived. I want that record to stand. If these Montagnards have been turned, they must think they are being approached by Hmong alone. That doesn't mean we're going to dump on the Hmong. Us six Westerners will spread out in three pairs and take advance firing positions. Then the Hmong go in like they would as if alone, taking whatever precautions they normally would. Let's go."

Campbell and Waller crept down in the central section of the fields, Murphy and Richards on the left flank and Nolan and Verdoux on the right. They were all reasonably certain they had not been seen. Three of the Hmong walked boldly forward and shouted loudly across the fields to those in the village. The other seven Hmong hung back, visible to the village and displaying a suspicious caution in marked contrast to the three men engaged in friendly shouting. The message was clear in any language—we're friendly fellows, but we carry a lot of clout just in case.

The men in the village clearing stood still for a few moments, looking at the distant newcomers, then spoke a few words among themselves and headed for several of the huts. After that, the only signs of life were the hens pecking in the ground around the huts.

The three Hmong shouted loudly and advanced farther. Mike would have worried about the safety of anyone else, but these teen-agers had already shown what they were made of. The seven other Hmong hung back.

A burst of automatic fire came through the wall of one of the huts. The three Hmong threw themselves flat on the dirt behind whatever cover they could find. Then fire from other huts was directed at the seven Hmong in the background, while about twenty men with automatic rifles and submachine guns poured out of the huts. They charged the three Hmong in the foreground while their companions pinned down the seven in the background. By now it was clear that they had not seen Mad Mike & Co. take up their positions.

The others waited for Mike's gunfire as their signal to start the carnage. Then Mike goofed. He underestimated the speed of the charge of the villagers—he had thought they were dealing with undisciplined peasant fighters, but these were highly trained men, moving quickly and accurately to overrun the position of the Hmong—and unknown to them, the positions of the Western mercs, also. The villagers had gained much more yardage than they ought to have—and were almost on top of Campbell—by the time he opened fire.

Mike saw their savage, triumphant snarls change to horrified surprise and craven fear as he mowed the nearest of them down at almost point-blank range. When your opponent is homing in on victory and you snatch it from him by surprise, it takes a little bit longer for his mind to sort out his reactions. This gift of a little extra time was all that saved Campbell and his team.

Verdoux heaved a grenade, and the fragments cut down some of those whose bodies protected the others. And still they came on.

The attacking Montagnards were firing wildly and shouting loudly, as if this were enough to make their adversaries turn tail and run. As it was, none of Mike's team could even raise their heads because of the fire of the three plus seven Hmong behind them, who were now sending an erratic hail of lead at a level of about three feet above the ground. As always when fire is heaviest and bullets fly in every direction, certain individuals seem blessed with a magic quality of survival. No matter how unprotected they are or what reckless things they do, nothing hits them. So it was with some of the Montagnards.

One big tribesman came right for Campbell, hollering and throwing short bursts from his rifle. Campbell ripped him apart from gut to head with his AK47. The Montagnard's body literally blew apart, scattering blood, pieces of tissue and bone splinters over Mike's face and hands. He spat out some fragments from his mouth.

He used the mangled carcass as cover to bring down another three of the Montagnards. The hill tribesmen suddenly realized that they were taking ninety-percent losses and ran back toward the village.

"Everyone OK?" Mike called.

They sounded off.

"Holy shit," Nolan added.

"Should never have happened this way," Campbell shouted back. "My fault. All the Hmong OK, Andre?"

"Yes. They want to wipe these bastards out."

"They got it."

They all moved slowly forward against the village. The remaining villagers joined the survivors of the charge, darting out of the bamboo and thatched huts, laden with weapons, to gain cover behind trees and earthen banks.

"If we let these bastards dig in, we'll be here for three days," Mike yelled. "Andre, tell the Hmong to continue this frontal assault, then you take Nolan and Richards advance on the left flank. I'll take Murphy and Waller on the right. Good luck."

"They'll be watching for us, Mike," Andre warned.

"They better be."

The two three-man teams drew fire as they ran from cover to cover on each flank. But the Montagnards couldn't concentrate on them, because now the ten Hmong no longer had Campbell's restraining hand to hold them back. Verdoux had translated the words "frontal assault" for them, and that was what they intended to deliver.

When Campbell saw the Hmong advance in this suicidal assault, he halted his own circling maneuvers and he, Murphy, and Waller provided covering fire. Verdoux and his men, on the left flank, followed suit. Although they only hit one villager, they stopped the others from massacring the advancing Hmong. Each time a Montagnard tried to shoot at them, he found himself ducking the cross fire of the two three-men teams. Nor could the Montagnards retreat. They found themselves pinned down and unable to return fire, while the murderous Hmong bore down on them with all the deadly certainty of a pride of hungry predators.

The ten Hmong threw caution to the winds. They ran forward in twos and threes, without shooting for fear of hitting one another, bayonets fixed and teeth bared. Three descended on the Montagnard in the most forward position, drove their bayonets into him repeatedly, and all together lifted him from the ground and threw his lifeless body aside, like farmers pitching straw with hayforks.

"Hold your fire!" Campbell yelled, as the Hmong overran the Montagnard's positions. "Waller, you want to kill commies? Go get 'em, boy!"

Waller took off like a thoroughbred from a starting gate, and in a matter of seconds was driving the shining steel of his bayonet in living communist flesh, withdrawing it covered in scarlet life's blood, waving the gory blade in a grotesque parody of a red flag while screaming obscenities about Marx, then plunging the tempered steel again and again into the writhing, screaming, turncoat tribesmen.

Chapter 19

THE party cadres looked expectantly at the cadre in charge of Eric Vanderhoven and the eleven other Amerasian youths at the reeducation camp. In a way they envied the fact he had been contacted about his wards from higher circles within the party—at least his existence had been acknowledged. Every one of them often wondered if anyone on a higher level either knew or cared what they did. But this was mere glorification of the personality—it was the sacred duty of a cadre to lose his or her identity and selfish motivations in his or her work for the party. The other side of the coin was that it was dangerous to have one's existence noticed, to have wards in the camp who attracted the attention of high-level functionaries. If something went wrong, the cadre would have to answer for it. And if the cadre blamed his fellow cadres for their lack of cooperation, they might all be in danger of being censured.

The stigma of being associated with any failure or error, no matter how indirectly, was enough to soothe their petty jealousies, rivalries, and personal dislikes and make them look down the long, woven wicker table with genuine concern at their colleague.

THE POINT TEAM

He stood to talk, and his face disappeared out of the bright light of the oil lamp on the table into the dark shadows above. He spoke in a quick hurried voice and made little effort to conceal his worry and agitation as he described his orders to allow the American crew to film Vanderhoven.

"I think this is a daring tactic on the part of our planners and one which will advance the party's interest," he concluded.

Everyone there knew that what he meant was that this was a mistake of some city bureaucrat and that whatever was planned would backfire. It went without saying that the nameless city bureaucrat would not accept responsibility for an ill-conceived plan, which of course left them holding the baby. The others present were inclined to agree with his implied judgment of the scheme.

A senior cadre took it upon himself to express the collective view. "This startling departure from accepted norms reflects knowledge and clearheadedness about future events beyond the abilities of all present here."

There was a gloomy murmur of assent to this, and they waited till the statement was carefully recorded by the secretary to be entered into the minutes of the meeting. More than this they could not do to register their opinions.

The cadre in charge of the Amerasian youths summed up. "The Americans will arrive in a government car with two interpreters. We are to distract the interpreters, giving the Americans time to wander at will."

"If we put Vanderhoven and the other boys out in the fields by the road, the Americans will notice them," one cadre suggested. "We could tell the boys they will be out there all week by themselves, without other workers nearby. When the Americans make contact with them, the boys will be able to tell them to come back and film them there. If necessary, we could detain the interpreters once again."

There was general acceptance of this suggestion.

"But the Americans must not suspect..."

THE POINT TEAM

* * *

Lt. Tranh Duc Pho walked over to his radioman and listened as the message was repeated through heavy static.

"Forty... repeat all forty... mountain pioneers killed. Weapons used by attackers seem to have been AK47s and American hand grenades. No survivors. No eyewitnesses. Reports of Hmong invading force of fifty men crossed Laos from Thailand. May be entering your area. Do not spread local alarm. Repeat. Do not declare emergency. Confirm."

The lieutenant nodded to the radioman, who transmitted, "Confirmed."

Tranh Duc Pho wandered away as a lot of patriotic palaver came to them over the airwaves—how it was essential to lay down their lives, if necessary, to stop the playfulness of these imperialist puppies, irresponsible agents of the malevolent foreign powers, hirelings of Peking and Washington bent on wanton destruction to besmirch the reputation of the workers' republic. The lieutenant normally made a point of dutifully listening to such claptrap in the presence of his men, but the news he had just heard caused a surge of anger and frustration in him that he found difficult to control and which would have made him lose face with his subordinates if he had revealed his emotions.

All forty of the men he had placed in the village dead! They had been the best Montagnard warriors he had ever convinced to join the new progressive forces. Nearly all the others had clung tenaciously to their outdated traditions and what they called their independence. Tranh Duc Pho himself had given them the name "mountain pioneers." Only two weeks previously he had presented the village to them as a reward for their efforts and help.

He had shipped the entire population of the village—men, women and children—to a distant reeducation camp as punishment for their smuggling activities, possession of weapons and contacts with outsiders. He had packed the

THE POINT TEAM

lamenting tribesmen into big helicopters and flown them beyond where they would ever find their way back. After a couple of rice harvests at the camp, they would be transported to an uninhabited mountain area well away from the border and allowed to make homes for themselves there. They would never see the good land and well-built homes of their old village again. These were now a prize for the mountain pioneers.

The lieutenant had expected that the forty friendly Montagnards would soon either entice or abduct women to their new property. Their sudden landed status and right to bear arms should send a clear message to the other mountain tribes of the advantages of cooperating with him and the Hanoi government. Tribesmen who didn't, disappeared.

Tranh Duc Pho believed in simple, forceful messages. Now these plundering Hmongs, no doubt on a smuggling mission to their old friends at the village, had come unexpectedly upon his mountain pioneers and had slaughtered them. These fools had wrecked his plan! His reward of the village now meant nothing! The other tribesmen would say this was the will of the Holy One and would become more firmly entrenched in their outmoded, mistaken ways!

His face twisted in rage, and he snapped close his fingers like the teeth of a rat trap. It was intolerable!

Yet he had a chance for vengeance. These marauding Hmong were advancing into his territory, by all accounts. They must have decided to deliver their smuggled goods elsewhere in Vietnam. The lieutenant knew that the estimate of fifty men was a gross exaggeration—it would not be permissible to admit that a much smaller force had defeated a greater force loyal to the government. From experience, the lieutenant knew the Hmong would number no more than fifteen men. They would be young and from this point operating in territory unknown to them, since they had always before returned into Laos from the Montagnard village.

He would capture and torture them to death, then nail

their mutilated bodies to trees as a warning to all who passed on the mountain trails.

A small smile of anticipation spread across Tranh Duc Pho's face.

Katie Nelson winked at Jake, the sound man, as their two interpreters were led off in voluble discussion by the camp cadres. Roger did a medium shot of their departing backs, then panned his camera on the thatched camp huts.

"I wish they had some barbed wire and guard towers," he complained. "This is going to look like a fucking Club Med."

As soon as their interpreters had gone out of sight, Katie drifted over to the car. "The key is in the ignition! I'd almost swear Eric was one of those kids we saw picking rice near the road."

"Katie, you don't pick rice—the kids were planting young shoots," Jake told her with a smile as he slid behind the wheel.

She got in beside him, and Roger took his camera off his shoulder and climbed in the back. In less than ten minutes they were at the edge of the flooded rice field in which the youths were working.

"Stay in the car," Katie said. "I'll be more inconspicuous if I go alone."

"Bullshit!" Roger exploded. "I came out here to get footage and that's what I'm getting."

He climbed out of the car and stared at her defiantly.

Katie sighed. "You'd better come too, Jake. I'd hate not to have sound if they machine-gun us."

The look on Eric Vanderhoven's face when he saw her made the whole trip worthwhile for Katie. He had stared up at the newcomers on the road above the rice field for an instant in his customary aggressive glare. This was replaced by a look of amazement, which in turn gave way to a smile of childlike delight.

"Beautiful, beautiful," Roger murmured as he squinted

through the viewfinder and rolled the tape. "I got the little fucker in a close-up that's real handkerchief material."

Eric had to make three separate approaches through the muddy water to Katie before Roger was satisfied with the shot.

"We've come to take you to America," Katie told him finally with a catch in her voice.

"Now?" Eric asked. "They'll let you?"

"*They* don't know about it. Someone is coming for you. He'll be here in a few days or maybe a week or more, I can't be sure. His name is Mike. He'll contact me and I'll bring him here to you."

"I'll be working in this field all week," Eric told her excitedly. "Any time he likes, I'm ready to go."

It had finally begun to dawn on Campbell's men that they were alone now, on a hillside in Vietnam, with no backing to rely on from the outside. Andre Verdoux was the first to put this feeling into words.

He said in private to Campbell, "God, I kind of miss the Hmong."

"I know what you mean, Andre, but I had to send them back to Thailand. They couldn't wait for us in these mountains, and anyway, we have to go back by some other route, so there would have been no way to rendezvous with them again. We'll go back the same way we came in, but it's going to be one hell of a lot tougher trip, and I don't want to commit us to any particular mountain pass in advance."

"The Hmong could have come with us," Andre said.

"What for? They don't know the country. If anything, we know Vietnam better than they do. Why do I need sixteen men? From here on in, I'm avoiding confrontation any way I can. Sixteen men are a lot harder to hide than the six we are now."

"The men are sort of jumpy."

"I like that," Mike said, half joking. "Nobody's going to creep up on them when they're edgy."

Verdoux could see he was getting nowhere with Campbell in his present frame of mind, so he grew quiet and moodily smoked a cigarette. The two men sat apart from the others as they all rested and sheltered from the midday heat.

The humid stillness was shattered by Harvey Waller's scream. Campbell had grabbed his rifle and flicked the selector to AUTOMATIC before he realized that Waller had not been stricken by an unseen enemy, but was howling in rage at Bob Murphy. The big Australian was sitting placidly on the ground, grinning up at the enraged Waller, who was now on his feet and jumping up and down like a crazed chimpanzee.

"You ought to be in a booby hatch," the Australian was telling him in a friendly way. "In there, the men in white coats would give you little pills to make you feel good and upholster the walls so you wouldn't hurt yourself climbing up them."

Waller was beyond speech. He took a few paces toward Murphy and tried to boot him in the face. The Australian jerked his head back, and the toe of the jungle boot grazed his nose.

Murphy threw an arm lock on Waller's leg, but the latter rabbit-punched him with the heel of his hand and worked his limb free.

The blow was enough to set Murphy off, and he bounded to his feet and charged Waller like a wounded grizzly. Waller stood his ground. He was picked up effortlessly and slammed to the ground.

Nolan and Richards looked on and laughed, making no effort to interfere.

Half stunned, Waller lay on his side and stared up at his tormentor, who now stood above him, hands on hips.

"I don't know why Mike brought along a rat like you, Waller," Murphy jeered. "We don't mind you being nuts,

THE POINT TEAM

what we do mind is you can't fight." He poked him in the side with his toe. "You run around ripping into dead bodies. Anyone stands up to you, mate, you flop over, belly up."

Waller snapped to his feet in a split second, whipping out his combat knife as he came. He shot a fast jab of the blade at Murphy, catching him a glancing blow on the left upper arm. The blade slashed his skin, and blood flowed. Murphy, outraged, ended it all with a straight right to the center of Waller's forehead, an instant anesthesia that dropped him to the ground.

Campbell hadn't reached them in time to stop the blow. Now he snarled at Murphy, "Bring him to. And be gentle or I'll kick your ass." He turned to Nolan and Richards. "What's wrong with you? Can't you see we have to stick together? When we get back to Thailand, you guys can make shish kebab of one another for all I care. While you're on my team, you look out for one another—and that means breaking up fights. Like you would if you were on a baseball or football team. Except none of those pro sports guys is getting paid a hundred thou for a few weeks' work like you guys are. So don't come on like some goofball just serving out his tour. You fucks are being better paid than Eisenhower, Patton and MacArthur all put together."

Waller seemed surprised to find Murphy helping him when he came to. He said nothing.

In order to pull the team together again, Campbell discussed their mission objectives. He passed about photos taken from satellites of Novgorod class and Poltava class Soviet merchant ships unloading military and other cargo at the docks in Ho Chi Minh City and of Soviet naval vessels at the old U.S. base on Cam Ranh Bay.

Campbell smiled at their puzzled looks. "We're not going to attack Soviet shipping. Those photos are intended only as disinformation in case we are captured." He held up a print. "This is the only one that counts."

THE POINT TEAM

Nolan glanced at it quickly. "Not from a satellite. Looks more like one of those pictures they used to take from a hundred thousand feet up on a Lockheed SR-71. Remember them? You could see a cigarette in a man's mouth and read the numbers on the license plate of a car."

"Yeah, I think you're right, Nolan," Campbell agreed. "It's a shot of the reeducation camp where the kid is detained. Old Grandpa Vanderhoven told me he got it from a pal at the Pentagon before his relations with Washington turned sour. Anyway, you see it's a low-security detention center, a kind of work farm, I guess, for nonpoliticals and dissidents the government is not much afraid of. Like kids. You see, here the jungle comes right down next to the rice fields. All the kid has to do is walk out and come along with us. It's going to be a piece of cake."

"I'd sure like to meet that Katie Nelson," Nolan said. "You can't see much of her on the TV, but I bet she's a nice piece of ass."

He gave Campbell an inquiring look, but before he could get the words "Did you score with her?" out of his mouth, Mike changed the subject.

"Those dumdums, Waller?"

"Yeah, Mike. I wasn't using any before, but I sure as shit am now. I kept shooting those mothers and they kept coming like I was using an air gun. You don't hit 'em in a bone, you don't stop 'em. These dumdums going to flatten on impact and tear huge holes in the fuckers. You'll be able to see the scenery through them."

"Go easy with them, Waller," Campbell said. "Put too many of them in your magazine, and you stand a good chance of jamming your gun."

"I'm using them one in five."

"That's OK."

Hollowing the point of the bullet to make it into a dumdum usually unbalanced the metal projectile. Any imbalance in the bullet jarred against the small tolerances of the precision rifling inside the barrel and was a potential cause of trouble.

Campbell said nothing but was surprised Waller had not been using doctored bullets up to this point. Campbell himself was, and he figured all the others were, too. Dumdums were illegal, according to the Geneva Convention, like a lot of other things in armed combat. Campbell didn't talk much about these aspects of warfare, as a matter of preference. He felt that people who talked usually ended up either excusing or denying what took place every day in some part of the world.

The bad feeling between Murphy and Waller and the amused unconcern of Nolan and Richards at their fight seemed to have evaporated as quickly as they had come into being. Campbell got the team under way while their mood was still good.

Joe Nolan was at point. Waller was ten yards behind him, then Campbell, Richards, Verdoux, Murphy. The spread-out line of men moved fast through the trees and undergrowth. They had too much ground to cover to use a more cautious approach. This way, if they ran into something unexpected and couldn't back off because of their pace, the opposing side was likely to be even more unpleasantly surprised than they, because as they traveled they were primed to react instantly and let loose at anything that stood in their way. Which was what happened.

They had been climbing ridge after ridge of the north-south-running mountains as they journeyed east. A stream in the valley at the base of one ridge cut through the next. If they followed it as far as it ran east, it would save them a lot of climbing. A well-worn path ran along the southern bank of the stream. Nolan waited for Campbell to give him the go-ahead.

It was tempting. After all their scrabbling up and down the loose rocks and undergrowth of the ridges, here was a level, smooth path to walk along—like a human being for a change, instead of a mountain goat. The vegetation on the north bank of the stream was too dense for them to make their way through, and the streambed, although nearly dry, was too rocky for easy walking. Campbell nodded to Nolan, but gestured with his Kalashnikov for them to be on extra alert.

Maybe Campbell should have slowed Nolan down. Maybe not, since it made sense that they should use the path for their greatest benefit, yet spend as little time upon it as possible. Fighting men don't spend a lot of time figuring out all the variations which might have occurred in any given situation because all that counts is what in fact did occur and what was done in response to its happening.

Nolan just walked into a group of armed men traveling in a tight bunch on the path, taking no precautions. At a glance, Nolan simultaneously saw that all of them had their rifles slung on their backs and correctly judged that he had no way out of the situation. He emptied the thirty 7.62-mm rounds in his AK47's magazine on the group, at chest level, then dropped to the ground on one side of the path, pressed the release button, discarded the empty magazine, and slapped a full one in the housing.

His burst of automatic fire cut down the leaders of the group. However, the entire burst was so rapid that the riddled bodies of those in front shielded those immediately behind.

Waller waited till Nolan dived out of the way, and while the leaders of the group were still staggering and falling, he emptied his AK47 magazine into the ones still wavering immobile from this sudden onslaught. He did not throw out his bullets in a sweep as Nolan had done, but in more accurate bursts, punctuated by dumdums.

The Viets looked like a bunch of lousy actors pretending to be poisoned—they suddenly clutched their bellies, rolled their eyes, made grotesque faces, keeled over slowly. Some screamed, others moaned, the rest fell silently.

Chapter 20

"HEY, Mitch, tell Red I want to see him," Eric Vanderhoven said in his usual tone of command.

Mitch ignored him.

Eric was alarmed by this. If one of the others had tried to defy him, he would have settled the rebellion right away, but Mitch and Red were his two buddies from Vo Veng's orphanage in Ho Chi Minh City, convicted with him of spying on Soviet ships with stolen video equipment. If one of them turned against him, he was in trouble. If both of them ganged up on him, he was finished.

"Hey, Mitch, you hear me?" he tried again.

No response.

Eric turned about to survey him carefully. Mitch was chopping up some vegetables he had stolen, and he concentrated on his task. Two of the other boys came into the hut.

"Get Red for me," Eric ordered one of them.

The boys paid no attention to him.

Eric stalked out of the hut, his instincts warning him to find out what was going on before he decided on a showdown. He was their leader. He would fight for that. It was a position he had earned, and he was going to hold onto it.

Another youth passed him, studiously avoiding looking him in the eye.

Eric saw Red's shock of bright ginger hair over by a drainage ditch, where he was gutting some frogs he had caught for their meal.

"What's up?" Eric demanded to know. "Have you turned against me, too?"

"No one's turned against you, Eric." Red's voice was cold.

"Don't pull this polite crap with me, Red. What's wrong?"

"Everything's great for you."

"Me?" Eric was genuinely puzzled. "Look, I'm your leader. Right? You tell me what's wrong and I'll fix it."

Red rinsed a freshly cleaned frog in the ditch water, placed it on the grass and looked at Eric. "You *were* our leader before you decided to cut out and leave us. Now we got to look for someone else."

Eric was silent for a while. Finally he asked humbly, "How did you know?"

"You talk in your sleep. We all heard you last night, about how Katie Nelson is getting someone here to rescue you. And leaving the rest of us behind. Oh, you didn't say that while you were asleep, but it wasn't hard for us to guess we weren't included."

They were quiet for a time while Red cleaned the final frog. When he had finished, he said, "We don't expect you to turn down this chance, Eric, but you got to understand you're not one of *us* anymore."

Red gathered up the frogs and headed for the cooking pot. He turned back to say, "You don't have to worry, Eric. None of us is going to give you away."

Eric felt so guilty, he stared at the ground between his feet.

THE POINT TEAM

* * *

"Yes, I want to go to the Buddhist temple," Katie Nelson said with finality.

Her senior Vietnamese interpreter shrugged resignedly. "You will give Americans the idea that the communists destroyed this temple we go to every morning. It has been a ruin for hundreds of years. Why do we have to go every day?"

"In America we interrupt the program for commercials— you've heard of them. We need shots to begin and end segments of the show, and the ruined temple and its intact statue of the Buddha is perfect for that. My cameraman needs to catch it in the varying light each day to match what we film later on."

This was barely disguised bullshit, but Katie knew from experience that people, even communists, are willing to believe anything they're told about television.

They made their way, as they did every morning, up the stone steps between the toppled stone columns amid a tide of jungle vegetation that swept over the broken walls and cracked paving. Some of the arches and walls still stood, giving them an idea of what had once stood in this place. Alone, and the only thing undamaged in this heap of defaced rubble, stood a fifteen-foot carved stone statue of the Buddha, in the sacred lotus position, one hand raised and the eyes staring outward, aware, passive, transcending the passage of time in its spiritual message.

Katie looked up at the smooth, rounded features of the stone face. In the iris of the right eye was propped a shiny new American quarter. Roger saw it too, and zoomed in on it with his camera lens while Katie distracted the interpreter.

Campbell had arrived! This had been the only meeting place they could be sure they would confuse with nothing else in the aerial photographs. The statue had shown up intact on them. Katie had not known what sign Mike would leave for her, but as soon as she set eyes on the coin she knew it was not the currency of any other country but her own. She did not have to see George Washington's head or the eagle with spread wings on its faces. She knew a Buddha when he winked.

Katie Nelson stared amazed at Eric Vanderhoven. "All eleven of them?"

"Right."

She took a deep breath and looked over at the eleven youths still busy planting rice shoots in the mud. Then she turned back to the determined thirteen-year-old who faced her on the roadway.

"I sympathize with you, Eric," she said, looking grave for the cameraman and wishing Jake was not picking this up on the microphone. "It's a matter of logistics. I don't think there's any way Mike could take you all. Perhaps one or two of your real close friends. I'll ask. But he'll say no to all of you coming. For sure."

"Then I'll stay."

Katie looked at him and felt like screaming, "You ungrateful little shit-head, you treat me like a fucking air-head and steal my equipment, and now when I come halfway round the world to save your ass, you say on tape that you won't come because you're too loyal to your buddies." Instead, after a nervous half-glance at the camera, she said, "I understand, Eric, you're being loyal to your friends. Everybody in America will know and understand that. I'll talk to Mike and see what he says. I'll try to persuade him. I promise you, I'll do my best."

Catch in her voice. A tear, perhaps, in her eyes. A sad smile. Change of focus. Roger panned on the laboring kids and turned off the camera. Jake cut the sound.

"Since when have you become a hero?" Katie rapped at Eric. "Up till now you've been a selfish, dictatorial little snot."

Eric grinned at her maliciously. "Say what you got to say to me on camera, lady. You be careful, or I'll say some things about you that you won't like."

He turned away and climbed down the earthen bank into

THE POINT TEAM

the rice field. He was soon at work again and, like the others, ignoring their presence.

Katie felt Roger's amused look, but did not acknowledge it. He knew what she was thinking—that he was too well-known as a cameraman for her to insist that she have a right to edit the contents of his film. If he ever got anything bad on her in the can, she knew he would insist on its being shown. Just to show her he could do as he pleased. No doubt he would call it artistic integrity or professional independence or some such. One word from him to a few producers that he had less-than-complimentary footage on Katie Nelson would set the mills of envy grinding. These were the dangers of live reporting in the field. The producers and their damn editors in the cutting room would make her look like less than star quality if she ever gave them the chance. While here she had been in Vietnam for a week already without being able to find a hairdresser!

Their interpreters were waiting for them in the car. Jake's opinion was that they had bored them so much, the interpreters no longer cared what they filmed or did. Roger claimed that boredom was a luxury no Vietnamese could afford under the communist regime, that if they were allowed to do something, there was a reason for it. Katie was inclined to agree. Yet, as news reporters, when given an opportunity they had to take it and ask questions later.

Katie noticed the interpreters were not so easy to shake off at places other than the reeducation camp. Except at the ruined Buddhist temple. They always followed the three Americans partway up the steps, then stopped and smoked while keeping an eye on them in the distance.

The day was baking hot, and Katie looked enviously at Roger stripped to the waist as he carried his camera on his shoulder. She could feel her blouse stuck to her back. She silently cursed the American TV audience which expected a woman to look primped, cool, and perfumed in the torrid tropics. There was no way Roger could get her to stand before a camera this afternoon.

Campbell stood concealed where he had been before. Roger quickly moved into the niche in the ruined stonework and passed his camera to Campbell. Mike was walking after a moment's delay alongside Katie Nelson in full view of the two interpreters, stripped to the waist as Roger had been, and the video camera on his shoulder blocking his face from their view.

"I'm not taking him on his terms," Mike said. "I'm taking him on mine."

"Eric said he won't go."

"We'll take him against his will if we have to."

"I really think Eric is right," she said. "I think you should take the other eleven with you."

"So now we know what you think," Mike snapped.

"At first I reacted the same way as you," Katie said earnestly. "Now I see it would be heartless to leave the others behind."

"It would be suicide not to. I can't take a goddamn school tour out of Vietnam across Laos."

"Talk to Eric."

"I don't have time."

Mike grew increasingly irritated at Katie, promised to meet her at the same place the next morning, and changed places with Roger.

Eric Vanderhoven and the others worked hard to meet their quota for the day's planting. It was essential to meet work requirements now to keep overseers away. None of the youths thought to question why they had been allowed to work together away from all the other workers and so conveniently located to meet with the American TV crew.

Eric, back in his position as leader, was taking his responsibilities as such with great integrity. He regarded himself as father-protector of the other eleven now, and his demands on their behalf had allowed him to cast himself in a role of glory. The others were willing to put up with this if it meant that they, too, could go along with him, as he assured them they could. He, Eric Vanderhoven, would insist.

As he worked, he watched out for the others—feeling himself to be an old male lion protecting know-nothing cubs. He saw the two Americans—they could be nothing else!—creep along the ditch near the rice field. He saw them unsling their rifles and place them on the earthen bank, then whisper urgently together as they looked at the working youths, heads lowered to their task. He was aware they had selected him, saw them grimace as they slid into the field and their boots filled with muddy water, was readying himself to bargain with them when he divined their intentions.

"Eric! Eric!" he yelled in warning to Mitch, who straightened and looked at him in a puzzled way.

The two Americans splashed across the rice field and hesitated.

"Run, Vanderhoven, run!" Eric shouted at the stupefied Mitch.

The Americans changed their minds, grabbed Mitch instead of him and led Mitch off struggling and kicking between them.

Barefooted and sure-footed in the familiar mud beneath him, Eric sped past the two sloshing mercs and their captive, climbed up on the bank, seized a Kalashnikov in each hand and disappeared over the far side of the bank.

Chapter 21

MIKE Campbell lay hidden along with deadly snakes and vermin among the roots of a great tree that had levered apart the ornamental carved stones of the abandoned temple as they swelled through decades of rapid tropical growth. The Buddha as usual was greeting the new day with his calm, impassive stare.

Campbell had decided the previous day, after meeting with Katie Nelson, to make a preventive strike. He knew Katie intended to film all sorts of sequences of Eric's rescue. Mike had no intention of allowing himself or any of his men to be caught on videotape. Now the damn kid was acting up, as if he and his pals were going on some kind of picnic or outing. Campbell felt sorry for the little turds he had to leave behind. There was no way he could drag a pack of kids through the jungles all the way back to Thailand. He decided to grab the Vanderhoven kid right away and strike out that night for Thailand, leaving Katie Nelson and all her demands behind him.

He put Richards and Nolan on the job, had them study drawings of Eric Vanderhoven made by an artist under Katie's direction. They unloaded their equipment, except for their Kalashnikovs and magazine pouches. Go in quickly, get out quicker and don't hurt any of the kids—those were Mike's instructions.

Mike observed the fiasco that followed through binoculars, saw one of the youths steal the AK47s, yet didn't realize that Richards and Nolan had bagged the wrong kid till they were much closer to him.

"I'm not Eric Vanderhoven!" Mitch was yelling as they carried him struggling.

"I know," Mike said and freed him from the grip of his men. "What's your name?"

"Mitch."

"Tell Eric I want to talk with him. I'll meet him at the temple statue at first light tomorrow. Know where it is?"

Mitch nodded.

"Wait a moment." Mike gave him a bagful of K and C rations. "And here's a half-dozen spare magazines for those rifles, to show there's no hard feelings. OK?"

Mitch disappeared with the food and ammo.

"Why did you give those kids ammo?" Murphy asked.

"I got an idea they may need it," Mike said.

Campbell had his men waiting to move out on the first streak of gray. He spread them through the heavy growth around the ruined temple with orders to grab the Vanderhoven kid but not to reveal themselves to any of the others if Eric didn't show. Campbell was satisfied that if Eric came, he would be trapped. They would take him and head for Thailand then and there. Too bad about the others. But he wasn't the International Red Cross. He had a dangerous job to do. The way Katie Nelson had talked, you would imagine he was the driver of a school bus.

All the same, Mike was bothered... In the future, he would stay out of this kind of deal, he decided. A merc's job was to go in and blow something or waste somebody, not these fucking mercy missions. No more missions like this. Of course, if this one worked out, he'd have a cool million. He'd never have to go on a mission again. But he knew he would...

He felt bad about the eleven kids who wouldn't be going. Too bad he couldn't take them. He knew he couldn't. The middle of a mission in enemy territory was no time for the leader to go sentimental. He steeled his mind and made his decision. Eric went. They stayed.

He heard the bushes part before he saw the figure come toward him. He knew it would not be Eric. Eric would not have gotten this far without being taken. It was the youth they had grabbed by mistake the previous day. Mitch.

"Where's Eric?"

"He's not coming. I'm his messenger."

"All right, Mitch. What's the message?"

"We've escaped from the reeducation camp. We're under Eric's command now. He's set up a camp in the jungle. We'll meet up with you if you want. If not, we'll make it to Thailand on our own."

"When did you take off? What time would you have been missed?"

"They left after you kidnapped me. They waited for me. We have guns and food and we sneaked down for water bottles during the night. We're ready to go."

Mike smiled at Mitch's confidence. He fished out a hand compass from his fatigues and handed it to him. "Know how to use it?"

"Eric does."

"I want to meet at high noon today."

Mitch pointed south. "You see that hill? On the far side, there's a path. We'll meet about halfway up. Right now they're searching for us that way." He pointed northwest. "They moved close by us before it was even light. The hill should be a safe meeting place. I'm going now. Mike, don't have me followed. We've got guys watching where I pass. If I have a tail, our meeting is off. We'll go it alone."

Mike nodded, allowing the twelve-year-old to see how impressed he was by his toughness. Fact was, Mike had no intention of trying to follow these kids while they were

THE POINT TEAM

being hunted as escapees. Mike & Co. would be the ones to blow their own cover. The mercs' great protection was that no one hostile knew they existed. Once they lost that, things would grow hot mighty fast.

Their two interpreters were icily polite, but uninformative.

"It is necessary that you return to Ho Chi Minh City today," the senior interpreter repeated as an answer to most of their questions.

Roger took up a line of attack that had worked against them before—speaking to Katie and Jake in English as if the interpreters couldn't understand a word of what they were saying. For some reason, this seemed to unnerve the two Vietnamese. This time it didn't work.

"It is necessary that you return to Ho Chi Minh City today."

Katie guessed that Mike had taken Eric and maybe even the others. Without telling her. Deliberately. Her keen sense for news told her there was nothing more for her here. She was disappointed. Yet she would forgive Mike if he had taken all the boys. She hoped she had made him feel guilty enough to do so. Katie was surprised to find herself so concerned about something that did not directly concern her TV career.

On the way to their car, they saw a big helicopter land on level ground not far off. Men in fighting gear poured from it and set off at a steady run. They seemed to be in a hurry.

Lt. Tranh Duc Pho and his fifteen-man unit had been picked up by chopper at their staging area at 0400 hours. The lieutenant now knew the objective of the Hmong marauders who had wiped out his mountain pioneers at the Montagnard village, massacred a militia group in a river valley and passed through his territory unscathed—much to his personal disgrace. To abduct twelve Amerasian

THE POINT TEAM

children! And no doubt attempt to take them back out of the area entrusted to him. Over his dead body...

His orders were clear. Bring his men in fast and get them into the jungle after the Hmong and the children. Return the children to the reeducation camp if possible. No Hmong prisoners were to be taken—none were to live to tell the story. If the children could not be brought back alive, dispose of them in the jungle. A party liaison officer had explained to him that the children's abduction from the reeducation camp was being kept secret, that such "aberrant behavior on the part of backward pirates" had no place in the life of a workers' progressive republic.

The message was plain. Keep quiet and get the job done.

The lieutenant saw that he was being given a chance to change his shame into glory. These Hmong had been disrespectful to him, had made him look ineffectual as a military man, had besmirched his honor. He could regain face only through their deaths and the failure of their mission. These hirelings of the American imperialists!

He and his men spent the morning cutting a huge half-circle between the camp and the foothills to the west. They beat the local peasants and threatened them with torture, so that they desperately recalled every useless incident in their lives for the past week, yet there was nothing. Troops stationed in the area and the local militias had been searching since dawn without turning up a sign of anything.

"You see the lay of the land," Tranh Duc Pho said to his sergeant as the sun climbed high in the sky and the full force of the equatorial midday heat bore down on them. He and the sergeant stepped into the shade of a tree, while the rest of the unit rested and drank from their canteens. "Ten to fifteen Hmong tribesmen, heavily armed and ethnically different from eveyone in this region, accompanied by twelve Amerasian kids from the camp, could not pass up into the mountains in daylight without being seen by someone! They couldn't have traveled up here in darkness, and we got here not long after dawn. You follow what I'm getting at."

"We've overreached them?" the sergeant queried. "They're somewhere between us and the camp?"

"I don't think so. It stands to reason they'd move out on the double. There's no reason for them to move more slowly than us. I think something may be keeping them close to the camp."

"You think they're still back there?"

The lieutenant nodded. "There's no other escape route for them to travel except due west. If they're not up here, chances are they are down there."

"There's a lot of thick jungle near the camp," the sergeant confirmed. "We could take our midday rest at the camp and comb the jungle on the way down."

The lieutenant smiled his hunter's smile. He had an instinct he was no longer threshing about in a vacuum. He could almost *feel* them down there somewhere near the camp. There was something going on here he did not understand. From the beginning, he had noticed peculiarities...

The sergeant spread his thirteen men out, side by side, with fifteen meters between each man, and he and the lieutenant placed themselves a few paces behind, more or less at the center. Then he ordered the men forward, and the sweep began. As they met obstacles and impassible patches, the line sometimes stretched out to four hundred meters and at times was condensed to one hundred and fifty meters—a tiny swathe of the Viet jungle, but not a random one. The lieutenant carefully studied the terrain ahead and constantly had the sweep cover a small hill to one side, search a hidden valley, investigate a stand of giant hardwoods...

Verdoux and Murphy heard a shouted order from the sergeant.

"They're searching for us," Verdoux translated. "I think they're coming this way."

"Damn."

The two men looked at each other. Mike's gamble had not paid off. He and Andre had discussed the pros and cons of stashing their equipment in one place and traveling light for their meeting with Eric. Since the search parties seemed to be off in the foothills, there was no apparent present danger in stockpiling the equipment and leaving a couple of men to guard it. Andre agreed with Mike that the less encumbered the men traveled, the less chance of their being detected. Still, it was a considered risk. As Andre and Bob were now finding out.

The two mercs could hear the Viet unit advancing through the undergrowth now. As usual in a typical sweep operation, they were making no effort to conceal their presence—depending, in fact, on the noise they were making to flush the enemy early enough so he could not harm them. Once they had him on the run, he could be methodically hunted down.

"They're coming this way," Murphy said grimly.

Verdoux strained his ears to listen for commands.

"We can't move all this shit." Murphy gestured at their equipment covered by camouflage tarpaulins. "I'm going to distract them. You hold out here."

He stopped when he heard the Viet sergeant shout commands in order to let Verdoux hear.

"The men are bunched up too much on his right, our left, and too spread out on his left, our right."

"I'll take the spread-out guys," Murphy said.

"Mike will be pissed because they'll see you're a Westerner," Andre warned.

"We got to trade them something if we want to keep our supplies," Murphy said. "Tell the bastard that if I don't come back."

"Good luck, Bob."

"You too, buddy."

THE POINT TEAM

The big Australian was gone, moving with amazing speed and stealth through the jungle growth. He barely made it to the far flank and hid only a few meters beyond the expected route of the outlying Viet trooper. The man passed without seeing him. Almost twenty meters separated him from the next soldier. Murphy crept up behind the outlying man. He could have bayoneted him, but a silent killing was not his purpose. Murphy blasted a single round into the man's spine, which snapped him backward, lifeless.

As the man fell and the shot rang through the jungle, Murphy switched the selector on his AK47 from semiautomatic to automatic and delivered a short burst which took the adjoining Viet trooper at gut level. The victim's legs buckled beneath him, and he sank to the ground clutching the leaking punctures in his midriff.

Bob Murphy saw the horrified stares of several other troopers, astounded to see what they assumed was an American attack and an attempt to kill them inside the borders of Vietnam. Bob sprayed fire in their direction and brought one of them down. Then he beat a hasty retreat, a fox followed by an eager pack of hounds.

Chapter 22

MITCH came with a delegation of three of the other youths. Mike waited alone and said nothing when they arrived.

"We've come to talk," Mitch announced.

Mike raised his eyebrows. He had heard from Katie that Eric Vanderhoven was a loud-mouthed, obnoxious kid. Apparently Mitch had taken to modeling himself on him.

"Where's Eric?" Campbell asked finally.

"First we want to hear your terms. Then we'll tell you ours. After that you meet Eric."

"No way."

"What?" Mitch seemed less sure of himself.

"I talk with Eric or nobody. Leader with leader, if you like. Go tell him that."

"We don't need you anymore, Mike. We got guns, a compass, food. We can make it to Thailand without you."

"You couldn't make it twenty kilometers from here without me. Now shut up and go get Eric. You're wasting my time."

Mitch was crestfallen, but he was not yet ready to back down.

Richards came up to where they were talking and winked at Campbell.

"I gotta go," Campbell informed the four youths and exited fast with Richards, leaving them standing nonplussed.

"Waller got the little bastard," Richards told Campbell.

Waller had tied the youth's thumbs together behind his back and was cuffing him on the ear when they arrived. Campbell looked carefully at the boy's face. No doubt this time, this one was Eric Vanderhoven.

Richards and Waller caught Eric beneath the armpits and frog-marched him between them, with Campbell leading the way back to their arms stash. Nolan brought up the rear. They were not too far away when they heard a single shot, a short burst and then a long rattle of automatic fire. This was answered by fire from a number of automatic rifles, fortunately moving away from them.

"Waller, stay with him in those boulders while Nolan, Richards and I check out Andre and Bob."

They ran forward and approached their supply dump cautiously. Campbell almost got shot by Verdoux. The Frenchman told them what Murphy had done.

"Crazy Aussie," Nolan said in admiration and went back to fetch Eric and Waller.

"They didn't get him, I'm sure of that," Andre told them. "He'll circle back here, but so will they to pick up their dead. They may even have guessed by now he was a decoy and be on their way back here to find out what they were led away from."

"Load up and move out," Mike snapped, draping himself with his armaments and other supplies.

The rest followed suit and in minutes they were under way.

"What happened to the rest of the kids?" Andre asked Mike.

Mike shot the Frenchman a dirty look. "Couldn't say."

For the first time Mike met Eric's eyes. He was surprised not to find them glaring out defiance and hatred, but simply submission and misery. It occurred to Campbell that Waller had been brutally insightful in his treatment of the youth as a detainee. Tie his thumbs together behind his back and clout him over the ear if he mouths off. Eric understood that approach. He was used to that treatment. And countered with meek obedience.

They moved on for a while until Campbell called a halt. The early afternoon heat was still at its most intense. Campbell untied Eric's hands, and the boy sat quietly. They rested a while before anyone spoke.

"We're not leaving Murphy behind," Campbell said with finality. "He put his ass on the line to save our supplies. Anyone got any ideas where he might show up?"

"Only landmark we have is that ruined temple," Nolan observed.

"Yes, that's it," Richards agreed. "I bet that's where he goes."

"You two want to wait for him there?" Campbell said, giving them a chance to volunteer.

Richards and Nolan unloaded their gear, taking only the essentials and traveling light.

"We may not be here when you get back," Campbell warned them. "Head for this spot if we're not." He showed them the place on a map and pointed up in the foothills. "On the north bank of this stream after it makes this elbow turn."

Campbell covered up the two men's gear with long grass after they had gone. "We better be ready to move at a second's notice."

The heavy thatch and windowless walls of the hut the youths had until lately occupied at the reeducation camp maintained a cool interior during the intense heat. Lt. Tranh Duc Pho sat with his sergeant on wicker chairs supplied by the party cadres. They sipped from two bottles of beer set on a card table between them in the semidarkness of the hut and stared reflectively at the bright, intense colors visible through the open doorway—as if watching a primitive form of television.

But the lieutenant's mind was dwelling on things not visible through the doorway. "The men resting? The helicopter ready to go?"

"Yes, sir." The sergeant was being more formal than usual until he discovered the officer's mood. They had lost three men and had failed to kill their assailant. He would have to be very careful with the lieutenant.

"All of the local troops and militias out searching the new area?"

"Yes, sir. We got them as they came in from the midday heat and dispatched them in pairs into the field. Each pair has a radio and calls in every twenty minutes. We divided up the wave bands, so there won't be more crossover and confusion than normal."

The lieutenant sipped on the bottle. "It's not ideal, but it's all we can do with limited manpower in this remote area. Sooner or later one of those pairs is going to stumble on something and call it in or get cut to pieces and go missing. We'll hustle our unit into the location by helicopter and flush them out."

The sergeant looked wary. "You think there's more than one American?"

The officer amazed his subordinate by smiling cheerfully. "I think they're *all* Americans. I don't think there are any Hmong here—this has not been the way they would have handled it. We're dealing with a small force of Americans. Perhaps only five or six men."

The sergeant gazed in awe of the lieutenant, for the likelihood of what he had said just dawned on him. "That was the coded radio message you sent to army HQ?"

"Correct." The lieutenant smiled happily and slugged down some beer. "We have them trapped down here. Along with twelve malcontent youths. They'll have their hands full taking care of those juvenile delinquents. We're going to nail them!"

THE POINT TEAM

The sergeant joined in the lieutenant's joy. He could see now what hero-citizens they were going to be after stamping out the imperialist vermin.

Bob Murphy had taken off at top speed with his pursuers hot on his trail. Their bullets whipped through the vegetation around him, rapped on heavy trunks like knuckles on a door, tore leaves from stems. But they were firing blindly or else on the run at a glimpse of his fleeing form. Murphy did not waste time zigzagging or in worrying about what was in front of him. His big body broke through the jungle growth with almost the force of a stampeding water buffalo. He ran wildly, with no tricks, no caution, no subterfuges. He ran and ran till his breath came in long, asthmatic wheezes of humid fetid air that seemed to hold no oxygen for his drowning lungs. He ran till his own heartbeat sounded in his ears so loudly he no longer heard the shots behind him, and he ran and ran till the sweat pouring into his eyes and stinging them had almost blinded him. Then he stopped, half doubled over, his chest heaving, his fatigues stuck to his body and his equipment dangling. He tried to listen. Above the sounds of his own body. There were snapping noises made by insects and the piping of a bird or small mammal. Otherwise the jungle was hot, still, motionless.

He stayed there till his body recovered. There was no point in going back to try to find Andre. He had led the troops away from him but they would return there to collect their dead. The others had come and taken the supplies, or Andre had been forced to abandon them. Either way, there was no reason to return there. The only other rendezvous point they had in the area was the one Campbell had set up with the TV crew—the statue of the Buddha. They would figure that out and meet up with him there. Unless they decided to abandon him and leave without him. Hell, they'd never do that. Not after he had sacrificed himself for them. Campbell would never do that to him. Some of the others, maybe. But not Campbell.

Murphy wandered about till he got his bearings and headed directly for the ruined temple. On the way he saw two Viet troopers searching through the jungle, making a hell of a noise and sticking nervously together as if they expected that at any moment a big tiger might jump out at them. Bob smiled. The team would not have much trouble eluding this kind of search. He worked his way around the noisy pair and had no more trouble on his way to the temple.

When he reached it, he did not approach it up the tiers of huge stone steps that Katie Nelson and her crew had climbed to meet them, but along a narrow, winding path through the undergrowth which a man of his height and bulk had to travel slowly to avoid rustling all the branches. He was moving carefully and reasonably quietly when his nostrils detected cigarette smoke. Murphy himself had given up cigarettes two years before, and he enjoyed a sneaky whiff of smoke from someone else's cigarette. Only Richards and Verdoux smoked. However, they were too professional to do so while waiting undercover for him.

It took him ten long minutes, step by silent step, to approach closer along the path and then circle around behind the smokers, who seemed to be lighting one cigarette from another. They were talking in Vietnamese. Two voices. From the way they talked quietly and the heavy smoke, Murphy recognized from his own experience what they were—two soldiers goofing off. He crept in closer behind them so that he could see them through the bushes. Their Kalashnikovs lay between them against the fallen slab upon which they sat. He maneuvered until he could see them clearly. They were dressed in fatigues but had no sidearms or grenades, only spare rifle magazines in a pouch on their belts and combat knives on their right hips. He couldn't understand what they said. When one spoke over a hand-held radio, Murphy knew he was calling in their codes and present location—and perhaps lying about the latter.

Murphy waited patiently and silently, gently uncoiling a length of cable from his shirt pocket. At last one of the soldiers stood and walked off ten paces to take a leak against a tree. Murphy waited till he had started urinating, then wrapped his length of cable once about the sitting man's neck as he placed his knee in the man's back and pulled on the garotte with all his strength, feeling the plastic-covered wire bite into his powerful, coarse hands.

The stricken soldier waved and kicked. His violent struggles only caused Murphy to pull tighter on the garotte while never taking his eyes off the second soldier, only a few meters away. One of the man's kicks knocked the rifles sideways, and his companion glanced back over his shoulder. He stiffened when he saw his friend's blue face and protruding tongue and eyeballs, his bloodied fingers clawing at the unforgiving roughness of the stone slab, while his Western round-eye tormentor pinned him to the rock with one knee and gazed calmly across at him.

The soldier was not a coward. He zipped the front of his fatigues and pulled the combat knife from its sheath on his right hip. He came fast at Murphy, holding the blade out flat in front of his belly, swift and sure in his footwork.

Murphy released the ends of the cable, pulled his own knife from its sheath and advanced to meet his foe. He didn't like what he saw one bit—the man was trained and sure of himself—but he could not risk a shot since he had to stay on in the place to wait for the others.

The Viet eased up in his onward rush when he saw the blade in Murphy's hand. They squared off against each other, each sizing up the other, trying to outstare, intimidate . . . catch off balance for one vulnerable instant by moving unexpectedly this way and that . . . looking for an opening into which to launch a deadly thrust.

It was heavyweight versus flyweight as the bulky Australian

THE POINT TEAM

lunged at the light-footed Asian. Although Bob weighed almost twice as much as the Viet, he was deceptively fast on his feet when he chose to be. He let his opponent see none of this and followed his first useless lunge with another and another.

Murphy waited till he saw a confident look on the Viet's face, then roared and lumbered forward at him. The trooper neatly sidestepped him, and as the big Aussie missed with his wild knife thrust, came in behind him ready to sink his blade into Murphy's right kidney. But the big man, while still in motion, whipped around 180 degrees like a fighting bull, threw four fast straight rights to the head and chest of the Viet soldier. The sharp tip of the steel blade cut through the Viet's left cheek, exposing his upper and lower clenched teeth, and penetrated his shoulder muscle once and chest twice, going in only a few inches, but agonizing and disorienting the soldier so much that he stumbled backward.

Murphy closed in on him and tried to drive his blade upward between the man's ribs and into his heart. He was repulsed by a kick to his right shoulder which almost caused him to drop his knife.

The merc managed to grab the wide tunic sleeve of the trooper's knife hand but missed the arm inside. He barged in and smothered the smaller Asian with his weight. Both men crashed to the ground, with Murphy on top rolling over on the Viet's right arm to prevent him using it and sending repeated upward stabs between the soldier's ribs which were slatted like a half-closed venetian blind. The blade cut through the muscle and fitted up between the ribs, rupturing blood vessels, lungs and connective tissue. The man's emaciated body vibrated and lay still.

Murphy drew the blade out of the soldier's side, and as he raised his head, he started with fear as he found himself looking at a pair of soldier's boots and the muzzle of a rifle a few inches from his nose.

He raised his head slowly and resignedly. He swore when he found himself looking fearfully up into Richards' grinning face.

Chapter 23

CAMPBELL, Verdoux, Waller and Eric Vanderhoven waited silently for the return of Richards and Nolan, hopefully in the company of Murphy. All three of the mercs kept a sharp eye on the youth, expecting him to pick up and run at any moment. Campbell wished he would try, because he had begun to suspect that Eric might have something more imaginative in mind, something that might be much more difficult for them to overcome. The youth sat sullenly and hardly moved, staring straight in front of him.

Once they heard voices, and Mike had them all ready to move in order to avoid discovery, leaving Richards' and Nolan's weapons concealed behind them. The voices grew fainter and in a little while died away altogether. They sat down again to wait.

Campbell passed around a can of insect repellent, which remained effective against the large, determined mosquitoes for only a short period of time before it had to be reapplied. He also passed out antimalaria pills.

Again, voices and sounds of searchers came within range, this time from two directions. Campbell ordered them to their feet. One search party was a considerable distance away, the other much nearer.

"Mike Campbell!"

Mike looked at Eric fast, since these were the first words he had spoken since they had grabbed him. He saw a hand grenade in the youth's right hand and the pulled safety pin in his left. Mike knew he had filched the grenade from Richards' or Nolan's kits.

"If you come near me, I'll release the lever," Eric threatened.

"Eric, if you loosen your hand on that lever, you have four seconds till it blows up," Campbell told him calmly. "Know what's inside? A spirally wound prefragmented steel coil. If you don't throw it far enough, both you and us will be cut to pieces by fragments of hot steel."

"Keep talkin', Mike," Eric drawled unconcernedly.

"Put the pin back," Campbell ordered.

"No way. If I don't kill us all, those search parties will hear the grenade explode. They'll finish the job."

Waller started to approach the boy.

"Come back, Waller," Campbell commanded. "What do you want, Eric?"

"For you to take my friends along."

"You got it."

Eric looked at Campbell suspiciously. "All eleven of them?"

"OK."

"I don't trust you."

"You have my word on it," Campbell offered.

"Why do you agree so easily?" the youth asked warily.

"You're not leaving me much choice, are you?" Campbell grinned. "Besides, maybe you've given me an excuse now to do something stupid which I couldn't justify otherwise."

Verdoux laughed. "I haven't said much up till now, Mike, but let me say this is the best thing to do. What do you say, Waller?"

Waller sneered at Eric. "You take one of these damn kids, you might as well take 'em all. I'd bet this one here will turn out to be a commie spy." He cackled to show he only half-meant what he said.

"Put the pin back, Eric," Campbell said.

"When we pick up my friends," Eric countered.

"Deal's off if you don't put that pin back," Campbell said. "Give me that grenade or throw it."

Eric took Mike's measure for a moment, listening to the voices of the searchers in the trees. Then he reinserted the safety pin in the grenade and handed it to Campbell.

The voices of the searchers faded into the distance after a time. When Nolan and Richards showed up along with Murphy, there were smiles and handshakes all round for the Australian.

"Let's go pick up your friends, Eric," Campbell said.

The youth looked relieved.

Eric led them to his secret camp. All of the boys except Mitch rushed to greet them, and Mike had trouble quieting them down.

Mitch didn't look too happy to be slipping from number one slot to second-in-command. "You arrived just in time," he told Mike. "We were just about to head out for Thailand on our own."

This was such a transparent lie that Mike slapped him on the shoulder and said, "Now you're with us, Mitch. On our team I call the shots, and my backup man is Andre. We don't have any other chain of command."

He did pay respect to Eric and Mitch's status by allowing them to keep the two AK47s they had swiped. The rest of the team had been sharing the four remaining AK47s among the six of them, but now, with the two rifles taken at the ruined temple, they had their full complement of six rifles again. Some of the boys asked to use the Ingram submachine gun each of the team carried, but Mike decided against it.

"It's too easy to wipe out your own men with an automatic weapon," he told them straightforwardly. "I

THE POINT TEAM

wouldn't feel safe standing in front of some of you guys with your itchy trigger fingers.''

They moved out for the foothills in a big group. If they had been women, very young children or very old people, Mike would have placed them at the center and guarded them on all sides. But these kids were agile as monkeys and could probably seek cover better than any of the adults in the event of a fire fight, so he let them go as they liked, as long as they did not wander too far in front or drop back too far behind. As he muttered aloud several times, school tours were not his speciality.

Three of the boys who had been making forays up front rushed back and in dumb show indicated that there were men with rifles directly in front of them.

"Get your pals together," Mike whispered to Eric. "You and Mitch stand guard over them. Not a sound."

The team had spread out with three to four meters between each man and were waiting tensely for Mike. When he joined them, they began to move forward cautiously, rifles ready.

They edged ahead, now one and now another slightly in the lead, each man acutely aware that he had no idea of what he was walking into—four unarmed peasants or forty crack troops. The silence maintained by their opponents boded ill. These were not loudly keeping contact with each other and beating the underbrush like baby elephants, as had the previous parties. Campbell asked himself questions. Had they heard his unit? Were they now lying in wait? Wondering why they had not yet walked into their ambush? Had they seen the kids who saw them? Mike told himself there were times when he had to forge ahead and be a fool, hopefully a lucky one. One of those times was right now.

It was like a mirror image—six men in fatigues with automatic rifles coming suddenly face to face with six men in fatigues with automatic rifles in the jungle vegetation. Campbell loosed off a burst of fire from the hip which blew the top of the skull away—peaked cap along with it—of the Viet trooper facing him at a meter's distance. The semidecapitated body jackknifed and slumped at his feet, and Campbell distinctly smelled the released bowels of his victim.

Verdoux was on his left and drilled four deliberate bullets into the Viet opposing him. The struck soldier's automatic fire passed between the Frenchman and Campbell, and as the trooper pitched forward, his rifle emptied itself into the ground before him.

Richards was on Campbell's right, a couple of meters away. Out of the corner of his eye, Campbell saw the Englishman being hit by a bullet and stumble backward. His assailant rushed headlong at him, firing but missing and attempting to skewer him on his bayonet. Mike got a side view of the Viet for a second and let loose a volley of lead aimed for his head. The bullets ripped the soldier's nose, eyes and lips clean off his face. For a moment the Viet turned in Campbell's direction and seemed to stare at him with the eyeless raw steak that was his face. Mike gave him a short burst in the rib cage to put him out of his misery, then emptied his magazine in the back of a Viet trooper who had dropped his rifle and was running away. Waller and Nolan were doing the same, and the force of all three streams of bullets picked up the Viet in a wild dance of death. When their bullets stopped, so did he. A shattered, life-size doll.

"Sound off!" Mike yelled as he rushed to Richards' assistance along with Verdoux.

No one was hurt except Larry Richards, who had taken two bullets, a few inches apart, in his right shoulder. It looked bad. Mike loaded a syringe with morphine and injected it into his right arm. Richards was semiconscious and moaning. Gradually his moans eased as his shoulder became numb to pain, and Mike waited another minute before investigating the damage.

He lifted him a little. "No exit wounds. We'll have to

THE POINT TEAM

take out those bullets before infection sets in." He pressed on the collarbone and upper ribs. "Doesn't seem to be any bones broken. But there's no way to tell how much he's bleeding internally. Let's move him out of here as far as we can while the going is good. Tell the kids if they want weapons and ammo to strip the bodies. Take any food or maps or anything else, too, but hurry it up."

Camp life and their hardships before it had taught the Amerasian boys not to be squeamish about corpses. Mike had barely finished giving the command when they were already expertly relieving the dead Viets of their weapons, plus two wristwatches and a ring.

The five team members agreed to support Richards among them, keeping him shot up on morphine. None of them mentioned the obvious—that a man with his injuries was not going to cross on foot the mountains and then the jungles of Laos all the way to Thailand. They were going to leave that one to Campbell to answer.

All Campbell allowed on his mind was the ways and means of moving his men out of this danger zone. The shooting had probably been heard, and he expected that a mobile force would be at the scene very soon. From here they would set out to track them down. There was less than two hours of daylight left. If they could get into the foothills before dark, bivouac wherever they found themselves and move on again before first light, they might stand a chance.

As Mike watched the twelve kids sling man-sized weapons from their narrow bony shoulders and hang grenades from outsized belts, he knew he had to try hard for their as well as his own precious skin.

A truck had arrived at 2100 hours with more helicopter fuel. Tranh Duc Pho had the pilot fuel up immediately to be ready to take off at first visibility in the morning. Another boost to the lieutenant's mood was a pretty peasant woman he had seen cooking the prisoners' food at the camp. He had forced her away from her tasks and now she was administering to his needs. Which were many in this time of stress. The cadres had warned the woman's husband she would be shot if he made a fuss now or complained later. He became reasonable when he heard this. Almost reeducated.

The sergeant and the rest of his unit were located somewhere behind the Americans and the escaped youths. They had disappeared by the time his men arrived on the scene of their latest slaughter. In the morning he would locate the escapees from his helicopter and direct his forces toward them.

The lieutenant had had his report to military headquarters confirmed. An American television crew—now deported—had acted in the locality as a contact for a group of American mercenaries. Unofficial apologies had been forthcoming from Washington through indirect channels, but no details on how many men or what their resources were.

They had come to rescue a rich man's grandson. Typical! Tranh Duc Pho took out the photo of Eric Vanderhoven he had obtained from the camp records. His orders were strict—bring this boy back alive. He would have to do that, he dare not disobey. But his orders said nothing about bringing him back uninjured. An oversight like that gave a lot of leeway to a man with a mind like Tranh Duc Pho.

The team began stirring with the first birds, in the darkness and stillness just before dawn. Campbell checked on Richards. The Englishman was fully conscious.

"Need a shot, Larry?"

"Yes."

"I'll scale down the amount," Mike said, "and if you need more, let me know *before* the pain gets bad. I dug out those two bullets last night and patched you up. No bones broken, and it seems like no major blood vessels were hit. You're going to be OK."

"Don't let them take me prisoner, Mike."

THE POINT TEAM

"I won't," Mike answered, recognizing in Richards' resigned tone that the man had assessed his chances and reached the obvious conclusion—he was not going to be able to undertake a week-long jungle trek, he was not going to walk out of this one alive.

Mike had operated on him by flashlight under local anesthetic. He had sterilized the blade with alcohol, cut out the two deformed bullets—both unfragmented, luckily—and had sewn up the wounds and shot him with antibiotics. Murphy and Verdoux had helped, while Waller and Nolan had trained the youths in the use of their newly acquired AK47s from the dead Viets and the light Ingram submachine guns from Mike's team.

With Andre holding the flashlight, Mike changed the dressing on Larry's wounds and shot him with penicillin.

"These look good, Larry," Mike said. "No drainage. You had a hell of a fever all night and a steady temperature of 102. You're down to a hundred now. That morphine taken care of things?"

"I'm all right."

They ate cold K rations in the darkness and then sat hunched up, chilled, waiting minute by slow minute for the weak light of the new day to filter through the heavy canopy of trees down to them. They climbed the moderate slopes of the foothills, and by the time it was full light they had emerged from the lowland jungle vegetation into pines and other conifers which covered the hills and, beyond them, the high mountains. As the sun rose higher, so too did the mist—till it was a thick, blanketing fog. They called to each other constantly when their dark figures vanished into the swirling grayness. When they cursed, Mike laughed and told them not to complain.

"We have a lot of open ground in this terrain," he said. "The mist is concealing us from the air. If we had this visibility all the way, we'd have nothing much to worry about."

Already, as the sun grew higher and hotter, the mist was

THE POINT TEAM

being burned away, growing thinner. They no longer had to shout to keep in contact with each other. After two hours, there was nothing left but miniature streaks of vapor within the heaviest and darkest conifers and a shining droplet of water on each of millions of pine needles. The air was cool, thin and sharp on the slopes, so different from the clammy, unmoving gas they breathed in the lowlands.

A helicopter systematically quartered the slopes north of them. It was as if the pilot had developed an obsession that they were in one particular area and kept returning and returning to search for what he knew must be below him somewhere. No one bothered to mention its presence, even jokingly, but the insistent throbbing of its engine served as a reminder to them and as a goad to keep up their pace as they climbed higher.

Then the chopper lifted and came flying sideways toward them.

"Everybody freeze!" Mike yelled. "Hug the ground! If he gets close enough without spotting us, I'll try to bring him down."

But the chopper eased its advance while still a thousand meters away, gained altitude and swooped in widening circles. There was no hiding from its surveillance.

"To hell with it," Mike said. "If he can't see us, he wants to keep us pinned down for his troops to catch up with us. This chopper's too big and unmaneuverable to try an air-to-ground attack on us. Let's go."

They were located by the helicopter almost immediately. The craft flew behind them, staying out of range of their weapons, and hovered there, gauging their pace. Then a dark object dropped from it to the ground, and the craft wheeled away down the hill slope and began to circle again. A column of orange-yellow smoke rose from the object the chopper had dropped.

"A smoke bomb to mark our position," Mike observed. "Don't bother with it. By the time he locates his men

THE POINT TEAM

down there, finds a landing place and gets them aboard, that marker will be worth shit."

Campbell gave Richards another shot of morphine, and he and Murphy, as the strongest members of the team, supported the wounded man between them and set out on a fast climb toward an area of stunted pines and bushy rhododendronlike shrubs.

"They won't be able to find us in there to do a direct airdrop on us," Mike explained as they went. "I want those troops on the ground again, searching for us. We can't fight heliborne troops. We gotta keep them on the ground, where they have to go through the same trauma and hard work as us. Stay away from areas a chopper can set down."

The kids swarmed ahead of the team, their very real weapons looking like plastic toys. Only their hard faces and calculating eyes would have alerted someone that these boys were not making believe. The chopper seemingly had located its forces, and its engine droned as it spiraled about them, searching for a landing place among the trees and rocks of the sloping ground. When they heard it finally set down, they quickened their pace even more. Eric and his friends had reached the area of dense pines and shrubs and were exploring its immediate interior while waiting for Campbell and Murphy to carry Richards there. Nolan and Waller formed an unhurried rearguard, looking like they would welcome the chance to take a helicopter load of commie troops out of the sky.

It was another half hour before the big Russian-designed helicopter was circling again higher up the slope from them, looking for a place to set down the Viet troops. They heard it land, then after a minute lift off again. They saw it fly down the slope and away.

"Back to base, refuel and wait for a radio call," Mike summed up. "Which means we've got everybody on the ground here."

"Unless that chopper's coming back with a second load of men," Verdoux added.

"Could be," Campbell conceded. "Which means we should take care of business here before they arrive."

They halted at a treeless, rocky hummock of land, a hundred meters in diameter and perhaps ten in height above the hill slope. Mike and Andre investigated it for its defensive possibilities, having transferred Richards to Waller and Nolan.

"I want them to have to come get us," Campbell told Verdoux. "We can defend this site from all sides from light weapons. If they have mortars, we'd have to move out. What do you say?"

"It's as good a place as any we'll find in the next five minutes," Andre said. "I reckon that's how long we have till we make contact."

Mike beckoned the others up. He spread the kids behind rocks in a kind of halo around the crown of the hummock. They were so arranged they couldn't do damage to others on their side by wild shooting. Mike was expecting the worst. Richards couldn't handle a weapon, but Mike deliberately did not make a big deal about him so he wouldn't feel himself too much of a burden and liability on the rest of them. The team members arranged themselves as they saw fit, staying flexible in order to handle an attack from any direction.

"Listen, you guys." Mike spoke in a loud reassuring voice. "We got eighteen men here. We probably outnumber these bastards. So all each of you has to do is bag himself one man and we got them beat." He was speaking for the benefit of the kids, of course, but honored them as full members of his unit by making his remarks seem applicable to all. "Keep your heads down. Bide your time. Don't try for him till you know you've got him. Never forget, we have the advantage here. They have to move on us. Hit 'em while they're moving. Quiet now! Good luck, men."

THE POINT TEAM

Mike ordered them to quiet down not to hide their positions, but to calm the kids' growing excitement at the prospect of battle. He could guess that their concept of a fire fight had little to do with the reality of one. Even with kids like these who had experienced the underside of life, when a gun was put in their hands and an enemy indicated— they forgot all the hard facts of survival they had learned and saw themselves as invulnerable conquering heroes. Mike had an uneasy feeling they were about to learn the hard way how things really were.

Verdoux had been wrong in his time estimate. It was almost twenty minutes before they saw the line of men coming down the slope. They suspected danger from the hillock right away, and slid around to the west of it, keeping their distance.

"I make it thirteen men," Mike said.

"Right," Andre confirmed.

"They haven't seen us. If they continue on downhill, we'll just sneak on up into these mountains. But I think they're going to investigate this rise of land."

He proved correct. A minute later, a lone trooper, presumably not too happy with his lot, ran toward them from cover to cover.

"Eric, this one is yours," Mike said in a hoarse whisper. "Nail him just as he rises from cover. A short burst. Don't empty your magazine at him."

The Viet was still zigzagging from rock to rock, never predictably moving in any particular direction—changing his pace and never presenting himself as an unmoving target. The soldier knew what he was doing, and Mike nodded to Andre to take him when the boy missed. But first, give the kid a chance.

The trooper dodged from behind a rock, went one way, then the other, walked into a couple of rifle bullets from Eric's gun and spun sideways, clutching his chest. His lifeless body rolled a little way downhill before coming to rest against a rock.

A loud cheer rose from Eric's friends. Their leader had done it! Killed one of their adult tormentors! Eric tried to smile for his fans, but looked more like he wanted to throw up.

Mike met Andre's eyes for a moment. They were both remembering their first day of combat—on different battlefields, in different years—when as raw recruits they had once cheered when the most daring or luckiest of them had first drawn enemy blood. Their cheerful mood had lasted till their side took its first casualty. After that, there was no more applause.

The remaining twelve Viets suddenly came forward, spread out and keeping well to cover.

"Mike, they're going to charge us!" Murphy warned.

"Grenades!" was all Verdoux said.

"You kids up front, come back here," Campbell ordered. "Don't let them see you."

Some of the boys were reluctant to abandon their front-row seats to the coming conflict, but the menacing advance of the Viets was enough to convince most of them. When they were all safely behind big rocks, Mike spoke rapidly to them.

"What they're going to try is this. They'll advance on us till they think they're within range, then throw hand grenades—offensive grenades with no fragmentation—so they can overrun us while we're stunned by the explosive shock. If they haven't seen you pull back, they may go for your forward positions with the grenades. Keep your heads down. When the grenades are finished, pop up and let them have it with all you've got. OK? Meanwhile, keep those Viets back well out of throwing range."

"Jesus, Mike, they're very good," Nolan muttered as they waited and watched their foe advance on them, making use of every rock and scrap of cover.

"Bullshit! They're just doing what they've been trained to do, like performing seals. They'll do what I said they'll do, and we'll waste 'em."

THE POINT TEAM

Some of the kids opened fire on the advancing men. Mike did not tell them to save their ammo till they got closer because he realized the boys needed to get the feel of their weapons—and there was nothing like shooting at something and missing to familiarize someone with his gun. The team let the kids make the running—they were keeping their guns cool till after the grenades went off. All twelve boys were blasting away now, without a single hit.

Then Campbell saw the overarm throws of the first incoming grenades.

"Heads down!" he yelled.

This time no one hesitated. The grenades went off among the forward positions the boys had occupied before retreating—just as Campbell had said. The hot air and dust traveling on the shock waves tore over the rocks behind which they were sheltering, so that they crouched in miniature sheltered pockets in the violent slipstreams of the explosions.

What Campbell had not said was that one of the attackers would have a superstrong pitching arm and overthrow the forward positions. The grenade came in as innocently as a flat rubber ball, bounced listlessly and spun on end where it lay.

It was perfectly placed from the enemy's point of view. Right in the center of them all. With maybe a fraction more than two seconds before it detonated. Probably less.

Larry Richards was slumped against a rock, looking drawn and with feverish eyes. The grenade lay in front of him like an apple at a picnic.

He said casually, "Carry on, fellows."

And flopped forward, covering the grenade with his body.

Its blast lifted his body into the air less than a second later. His flesh absorbed the major impact of the explosion. The rest were hit by a blow resembling a human punch. Next thing they knew, Campbell was yelling.

"Drill the fuckers! Give it to 'em! Kill! Kill! Kill!"

They rose simultaneously to their feet, like a crowd at a stadium, and hammered home good ol' USA holes in the communist attackers.

The Viets died out in the open like moths on a summer's evening.

Mike, businesslike as always, counted the dead Viets and found one missing. One must have gotten away. He instructed the youths to pick over the bodies for weapons and ammo. Meanwhile, he and the other team members dug a shallow grave for Richards. To make up for the lack of depth, Campbell had everyone pile rocks over the mound of earth covering the merc's body.

Bob Murphy, as Larry Richards' friend, placed the last rock on his cairn. He looked around them all, with a single tear trickling down his left cheek. "I don't need to tell you that he saved every one of us here. And he was the only one of us who was not in Vietnam during the war. He and I joked about this—I always swore I would attend his funeral, that the Irish would get him. He thought so, too. As usual, we were only half right."

Chapter 24

THEY climbed for a day and a half up the mountains without seeing a human. Whether they themselves were seen, they could not tell. At the opening of a mountain defile, they met two Montagnards. Campbell felt that the two tribesmen were waiting for them, and Verdoux could neither confirm or disprove this in his very dislocated conversation with them. He made a gift of three filled AK47 magazines to each man and listened carefully to what they said.

"So far as I can make out," he told Campbell, "they're telling us not to cross the mountains due west of this point. They say we should travel north half a day and then head northwest, where we will be in territory not controlled by the Hanoi government."

"Any reason we shouldn't take their advice?"

"I'd take it," Verdoux said.

"Done," Campbell confirmed. "What else do they say?"

"That we stick to paths marked with blazes on tree trunks. I think we both know what that means."

Campbell nodded.

They bowed in farewell to the two Montagnards. Mike

thought he detected a glimmer of amusement on their stone expressions—like they were thinking their equivalent of the Yanks are back in town with their crazy goings-on, such as five mercs and twelve heavily armed children crossing the mountains from Vietnam into Laos. Mike could see a grim humor in the situation.

Tranh Duc Pho scraped off the encrusted blood which was almost closing his right eye. He could feel with his fingers that his right ear had been cut almost cleanly off his head by a bullet. He had dropped his rifle, he supposed, and staggered away—crazed and blinded by the fierce pain coursing through his head. He had run wildly, trying to escape from the demon ripping his brain and soul apart in an agony so powerful it took over his being like an independent spirit. Then he had fallen face down in the pine needles—he remembered the way the dry brown needles looked two centimeters before his eyes—and screamed in pain into the earth.

He was a soldier. Tranh Duc Pho was a warrior. A proud man. The essential part of that bargain with existence, in his view, was that he die rather than accept defeat. It was a fighting man's only excuse for failure—his own death offered in recompense, along with as many enemy lives as he could bring along with him.

Tranh Duc Pho admitted failure. It was more serious than having his unit wiped out and his remaining as the only survivor—although this was a disgrace in itself. He was in much deeper trouble than this. His orders from Hanoi were clear as a mountain stream—locate the American invaders and inform military HQ so they could send a party-selected senior officer to finish them off and take the credit. Of course, if the invading party turned out to be simply Hmong—Hanoi was still not accepting his word that Americans were involved, even after Washington's acknowledgement of the fact (party regulars were accustomed to regard all American news as CIA disinformation) —no army brass was going to bother to make the trip.

The lieutenant was tired of being a lieutenant. He had just seen half a year's work with the Montagnards reduced to zero by the slaughter of his mountain pioneers. Achievement in the field of battle was transitory... He had laughed before at suggestions that he think of himself. For the first time, he had tried to do that. Claim the credit that was rightfully his. By not calling in the reinforcements that the situation demanded. He had taken a chance. And failed. He would be held responsible. Now he must die. Honorably.

Strangely to him, he felt no animosity to the American soldiers of fortune. They were like him, in a way—like every warrior since history began, regardless of cause, of right or wrong. He channeled his hatred, he focused all his spleen and frustration on a single target. Eric Vanderhoven.

He had to destroy this spawn of gold bullion, this grandson of a decrepit capitalist who could buy healthy men to do his dirty deeds in impoverished countries. The boy was the larva of a greedy monopolistic toad, and he would metamorphose into a killer adult.

What he was doing was comparable to spraying malarial swamps. He was ridding mankind of a potential future parasite. Tranh Duc Pho would die a hero.

Tranh Duc Pho followed the Westerners and the children from the hill where they had slain his men. The rifles they had not taken with them, they had damaged beyond repair. They left no grenades behind, and threw other weapons and ammunition among the rocks. The lieutenant had lost his own rifle, but still possessed his 9-mm Pindad pistol, an Indonesian-made copy of the FN Browning HP, which carried thirteen rounds in its magazine. He had seven spare magazines, a combat knife, and a canteen of fresh water. He had all he would need.

One of the Western mercenaries kept a constant watch on their rear, and Tranh Duc Pho was careful to keep his

THE POINT TEAM

distance behind. There were so many in the group, they were easy to follow. He watched while they talked to two Montagnards, apparently receiving directions from them, because now they turned north instead of continuing east. The lieutenant raged inwardly at this treachery, for that advice was good. If ever he had armed men under his command again, he would return to this place and destroy the village of those two Montagnards who had given assistance to foreigners. If ever he had men under his command again...

They were moving now into territory hostile to the government, where the mountain tribesmen went to great lengths to maintain their fierce independence. He should strike soon.

They came to a perfect place for his attack—great clumps of flowering bushes obscured vision, and often three and sometimes five paths ran more or less parallel to each other. While the Westerners fussed over which path they would take and paused at every branching of the ways to make new decisions, he caught up with them rapidly, took a path that branched off from theirs and almost certainly rejoined it a little farther on. He would wait there, kill the Vanderhoven boy and disappear into the bushes.

Tranh Duc Pho could hear them, perhaps only twenty meters away through the bushes on his right, as he sped silently along the parallel path. His heart beat fast in anticipation. He felt a gentle pressure and then a snap against his ankle as he broke the trip wire. He heard the bent-back tree branch spring loose, and for an instant he saw the five six-inch hardwood darts, thick as his little finger and sharpened to a point at either end, fly in formation at his chest. Two glanced off the tough cloth of his army shirt, three penetrated his chest the length of a finger deep.

The lieutenant's agonized howl from so close by in the thick bushes caused the hair to stand up on the nape of

THE POINT TEAM

Campbell's neck. Seconds passed before he even recognized it as a human sound. The dozen boys bunched close together and looked around them with fear-widened eyes, obviously expecting to see some kind of Oriental demon bear down on them out of the bushes.

The Montagnard village was the typical collection of thatched huts—these were well-made and cared for. Crops grew in the well-tended fields about the houses. Domestic animals wandered freely all over the place, children ran up to look at them, women hurried past with openly curious looks.

"Every man in the village is peering along the sights of a barrel at us right now," Mike warned, "so keep your movements slow and your hands off your weapons."

A dried-up old man, though sprightly enough on his feet, emerged from one hut. Andre greeted him. He greeted Andre. They seemed to be spending some time complimenting each other, judging by the old man's smile and a wink to Mike from Andre. The Frenchman was handling the village language well.

"He says he's heard of us," Andre finally informed the rest of them. "Apparently the Montagnards we and the Hmong killed when we first crossed the border into Vietnam were some kind of procommunist renegades. Mike, you want to show him the ID you took off the lieutenant who skewered himself on the booby trap?"

The old man looked at the papers for a moment. Mike wondered whether he could read Vietnamese—he certainly didn't seem able to speak it. The Montagnard's face remained expressionless, and he went into the hut. They waited where they were in the hot, dusty street of the village. The sun beat down but was not unbearably hot at this altitude. Baby pigs, dogs of all sorts and hens competed with each other to sniff or peck at their feet. The children and women had by now formed a silent half-circle about them, but for some giggling and pushing.

A young man now emerged from the hut, carrying the lieutenant's ID papers. He was in traditional Montagnard dress, except for a Los Angeles Angels T-shirt he had obviously just pulled on for their benefit. He smiled at them all and spoke fast to Andre first in Vietnamese, then in his Montagnard language.

From him they learned that they were heroes because they were credited with the death of the notorious Tranh Duc Pho, who had always promised to "bring progress to these backward communities." They were given a feast, attended by the whole village, of pork stew, rice, bamboo shoots, tubers and many unidentified odds and ends, followed by fruit and cheese. They slept the night in hammocks strung in a large, clean hut and woke the next day never wanting to trek through the jungle and sleep with night creatures on the forest floor again. The Montagnards provided them with two guides who would take them safely across the border into Laos and two day's march into that country along a mountain spur. As a parting gift, Mike presented the headman's two teen-age sons with an AK47 each. Every man in the village got some kind of gift—a knife, a pistol, a compass, ammo... They had become quite loaded down before arriving in the village with the spoils of their victories and were happy to lighten their load among friends.

They spent the two succeeding nights in Montagnard villages on their journey, and these basic, not to say primitive, comforts buoyed the five mercs in both mind and body. The twelve- and thirteen-year-olds couldn't have cared less if they'd been told to sleep high in the trees. However, everyone's good spirits slowly wore off after their two Montagnard guides left them and they continued into the hot, jungle-clad hills of Laos. Mike reckoned they had a four-day march in front of them, all going well, till they reached the Mekong river. Once they crossed the Mekong, they were in Thailand and home free. Four days, covering twenty miles a day...

THE POINT TEAM

At an easy walk, over level open ground and with no need for concealment, a man can travel twenty miles in four hours. Crossing hills, valleys, swamps, jungles, avoiding populated areas and chance meetings, plodding forward with equipment in equatorial heat, a man traveling at the limits of his physical endurance can travel two miles in the same four hours. Things were not that bad all the time. Only some of the time.

The worst parts were the swamps, where they waded through stagnant black water, raising clouds of mosquitoes from the aquatic plants and feeling primitive life forms slither against their legs. Humid jungles were the next worst, because not only did plentiful varieties of insects attack, but so did just about every kind of animal. They had to watch especially for a light green snake with a white belly and orange eyes that curled up in the leaves of overhanging branches and dropped on its victims as they passed beneath. Andre said its bite was deadly—he had known it in Cambodia, where it was called the *hanuman*.

They had to avoid the coral snakes, whose venom glands were so large that in some they extended for one-third the length of the body, displacing the heart backward to make room for them. The cobras were dangerous because they were so aggressive—they did not bite in defense only, they came chasing after you. However, most of them were nocturnal, and since the group did not travel in the dark, they did not come across many. Pit vipers were among many other kinds they had to watch for, but their main problem was with kraits. These snakes ate other snakes, but struck at humans without warning and were highly venomous. Murphy managed to stand on one over three feet long. He realized what he had done only when he looked down to see what was hitting the upper surface of his boot. The snake was trying to drive its fangs through the leather, and Murphy jumped high in the air like a Russian ballet dancer before the reptile got around to trying his ankle instead. By the time Murphy came back to ground, the snake was gone.

Campbell's mania was disease. He repeated his claim several times a day that in the tropics disease killed more soldiers than enemy bullets. He doled out pills each night, and every morning he gave everyone a close look to search for telltale symptoms of fever. Leeches were his special worry—he claimed they transmitted more disease than anything else. The leeches clung to their bodies while they waded through water, they picked them up by brushing against damp leaves or long grass, and some, like the deadly green snakes, dropped from branches overhead— and these slipped down inside the collars of their shirts to begin their blood-sucking meal. Campbell didn't smoke, but for hours on end he kept cigarette after cigarette going to burn off these pests with its glowing tip.

There were also deadly spiders, leaves that caused skin rashes on contact, thorns whose punctures swelled into little abscesses, dysentery, two of the boys sick with mild malaria, depression, exhaustion, at times despair...

For the first two days they saw no one. It was with a kind of savage delight that they surprised three armed militia men at the edge of a settled area, mowed them down and took their valuables as well as their weapons to make it look like bandits had attacked them.

Then they saw soldiers by the side of a highway they had to cross.

"They're Vietnamese," Andre hissed.

They seemed to be anchoring timber poles floating in the water to the edge of the small canal that ran alongside the road.

"They're setting up an ambush," Nolan warned.

"No," Andre disagreed. "When rebels blow a hole in the road with explosives, they use these poles to bridge the gap and keep the traffic moving. The Viets are very efficient at this, since they themselves invented most of the tricks the rebels now use."

THE POINT TEAM

In a short while the soldiers finished their work, paused to smoke a cigarette on the roadside and then mounted their bicycles and headed south. After they had gone, Mike & Co. used the poles to cross the canal.

They spent a lot of time skirting areas where the rural population was heavy and people streamed along the country roads in throngs found only in cities in the West. Campbell and Waller felt their large frames to be so out of place here, they were freaks. Even at a great distance, they knew they could not pass without drawing attention to themselves. Yet Campbell held ruthlessly to his twenty miles per day minimum, and no one dared question him on how the hell he was measuring it, since it felt more like forty miles per day to everyone else.

When they were totally exhausted and felt they could go no farther, Campbell would turn and say things like, "This is too good to last. We're having things too easy. Enjoy it now while you can, there's rougher times ahead."

With his rough laugh, he would stride forward energetically, shaming the rest of them into trailing after him as best they could.

Late in the afternoon of the third day, they heard the drone of a small plane. Then another. Or it might have been the same one. The plane was flying low, clearly on an aerial reconnaissance of the terrain beneath. That evening, just before dusk, while they were looking for a secluded place to bivouac not far from a highway, a convoy of eighteen military trucks went north on the road. No one made direct remarks about this new military presence, but already they were recalling their adventures with bird-eating spiders and vampire bats in inaccessible jungles with a warm nostalgia. Campbell said very little.

The next dawn he was a different man, checking equipment, lecturing the slow-moving, all the time repeating variations on the magic phrase, "Tonight we cross the Mekong, at dawn tomorrow you will see the sun rise in the free world."

THE POINT TEAM

After only a limited time in the oppressive communist world, the team members were beginning to see the beauty of this statement. As for the boys, it electrified them into a frenzy of action. Each time Mike urged them on, they grew wilder. No one could stop them now! Murphy and Verdoux laughed together at the simple, direct power Campbell held over people as a leader. Yet in spite of their knowledge of what he was doing and how he did it, they admitted he infected them, too. Waller and Nolan, less complex individuals, joined with the Amerasian youths in their heightened, fierce determination to cross over into Thailand.

Not long after they set out on what they expected to be the final leg of their journey, a small single-engined recon plane crossed their path. They froze till it was out of visual range. In the next two hours, seven more of the small planes crossed the sky.

"Bastards know we're coming somehow," Waller ground out.

"All they got to do is follow the dead bodies we leave behind," Murphy said jokingly.

"We ain't been so bad recently," Waller said defensively. He grinned his loony grin. "I can hardly remember when I killed my last commie, it's been so long ago."

Murphy laughed. "Holy shit, Waller, you're going to miss it when you get out of here."

"Naw. There's always work to be done, no matter where a willing fella like me finds himself."

Waller was not joking now. Murphy let it pass.

They had a break when the country turned to forest with a high canopy, giant trunks and relatively passable vegetation on ground level. In a large, clear-cut, lumbered area, as they threaded their way among the three-foot stumps, they met a ground-search unit of Lao troops. Campbell had a big eye-opener about the fighters under his command. While the Lao troops broke for cover, the kids and the team members never missed a step in their implacable forward pace. They advanced in an even line and threw lead from the hip as they came. One by one, the Lao troops flopped down like targets struck at a fairground booth.

They moved on without delay, pausing only to dispatch the wounded with a pistol shot to the head.

"I don't want anyone talking about who we are at this stage," Campbell declared. "We can't afford it. So anyone who sees you—man, woman or child—kill them. You want to be kind to them, make sure they don't get to see you."

Campbell himself saw the effect of his leadership on the kids. He had turned them into monsters! Now even his own men (mercenaries!) had to strive to compete with these ravening little savages.

Verdoux muttered something wise in French about the hunger or thirst for liberty turning its holder into something else.

"Ah, the frog is thinking about wine and women again," Murphy said.

"I'm so desperate now, Bob," Andre said sarcastically, "I'd even settle for Australian wine and an Australian woman."

Nolan joined the conversation. "You know what they say about Australian girls, frog? They got what it takes down under." He indicated the area of the body he meant, in case they didn't get the joke.

Andre sighed dramatically and moved away.

They wiped out two small armed parties and hid the bodies in the undergrowth. So far they had not received a scratch themselves. Their frenzy rose with the killing, and all of them began to feel that nothing could stop them now. They were nearing the Mekong, only hours away. Verdoux claimed he could already *smell* Thailand!

Then things took a different turn. First Campbell realized that he had driven his unit harder than he thought. With three hours of daylight remaining, they were descending

THE POINT TEAM

ahead of schedule into the broad valley of the Mekong. There was no holding back now. They had not been precisely located, but the military was closing in. Campbell saw their best chance as establishing a position on the bank of the Mekong and holding out till dark. He had only one objective now—get to the river. When he got there, he would decide what to do.

The next happening that changed their circumstances was a run-in with a Lao unit of forty-eight or more men. The two Lao platoons exchanged fire with them beyond effective range, and then fled before either side had taken any casualties!

Murphy roared with laughter. "They're the first ones we've met with any sense!"

Campbell was dour. "They'll radio in our position. Those were probably a bunch of peasant conscripts who didn't want to tangle with us. Now they'll call in hardened troops. I reckon we're no more than forty minutes from the riverbank. Let's make an all-out break for it and try for a quick daylight crossing. That means *run,* you bastards, run, run, run!"

He didn't give them time to think—kept them on the move. Now they ran across fields in which peasants were working, passed women carrying pitchers of water from a well, stopped bicycle and ox-cart traffic on a dirt road as they crossed it in a pack, and ran down among fishermen repairing nets on the muddy bank of the wide river.

Mike picked on two of the fishermen, who looked like father and son. He forced them to stand at gunpoint with their hands clasped behind their necks.

"Ask them if we can wade across the river here," he told Andre.

The older man replied to the Frenchman's question. Andre translated, "He says we can."

Campbell barked, "Tell him that both of them lead the way and if the water gets above their waists, I'll gun them down."

THE POINT TEAM

Andre conveyed this information to the two men, listened to their reply and translated, "They say it would be quicker to cross in their boats. The boats are hidden in the bushes fifty meters down the bank. But they complain it is dangerous for them—"

Mike held up a hand for him to stop. He took a wad of Thai bahts from his shirt pocket and let the two fishermen look at the bills. They nodded, unclasped their hands from behind their necks with a smile, and set off down the riverbank at a half-run.

What Andre translated as "boats" turned out to be two canoes. Mike didn't have time to go back and force other fishermen to cooperate with him. There were other canoes, but he guessed they were better off overloading two craft with experienced boatmen than trying to handle the temperamental, fragile craft themselves in the fast-flowing river currents.

The canoes sank in the water almost to the gunwales under their weight, and every time anyone moved out of sync with the others, the craft threatened to tip over. They finally all piled into the canoes in shallow water and stabilized their loads. With a few expert strokes, the fishermen shot their craft into the currents and maneuvered across the river at a 45-degree angle, using the swift waters and the calms like a car driver weaving in and out of crowded traffic lanes on an interstate highway.

Even Campbell thought they had it made, with three-fourths of the river covered, when a big chopper swept over the waters from upstream and touched down on its skids on a gravel bank in a foot of water behind them.

"Go! Go!" Campbell yelled to the boatmen.

They did not need his message to be translated for them. They paddled the canoes into the fastest downstream rushes of water they could find. The helicopter landing was sloppy. The unloaded troopers could not fire at them because the chopper rotors whipped up the river water and obscured their vision. They took longer than they should have to unload a heavy machine gun, keep it out of the water, set up its tripod on the gravel bank and mount it. The chopper lifted off.

Campbell's canoe, paddled by the old man, hit the shore. Mike threw the notes to him and, as they jumped out, yelled for him to head downstream as fast as he could. Another message that needed no translation.

The younger Laotian's canoe was farther out. Mike gestured to its occupants to abandon it and get to shore. They wasted valuable time in trying not to upset the craft—which they didn't—and the first wild burst of heavy machine-gun fire whipped over their heads as the soldiers adjusted their weapon out on the gravel bank.

Verdoux and Nolan, who had also been in Campbell's canoe, returned fire but ineffectively. The troops were crouched behind the machine gun, and their support lay in the water and presented little in the way of a target.

The next foray of the machine gunner was more successful. As they splashed toward shore, the bullets danced off the water just downstream from them. Murphy yelled for all of them to lie behind a sandy shoal before the gunner zeroed in on them.

Two of Eric's friends panicked. They saw the shore of Thailand only fifty yards away—freedom!—and they ignored Murphy's command. The stream of bullets found them a few seconds later as they splashed toward shore hysterically, cutting them down in the water... It's especially pathetic the way an automatic stream of heavy bullets chops up a child's body, which does not have the bulk to absorb the impact of the high-velocity slugs.

Their butchered bodies were dragged over the shallows by the blood-stained river waters, carrying the tragic burdens downstream.

Mike raged. His blood boiled. He had to strive to clear his head so he could think. Opening his eyes, he saw the solution right before him on the riverside highway. A Thai farmer with a truck bearing a transverse 500-gallon tank.

THE POINT TEAM

Mike had thought it was agricultural fertilizer till he heard the farmer, who had abandoned the vehicle in a panic as bullets ricocheted around him.

"Gasoline! Petrol!" he screamed, pointing at the tank.

He only recovered his senses when Mike showed him a wad of dollar bills and the muzzle of his AK47.

"*Deux mille litres*!" the farmer squeaked.

Mike hoped so, and counted out twenty hundred-dollar bills before he seized the ignition keys.

Verdoux nodded and hauled out a spare magazine from his pouch as he ran back to the riverbank.

As Mike drove the truck upriver on the road, he looked out at the machine gunner who had Murphy, Nolan and half the kids pinned behind the shelter of a gravel shoal fifty yards from the bank.

At a boat landing, he drove the truck out into the river. The late 1960s truck operated well till the water got above the wheel hubs. Then the engine cut out. And would not restart. Mike figured he was OK where he was and did not fight it.

He did not bother with the fuel hose but released two emergency valves on the tank that sent the fuel spilling onto the river water. In a minute, a wide slick of gasoline spread over the surface. The currents were bringing the slick in the general direction he needed, yet it was too early to tell if it would reach its goal.

Verdoux waited till the slick, in its rainbow colors, had reached the machine-gun position before firing his magazine full of tracer bullets into it. The burning phosphorus on the bullets ignited the gasoline slick in a carpet of blue flame.

Although the water the soldiers were in was only about a foot deep, the sea of flames rose three feet high above it. When they jumped up to try to escape, only their heads and shoulders were clear of the consuming tongues of flame. Their awful cries of agony and screams for help to

"No one's going to complain about that," she said. "One moment, Roger is saying something." She came back on the line. "Remember Roger? He's the cameraman. He wants you to delay your arrival to Bangkok till daylight tomorrow."

"Tell Roger from me where he can stick his video camera."

Katie laughed. "I thought that would be your reaction. What time can we expect you?"

"About one or two in the morning, if our driver doesn't kill us."

All of them, including the kids, were now feeling the effects of their weariness and the strong Thai beer they had drunk. And all, except the ever-vigilant Campbell, dozed off from time to time. Mike roused them as the bus hurtled through the nearly deserted, early-morning outskirts of Bangkok. Andre translated his instructions for the driver.

The kids, with their too-large weapons slung about their puny bodies, stepped one by one from the bus door, led by Eric, into the incandescent white glare of Roger's portable TV lights. A large crowd had collected to see what was going on. Katie was interviewing them, Jake was creeping around with microphones out of the camera's line of sight, Roger was moving this way and that with his shoulder-held camera, old man Vanderhoven—whose presence surprised Campbell—seemed to be making some kind of speech.

"This is where we get off," Mike said to the other four mercs.

They piled their weapons and ammo on a double seat under the watchful eyes of the driver, who was accepting them as payment for the hire of his bus. The mercs slipped off the bus quietly and were noticed by hardly anyone. They grinned as they heard Eric boasting before the cameras how he alone had led his pals out of the bondage of communism into freedom.

"You coming along with us, Mike?" Nolan asked.

the people they had been machine-gunning seconds before rang clearly across the water surface.

Murphy, Nolan and the surviving kids who had been marooned behind the shelter of the gravel shoal ran like crazy for the Thai shore.

The gasoline combustion lasted a few seconds more, then suddenly, the fuel almost spent, the flames on the surface of the water died down to a shimmering topaz glimmer on the river. Some of the soldiers were still staggering about, burning and smoldering. Others had fallen into the flaming water and flopped about like dying fish, blinded, half drowned, half burned to death.

The ancient bus bumped at terrifying speeds along the roads, driven maniacally by the brother of the Thai whose gasoline Campbell had bought. In the weak yellow headlights, they had glimpses of people jumping out of their way into the darkness, and every so often they would compete with an approaching pair of undimmed headlights for supremacy on the narrow roadway.

Mike yelled to Andre over the rattles and squeaks, "Tell him to ease up. We haven't come this far to die in a goddamn traffic accident."

Whatever the Frenchman said to him, the Thai thought it was hugely funny and drove all the faster. They made only one stop, at a roadside eating place, for Campbell to telephone the TV network bureau in Bangkok. He couldn't have cared less if no one was there, but it was part of his bargain with Katie Nelson, so he waited nearly fifteen minutes for the call to go through. He and the others ate a huge dinner of pork slivers barbecued on small wood skewers, served in a thick, hot peanut sauce over rice.

"Mike, you've done it!" Katie Nelson's voice finally came over the wire.

"We lost one man and two of the kids, but we're here and in good shape. Except, I think you'll find Eric Vanderhoven quieted down a lot."

"We're going back to that place I found last time here with all the pretty girls."

Mike grinned. "Whatever you say, chief."

A great rush of contentment passed over him. He had no more orders to give now. Mission was complete. Objective achieved.

GREAT MEN'S ADVENTURE

___DIRTY HARRY
by Dane Hartman

Never before published or seen on screen.

He's "Dirty Harry" Callahan—tough, unorthodox, no-nonsense plain-clothesman extraordinaire of the San Francisco Police Department . . . Inspector #71 assigned to the bruising, thankless homicide detail . . . A consummate crimebuster nothing can stop—not even the law!

___DEATH ON THE DOCKS (C90-792, $1.95)

___MASSACRE AT RUSSIAN RIVER (C30-052, $1.95)

___NINJA MASTER
by Wade Barker

Committed to avenging injustice, Brett Wallace uses the ancient Japanese art of killing as he stalks the evildoers of the world in his mission.

___SKIN SWINDLE (C30-227, $1.95)

___ONLY THE GOOD DIE (C30-239, $2.25, U.S.A.)
(C30-695, $2.95, Canada)

WARNER BOOKS
P.O. Box 690
New York, N.Y. 10019

Please send me the books I have checked. I enclose a check or money order (not cash), plus 50¢ per order and 50¢ per copy to cover postage and handling.*
(Allow 4 weeks for delivery.)

_____ Please send me your free mail order catalog. (If ordering only the catalog, include a large self-addressed, stamped envelope.)

Name _____
Address _____
City _____
State _____ Zip _____
*N.Y. State and California residents add applicable sales tax.

14